THE CREATURE FROM THE GRIM MIRE

JEANNIE ALDERDICE
PETER ALDERSON SHARP

The Creature from the Grim Mire
by
JEANNIE WYCHERLEY and Peter Alderson Sharp

Copyright © 2020 Jeannie Wycherley
Bark at the Moon Books
All rights reserved

Publishers note: This is a work of fiction. All characters, names, places and incidents are either products of the author's imagination or are used fictitiously and for effect or are used with permission. Any other resemblance to actual persons, either living or dead, is entirely coincidental.

No part of this book may be reproduced, distributed or transmitted in any form or by any means, including photocopying, recording, or other electronic or mechanical methods, or by any information storage and retrieval system without the prior written permission of the publisher, except in the case of very brief quotations embodied in critical reviews and certain other non-commercial uses permitted by copyright law.

Sign up for Jeannie's newsletter:
eepurl.com/cN3Q6L

The Creature from the Grim Mire was edited by Christine L Baker
Cover design by Taurus Colosseum.
Formatting by Tammy
Proofing by Johnny Bon Bon

Please note: This book is set in England in the United Kingdom. It uses British English spellings and idioms and Devon vernacular.

AUTHORS' NOTE

This novel came about after I (Jeannie) bought the cover but didn't know what to do with it! At the start of the pandemic, I mentioned it to my Dad, Peter Alderson Sharp, who along with my Mum was shielding at home. I suggested—vaguely—we might work together on something ....

I knew he was bored, and I wouldn't be able to see my folks for a few months, so this seemed like a great way to interact.

With return of email Peter had concocted a story idea that I loved. After that we used collaborative documents – without ever having to see each other!

2020 has been a very strange year but we're grateful to have had this opportunity to work together.

We hope you enjoy the finished project as much as we enjoyed creating it!

#staysafe
Jeannie and Peter (father and daughter)
xoXox

CHAPTER ONE

The mist swirled like a living entity, rolling and tumbling as it crossed the marsh. Maud Wells shivered and tugged at her shawl, wrapping it more tightly around her shoulders. At her grand old age—she'd be ninety next birthday, after all—she suffered with the cold. The damp air had started to seep through her clothing, chilling her to the bone. The sky above the vast moor was dark with foreboding and, in truth, it was a horrible night to be abroad.

Maud clucked. *Needs must.*

Fossy had to have her evening stroll. Dogs need to do what dogs need to do.

"We don't want any more little accidents, do we Fossy?" she called.

The little terrier-like dog scampered happily around, zigzagging left to right and back again, favouring Maud with a glance. Her large, intelligent eyes shone brightly in the light cast from Maud's torch but then, picking up a new scent, she trotted away once more.

Maud directed the cumbersome torch onto the path they were negotiating. It wouldn't do to stray from it. Not with the marsh so close. There were endless stories of travellers coming to grief in Foxtor Mire, disappearing beneath sinking sand or being sucked deep into a bog, nevermore to rise.

Folklore nonsense, thought Maud. But then again, on a night like this, it wasn't beyond the realms of possibility that anything might happen to a stray wanderer.

You needed to keep your wits about you. And Maud had a full complement of those.

Fossy ran up to her, barking and wagging what passed for her tail. With a skip and a woof she was off again, dashing along the path with a merry bounce in her step.

"Careful, Fossy! Stay on the path!" Maud reminded her.

Maud loved all the little 'children' who waited patiently at home for her return, but there was a special place in her heart for Fossy. The darling creature had been near to death when Maud had first taken her in, and she'd become the old woman's favourite companion. Maud didn't want to give Fossy up. She knew she would miss her terribly when she had to be returned.

"Come on, my girl! We'd better go back now. Let's go home."

As Maud spoke, the sky suddenly lit up overhead. A searing flash of light was closely followed by a heavy thud, and the earth beneath Maud's feet began to vibrate. She gasped, casting the light of her torch around to see what might have caused the violent disturbance. A loud splash somewhere to her right made Maud jump. Something had crash-landed near the edge of the mire and spewed clods of earth and jets of water high into the air.

Maud, startled, stumbled backwards, nearly falling in her haste to get away. She clamped her hand to her chest where her heart thumped hard enough to break her ribs, then fought to regain her balance.

"My God, Fossy, what on earth was that?" she asked, her voice hushed almost to a whisper.

The little dog rushed back to her feet, cowering and quietly whimpering beside her. Maud lifted her torch in shaking hands and shone it along the path towards the marsh. Ahead of her, at a distance of a hundred yards or so, she could discern a red glow in the dark, but her torch didn't have the range to see the object more clearly. The red didn't glow steadily; in fact, the intensity seemed to wax and wane, pulsating in the darkness. She cocked her head, watching anxiously. When the light was at its strongest, she thought she could see movement near the object.

She remained still, her mind a maelstrom of confusion. Should she hurry back to the house and phone the police? Or should she approach what she supposed was the wreckage? What if this was a light aircraft that had crashed? Someone might urgently require her assistance.

The decision was made for her by Fossy. With a snarl, she sprinted towards the glowing object.

"Fossy!" Maud took a few faltering steps forwards, fearing the dog would be burned or injure herself some other way on jagged shards of debris. "Fossy!" she called again, full of despair. "Come back here, you naughty girl!"

Maud pulled up sharply, her sixth sense sounding alarm bells. Trembling violently, she attempted to angle the torch closer to the scene, finding it difficult even to grip the handle. Ahead of her, Fossy was standing her ground, all four paws firmly planted, noisily confronting whatever lay in front of them.

Not a person ... a thing.

A thing that appeared to be some shapeless mass. Black and slimy. It didn't crawl or creep. It ... slithered.

Maud shifted the torch, highlighting another such creature lying next to the first. This one wasn't moving.

Fossy continued to bark and snarl, half-circling the moving mass, dancing first one way then the other. Unexpectedly the object reared up. Fossy leapt backwards, squealing in shock, then took off for the far end of the mire, yelping as she went. Maud reached for her, her fingers finding only air, as though this movement alone would bring her back. "Fossy, no!" she cried, but to no avail. Maud's favourite friend kept going, solely intent on getting away.

Maud frowned as she watched Fossy disappear.

Was it a trick of the light? Or was the mist distorting her view of the world? She leaned forward, squinting into the darkness. As Fossy vanished into the fog, she seemed to be growing larger.

The black mass flopped back to earth with a disgusting splat and then, with a tremor, it slithered to the edge of the mire. Maud grimaced, watching as it slipped gracefully into the water without creating so much as a splash. The other creature remained motionless.

Maud watched it, holding her breath. It didn't even twitch.

Shuddering, she decided not to hang around to see what would happen next. She scurried for home with as much haste as she could manage given her advanced age, overwhelmed by guilt, hating to leave Fossy alone on Foxtor Mire. But what was the alternative? There was no way she could have kept pace with the little dog. Fossy had disappeared like a bat out of hell.

She was an intelligent creature. Maud, although desperately worried, was confident Fossy would find her way home in daylight.

Maud reached Prior's Cross, her home, and stood in the doorway looking out over the dark and desolate moor. She considered calling the police, but she had a bad feeling about the incident. Somewhere and somehow, she sensed her father's involvement.

It really wouldn't do for him to be mixed up with the police.

CHAPTER TWO

Tap, tap, slap, tap.
Felicity shot bolt upright in her bed, her heart pounding, nerves jangling.

Tap, tap, slap, tap.

There they were again. The sounds that interrupted her dreams.

Tap, tap, slap, tap.

Not loud noises, but crisp. Clear. Originating from somewhere close by.

Downstairs?

Breathing heavily, she leaned over and switched on the bedside light before fumbling for the poker which she had stored by her bedside ever since she'd moved into the old house. She had quickly become used to most of the bumps in the night, the creaking rafters and joists and such. The old timbers adjusted themselves, especially on windy nights—and there were lots of those out here on the moor. She had also become more familiar with the crying of foxes—which had freaked her out completely in the beginning—as well as owls calling and the pitter-patter of mice searching for food.

It surprised her that she didn't mind the mice as much as she had thought she would, but at the end of the day, she was an animal lover and couldn't bring herself to put down traps. *Live and let live,* she thought. *If they don't bother me, I won't bother them.*

But she couldn't blame this sound on the mice.

Mice *might* on occasion produce some kind of tapping sound, but there was no way, to Felicity's mind at least, that they could create the slapping sound. It sounded like a large wet dishcloth being dropped from a height onto a work surface.

And Felicity had checked for dishcloths on work surfaces when she'd heard these noises before. It had come as no surprise when she hadn't found any.

She slipped out of bed and rammed her feet into her slippers. Mister Ogilvy, Aunt Maud's old ginger tom, glared at the bedroom door. Not a happy cat, he stood rigid, perfectly still, his hackles raised and back arched, his tail as stiff as a ramrod, claws out and fangs on display. Felicity could just about hear his virtually inaudible keening.

She tiptoed to the door and raised her poker high. Grasping the handle with her free hand, she yanked it open, creating a rush of air.

Nothing!

Light from her bedroom spilled onto the empty landing. She crept to the head of the stairs where Mister

Ogilvy had taken up a new position. Together they peered into the hall below. The downstairs was pitch black, but Felicity was certain that she could make out the shapes of people moving around.

People?

Felicity started in horror. *Stop it! There's no one down there. It's all my imagination.*

She fumbled for the two-way switch at the top of the stairs and flicked both lights on. The downstairs hall was instantly flooded with light. Coats, hats and scarves hung from the hooks on the wall, but there was nothing sinister. No burglars, no demons. Everything was as it should be.

Still gripping the poker, she clapped her free hand to her cheek. *What on earth is up with me? This is the person who has written gothic horror novels. One a bestseller! And here I am behaving like a frightened schoolgirl. I really need to get a grip!*

The tapping noise had stopped, at least temporarily. It had been replaced instead by a quiet, high-pitched whine. Felicity cocked her head and listened.

"Okay," she said aloud. "There's absolutely nothing sinister about that. It *has* to be some sort of machine on the Gurneys' farm." The Gurneys lived just up the lane and were her nearest neighbours.

Felicity loosened her tight grip on the poker and returned to the bedroom to look at the time. Just after four. An obscene time to be awake.

Bit early for old man Gurney, Felicity thought. *I know he's an early riser, but surely not even* he *would get up at four in the morning and start up a machine that could wake the dead?*

Gradually, the frequency of the whine increased. The pitch rose until, despite still being barely discernible to the ear, she could feel it in her head. It became increasingly uncomfortable. At the point at which she knew she could no longer stand it, the sound abruptly halted.

She sagged with relief, just as the night sky was lit up by a brilliant flash.

Shrieking, Felicity dropped her poker.

Lightning?

Is that all it was?

She laughed shakily, bending to retrieve her weapon of choice. She started to count, an automatic reflex, something Aunt Maud had taught her. *One thousand, two thousand, three thousand, four thousand, five thousand ... that's a mile ... six thousand ... seven thousand ...*

By the time she reached twelve thousand—representing two-and-a-half miles—she had yet to hear the expected clap of thunder. Felicity frowned, certain that the lightning had been very close by. *Probably on the high moor*, she mused. Perhaps the military radio mast on top of Yes Tor had been struck. It wouldn't be the first time.

Pulling herself together she made her way down the old, uneven stairs. They creaked and whinged with every step she took. She turned into the narrow, whitewashed corridor at the bottom and shuffled dozily towards the kitchen at the rear of the house. Switching on the fluorescent light, she waited a few seconds until her eyes became accustomed to the intrusive brightness then, blinking, she performed a comic half-asleep double take.

Earlier the previous evening she had made herself a sandwich, intending to have it for her supper. However, she'd been so tired that she had decided not to bother, turning in early instead. She'd left the sandwich on a plate on the kitchen table, covered by a tea towel. But now the tea towel had been pulled away and more than half of the sandwich was missing.

Felicity wheeled round and stared at Mister Ogilvy, who had dutifully followed her down the stairs.

He looked back at her, his face sheepish.

"I think we know who the culprit is, don't we, Oggy?" She smiled. "Don't I feed you enough?"

She switched the kettle on. While waiting for it to come to the boil, she disposed of the rest of the sandwich and wiped down the table. She popped a teabag in a mug and added sugar and milk. Sweet milky tea would help to settle her nerves, and then maybe she could either go back to bed and sleep or sit down and do some writing. Grabbing a packet of Digestive biscuits, she padded back down the hallway and into the living room, settling herself on the old settee in front of the log fire.

The fire had mostly burned down to ash, but there was just an inkling of a glowing ember on one of the burnt-out logs. Her heart squeezed and she smiled, remembering how she would sit in this exact place as a child. What wonderful days they'd been.

She had pestered her parents to take her to Aunt Maud's whenever the opportunity arose. She loved Dartmoor and she loved Prior's Cross, so it had been a treat to spend most of her school holidays in this centuries-old house. Moreover, dear Aunt Maud was always delighted to see her and made such a fuss of her, spoiling her terribly. Once Felicity's parents had left— and that happened on most visits, as they preferred to leave her to her own devices while they travelled abroad for a week or so—young Flick, as she called herself out of their earshot, had total freedom to do what she wanted and go where she liked.

Within reason, that was. She could still hear Aunt Maud's admonition, oft repeated, especially as Felicity first arrived for her stay. "You can do what you like here, my dear," she would say in her broad Devon accent, "as long as you keeps yourself clean and tidy and presentable, and don't 'ee go near that there bog!"

'That there bog' referred to Foxtor Mire, situated just south of the house. It had a fearsome reputation and was generally believed to be the model for the notorious 'Grimpen Mire' of Arthur Conan Doyle's *The Hound of the Baskervilles* fame. It had earned the nickname among locals as the grim mire, but Felicity had always rather loved it and its lonely desolation.

As for keeping herself 'clean and tidy and presentable', unfortunately that rarely went well. Young Flick had been a real tomboy as a child and, given the freedom afforded by Aunt Maud, had scoured the area around the house and often visited the Gurney Farm just up the lane, getting into scrapes with the boys who lived there and coming home covered in muck.

The Gurney farm offered no end of opportunities for adventures. Mrs Gurney would let her feed the chickens and, in spring, she could hold the new-born lambs. The Gurneys had two sons, Daniel—or Dan'l—who was three years Felicity's senior, and John—or Jan—who was the same age and had become her playmate when they were young. They had particularly enjoyed playing in the small wood north of the farm and climbing the trees. Some days they might choose to be outlaws in Sherwood Forest, another day they were members of a smuggling gang on the run from the excise men.

As they grew older, she saw less of the boys, until eventually she didn't see them at all. When not at school, the boys devoted all of their time to the farm, becoming heavily involved once their formal education had ended.

When Felicity eventually returned to Prior's Cross at sundown, hungry and tired naturally, Aunt Maud would take one look at the dishevelled, dirty waif that had sheepishly entered her house and raise her eyes to heaven. There would never be any scolding, however. She might sigh or tut, but then Flick would be directed into Aunt Maud's enormous bath, full to the brim with hot soapy water, the overflow of bubbles generated by some strange, though not unpleasant-smelling crystals tipped into the tub.

And yes, after supper they would settle down on this very sofa in front of a roaring fire and Aunt Maud would read to her. Initially, she had read children's stories: *Peter*

Pan, *Heidi*, *Black Beauty* and, later, *Little Women*. Then, after a couple of years, the emphasis changed. Aunt Maud began reading to her from adventure and fantasy stories: *The Time Machine*, *War of the Worlds*, *The Lost World*—and later still came *Dracula* and *Frankenstein*.

Felicity was convinced that these latter stories had ignited a spark in her which grew to be an overwhelming interest in all things gothic and scary. Her own writing, and she had published three books to date, had all been of that genre.

Felicity had been immensely sad to hear of her dear aunt's passing just a few months ago. She had hardly begun the grieving process when, a few days later, a firm of solicitors in Tavistock had contacted her to inform her that Aunt Maud had thought to provide for her in her will. Felicity had been astonished. Aunt Maud had, in fact, bequeathed Prior's Cross House, together with a small legacy comprising a meagre share portfolio, generating a small yearly income to be spent on the upkeep of the house if Felicity so chose.

Grief-stricken at the loss of her aunt, she had barely cared at first, but when she thought it through afterwards, she supposed the inheritance made sense. Aunt Maud was in reality her great-aunt, being the half-sister of Felicity's grandmother, Mary, or Granny Gannicott as she had known her. Maud had no children of her own and her only other living relative was Flick's mother, who she rarely saw. Flick and Maud, on the other hand, had spent many, many happy days in this beautiful old house, and far too many evenings to count, cuddled up together sharing their love of adventure stories.

Felicity still hadn't fully awoken to the realisation that she now owned this beautiful building. Set in the centre of Dartmoor, Prior's Cross lay a mile or so from the village of Princetown, down a very narrow and bumpy unmetalled track. Her nearest neighbour was the aforementioned Farmer Tom Gurney, a quarter of a mile back up the track towards Princetown. Originally the house had been four-bedroomed, but the downstairs bedroom had been converted at some time in the past into a wonderful study.

Sitting somewhat incongruously at the back of the house was a two-storey wooden barn. The house had never been a farm or, as far as Aunt Maud knew, never even a smallholding, so why a barn had been built in the grounds was a complete mystery. Even so, it was a place of enchantment; full of antiques, knick-knacks, old paintings, ancient tools, electrical equipment, valves and tubes. As a child, Felicity had often amused herself in the barn on rainy days. Since moving in recently, she had promised herself that one day she would go through it all and sort it out. She suspected that most of the stuff in the barn was junk, but there might be one or two little treasures lurking in there. You could never know.

Sitting in front of the dying fire now, she recalled how, on one occasion, she had asked Aunt Maud whether she might be allowed to climb up to the top floor. Felicity had spied a trapdoor in the ceiling, but there was no ladder and apparently no other way to reach it.

That had been one of the few occasions Felicity could remember Aunt Maud being stern with her. She had held Felicity by the shoulders. "Promise me you'll never attempt to get into the upper barn," she had said. "You could hurt yourself very badly. It's full of electrical equipment which could be extremely dangerous!" She had ducked her head and stared into the child's eyes. "You must promise!"

So Felicity had promised.

Now she blinked the memories away. Dear Aunt Maud.

How I miss you.

On impulse, Felicity jumped to her feet and crossed the living room to the door that opened into the study. This was her favourite room of all.

How I love this place, she thought as she entered. The room was richly carpeted, and in the centre was a well-used, but still beautiful, oak desk. The desk faced a large bow window looking out towards the mire. On a fine day, Felicity was afforded an extraordinary and breath-taking view of the rolling hills of the south moor. The study walls were completely lined with shelves bearing Aunt Maud's library—of which she had been justifiably proud. Many of the volumes were leather-bound first editions, and a number of these—as Aunt Maud had often boasted—had been signed by the author.

Felicity plonked herself down into the comfortable leather upholstered captain's chair at the desk. Gone were the blotting pad and inkstand. In front of her on the desk was her laptop, a decent model she'd invested a lot of money in, and to the side, her mouse. With a nod to tradition, Felicity had positioned an old-fashioned scribble pad on the left of the desk, and on this rested the gold fountain pen Aunt Maud had given her for her twenty-first birthday.

She parted the curtains and looked out of the window. Not much to see. The sun had yet to struggle up the side of Ter Hill and, for now, the hills and mire were still shrouded in Dartmoor's famous mist. If you stared at it long enough you would see men, horses, dogs and all manner of creatures appear and disappear. According to local legend, the creatures were created by the pixies. Felicity always found herself half-believing such stories. There was no doubt in her mind that Dartmoor was a magical and enchanted place.

Thinking of which ...

She switched on her laptop. Publishers don't make allowances for ghosts and ghouls and things that go bump in the night and keep you awake. Felicity needed to write and deliver words to her agent.

ASAP.

She opened a document, picking up the strands of a story she'd started fleshing out a few weeks ago, but this morning, inspiration wouldn't come.

I'm too tired.

Concentrate!

She made herself write a full paragraph, but on reading it through, she realised it was complete tosh. She tried again. She punctuated every line with a yawn, her head occasionally nodding, and she quickly realised she'd have to give it up as a bad job. Rising, she stretched and tousled her hair.

She'd lost this battle. Sleep was winning. She might as well surrender to it.

Switching off the computer, she trudged wearily upstairs, Mister Ogilvy under her feet. She chucked her robe to the floor and collapsed into bed. She'd had two disturbed nights in a row and now felt exhausted enough to make up for it.

"Come on, Oggy, cuddle in," she murmured. "I always sleep better when I can feel you near me."

The cat obliged, pushing himself into her back. Within seconds Flick had fallen fast asleep, her gentle breathing the only sound in the room.

But Mister Ogilvy did not sleep.

He had unfinished business. Downstairs.

Leaping lightly from the bed, he padded to the top of the stairs and halted there, listening attentively. After a moment, he slipped down the top three steps and stopped again, his ears constantly pivoting front and rear. He took the next three and waited once more, listening hard. And the next three. This time when he paused, he hissed to warn those unfortunate enough to be in his path to move.

The Great Mister Ogilvy, do-er of daring things, fearless night hunter extraordinaire, was coming!

He slunk into the kitchen, knowing full well what he would see and not surprised in the slightest. Standing on the table was a green five-legged creature with a bulbous head and large round eyes. It had virtually no body but its five limbs, or rather tentacles, extended from what little there was. The creature balanced on three of its tentacles while the other two tore apart the remnants of the sandwich it had evidently stolen from the bin. It rapidly stuffed the pieces into its beak-like mouth.

A furious Mister Ogilvy meowed aggressively and pounced. He shot out a paw, claws extended, and only narrowly missed his target. In response, the creature flicked one of its tentacles towards him. The tip clipped the cat's nose, sending him flying, snarling and sneezing as he went. Mister Ogilvy had had dealings with this creature before.

He hated the thing.

Refusing to give up, he shot his paw out again, this time catching the creature on the side of one of its standing tentacles. With the grace of a ballerina en pointe, the creature danced away from him, slipping into one of the store cupboards. Mister Ogilvy tried to follow, but the creature had disappeared.

The cat stared up in confusion. *How? Where?* The only escape route appeared to be a very small window high up in the wall. He leapt up onto one of the narrow shelves but couldn't find enough purchase for a second jump from there in the direction of the window.

He gave up the chase—for now—and scrambled down to the floor once more, scattering a few of the tins as he did so. He sat neatly, his tail curled around his body, licking a paw and preparing to groom himself, basking in his almost-victory. He had successfully chased off his enemy.

His euphoria didn't last long. His sensitive ears pricked up. From somewhere outside, quite nearby, he detected the low snarl of a dog. There weren't many things in this world that frightened Mister Ogilvy, but dogs were one of them. He decided to investigate, but from the relative safety of the window. He jumped up onto the draining board, from where he had the best vantage point for the yard outside. What he spotted there made his blood freeze.

Standing just outside the door was the largest, most fearsome-looking hound he had ever had the dissatisfaction of clapping eyes on.

Ooh no. No, no, no.

Regaining his senses, he leapt off the draining board, shot down the hall and scrambled up the stairs. He threw himself onto Flick's bed, pushing himself into her back as far as he could.

He lay there shivering for a long, long time.

CHAPTER THREE

Felicity dragged herself out of bed much later that morning, in fact so late, it was almost afternoon before she managed to separate herself from her duvet and crawl into the shower. She had slept relatively well in the end, all things considered. She recalled odd snippets of a dream, where she'd been running on the moor like some kind of animal, but it hadn't disturbed her. She skipped down to the kitchen, feeling more rested and relaxed than she had for days, only then to be faced by the slight disruption she found there.

Mister Ogilvy had seemingly decided to fish out the sandwich from the bin and finish it off, but that didn't really explain the scattered tins in the store cupboard. She restacked them, puzzling over how they'd ended up that way.

What on earth had he been up to?

Oggy, she thought, *what am I to do with you? You're a dear little chap, but you're a bit of a liability!*

She sat down to a brunch of Rice Krispies swimming in ice-cold milk and with a very generous sprinkling of sugar, eyeing the store cupboards. They needed sorting out. There were dozens of tins of cat food in there. She could understand that. She supposed Aunt Maud had probably bought in bulk to save money. But there were several dozen cartons of dog food too. What on earth had possessed Aunt Maud to buy dog food?

Maybe Felicity should offer it all to a foodbank.

After breakfast she moved into the study with her cup of tea, sat down at the desk and began to sketch out a new idea. She had hoped this morning, after a better few hours of sleep, that the words would flow out of her. But they didn't.

Why won't they? What better conditions to write in than these?

Feeling slightly dejected, she glanced up from the screen to take in the amazing view. It was a crisp autumn day with not a hint of mist to be seen. The sun was playing hide and seek behind a few clouds, but when it did emerge from time to time, it lit up the stunning landscape with a plethora of colours: the reds, blues and purples of the heather, the lush green of the rolling downs and the faint blue of the distant tors.

Concentrate, Felicity, concentrate!

After a brief pause for lunch—a mug of tea and two slices of toast—followed by a brisk walk down to the edge of the mire and back, Felicity tried again. She pulled out her notebook and wrote longhand. At five o'clock she leaned back in her chair and threw her pen down in disgust. She had managed a paltry two hundred words, and the content was so bad, so derivative and generic, that she reckoned she might as well burn it.

She stretched the creases out of her back wondering what could be the matter with her. Where had this writer's block come from? Once upon a time she'd regularly managed four thousand words a day. *Good* words. If the landscape here didn't afford her any inspiration, she didn't know what would.

Tomorrow is another day, she reminded herself. *What I need now is a nice dinner and a glass of plonk.*

Supplies were scarce. Opening the fridge, she found milk, butter, cheese, a tatty old lettuce and a few slices of bacon wrapped in cling film. If she didn't throw the bacon away soon it would walk to the bin on its own. The freezer contained a number of frozen instant meals but none of them appealed to her. After a day that had consisted of Rice Krispies, toast and a couple of Custard Creams, she had a craving for proper food.

Proper food? That's it! I'll walk up to the Plume and have a meal there; let someone else cook for me!

The 'Plume' was the pet name the local community had given to their pub. The Plume of Feathers, a charming old eighteenth-century inn in Princetown, had a decent reputation locally for food and drink.

After a quick wash and brush up, Felicity donned a clean pair of jeans, a heavy sweater and her best Dr Martens and set off up the lane. She strolled past the

Gurney Farm, then stopped. On impulse she walked back to the gate, opened it—remembering to close it behind herself, of course; she didn't want the chickens getting out—and slid across the yard. Given the slipperiness of the mud beneath her feet, the pervading countryside smell of livestock and the failing light, she instantly wished she'd chosen to wear her oldest walking boots.

She paused outside the battered front door and pushed it open a fraction—it was never locked—and called out. "Yoo-hoo! It's me! Flick! Alright if I come in?"

Mrs Gurney, who had a voice like a Brixham fishwife, called back, "Course it is! Get in 'ere, you silly maid!"

Mary Gurney often referred to Felicity as a 'silly maid'. She had done so ever since Felicity had been a tot. Felicity didn't mind, knowing that coming from Mary, it was a term of endearment. She scraped her boots clean and poked her head into the kitchen. Mary and her husband Tom, sitting in chairs opposite each other in front of a roaring fire, had been listening to the early evening news on the radio over a cup of tea. Now Mary was on her feet and rushing towards her. Throwing her arms about Felicity, Mary kissed her on the cheek and then held her at arm's length, appraising her.

"Look at you, my lovely! We'd heard you'd taken Prior's Cross, so we've been expecting you. Why haven't you come sooner, you bad girl?"

Felicity fidgeted. "I'm sorry, Mary, truly. There is just

so much sorting out to do. And what with that and my writing ... you know how it is."

"Don't you be apologising, Flick," said Tom, enveloping Felicity in an enormous—if slightly whiffy—bear hug. Tom, or Farmer Tom as Felicity had called him when she was a child, much to his amusement, always stank of the farm. "We guessed you'd have a lot on your hands at the moment. Pay no mind to Mary." He let her go. "Look who's 'ere," he said, indicating the young man hovering behind him.

Jan, Felicity's childhood playmate, had pushed himself up from the dining room table where he'd been reading and taken a step towards her. He hesitated, slightly pink in the face.

"Hello, Flick," he said shyly, extending his hand. "It's good to see you."

Felicity grinned and knocked his hand away. Stepping forward she took him in her arms and gave him a hug. "Come here, you big lug. I've missed you."

As she stepped back, she reached up to ruffle his blond hair. "You need a haircut, mate."

Jan's blush deepened, but his smile told of his pleasure.

The Gurneys engaged in pleasant small talk for a while before Felicity told them, "I really came to say that I'm on my way up to the Plume for a meal. Anyone care to join me?" By anyone, of course, she meant Jan, but felt it would be impolite not to include Tom and Mary.

"That sounds good," said Jan eagerly. "I could murder a pint. Let me get my jacket."

Felicity raised her eyebrows at Tom and Mary.

"Ooh, a pint sounds smashing—"

Mary elbowed her husband. "But not tonight, dear. You've an early start tomorrow."

"Have I?" Tom frowned; it had obviously slipped his mind.

"Yes, you have," Mary replied firmly.

"Oh." Tom's mouth turned down at the corners.

"Another time?" Felicity offered, and the older Gurneys agreed that any time in the future would be perfect.

Jan and Felicity enjoyed their meal and a little banter with the locals. The Plume boasted a campsite in the field behind, but this time of year there were only a few hardy visitors. The local clientele was a mixture of farmers, prison officers from the nearby Dartmoor Prison, workers from the brewery and a miscellany of people who lived in Princetown but commuted to their various jobs in Plymouth or Exeter. They were a good crowd and fun to be around.

Jan and Felicity's conversation in the main dwelled on reminiscences of times past. "Do you remember when …?" and "Was it you or Daniel that …?" and "I wonder what happened to …"

As the bell rang for last orders and Jan returned from

the bar with their final round, Felicity changed the subject and mentioned the strange flash of light she had seen the previous night. "Did you see it?" she asked.

"No, I was asleep," Jan replied. "But Father did. He told me about it this morning. Thing is, it's not the first time."

Felicity looked surprised. "It's happened before?"

"Yes, apparently. Again, I haven't seen it, but I do recall Aunt Maud told me about an incident that happened to her once."

Jan had always referred to Maud as 'Aunt Maud'. She'd encouraged it when Jan and Felicity played together as children, and he had come to accept her as *his* Aunt Maud.

"When was this? Can you remember?" Felicity's interest had been piqued.

"Thinking about it, it can't have been long before she died. I used to pop in and see her on a regular basis, just to make sure she was alright and whatnot. You know, to see if she needed anything."

Felicity nodded. She placed her hand on his arm, silently thanking him, her eyes filling with unexpected tears. Jan offered a sympathetic smile in return and continued, "She was out with Fossy one night—"

"Fossy?"

"Oh! Of course. You probably didn't know. Aunt Maud 'acquired' a little terrier called Fossy. No idea where from. Kind of cute, in an ugly sort of way."

Felicity laughed. "That's cruel!"

"Listen, you didn't have the pleasure of meeting her."

"No, that's true." Felicity frowned. Aunt Maud had never mentioned a dog, but that explained all the dog food in the cupboard. "But that's sad. What happened to her?"

"One of the last times I saw Maud," he grimaced, "one of our last conversations ... she told me that she'd been walking with Fossy by the mire when this flash occurred. Aunt Maud was absolutely convinced that something had crashed into the mire, she was, and she was equally adamant that something had slid out of the wreckage and into the water."

"Eh?" Felicity wasn't following.

"I know. But that's what Aunt Maud said, bless her. Anyway, poor Fossy took off with the fright of it and was never seen again."

"Oh no! poor Fossy."

"Yes. Beside herself, Aunt Maud was. Expected Fossy to come home the next day but she never did." Jan pulled a face. "I went looking for her the day after Aunt Maud told me, but there was no sign of her. Such a shame. She probably got trapped in a bog. Aunt Maud was really fond of her. As I say, she was a bit ugly, but she was a lovely little dog. Very intelligent. Big black eyes."

"That's heartbreaking! Did you find any wreckage?"

"No." Jan shrugged. "To be honest, I didn't even look. Let's face it, if an aircraft had come down, the sky would have been filled with helicopters and the moor would have been crawling with air investigators." He picked up his pint. "There was none of that. I just think it was the fog playing tricks with her eyes."

"Maybe it was the pixies," smiled Felicity.

Jan laughed, "Yes! That would be it! She was being 'pixie led', as Mother would say."

They finished their drinks, bade a merry farewell to the landlord and those still slumped at the bar and stepped out into the cool night air. Walking back down the lane, Jan lapsed into silence. Felicity, puzzled, linked her arm through his and tugged him towards her. "I haven't said anything wrong, have I?" she asked.

Jan pulled up and stared in surprise. "Of course not. Why do you ask?"

"It's just that, well, you suddenly seem a bit distant?"

"Sorry, Flick, sorry," he laughed. "I don't mean to be. It's just me, you know what I'm like. You're my best mate. You always have been and always will be, no matter what happens to the two of us in later life."

Felicity squeezed his arm but kept her head averted lest he saw the sudden tears forming in her eyes. At the Gurneys' gate, with her emotions now back under control, Felicity finally looked up at him. "You go on in, big fella. I know you have to be up early tomorrow. I can walk the rest of the way on my own."

"Don't be daft. I won't let you do that at this time of night! I'll walk down with you."

"Very gallant of you, kind sir, but I'm a big girl now. I can look after myself."

Jan laughed, "You always could, mate. You always could."

With a gentle peck on his cheek, she left him and dawdled towards Prior's Cross, musing as she went. She had really enjoyed the evening. It had been wonderful to see the Gurneys again, particularly Jan. She thought of the two of them playing together in the garden while Aunt Maud sat in her rocker on the patio, watching and smiling indulgently. Jan had been a thin lad in those days, tough and wiry but skinny as a lath. Now he had filled out, standing a good six feet in height and was broad with thick, strong arms too. His skin, tanned brown by constant exposure to the elements, contrasted with his blond wavy hair. There was no doubt about it, Jan Gurney was a big handsome man. It obviously ran in the family, because both his father Tom and his brother Dan'l were similar.

Felicity recalled, once as a child, remarking to Tom on the thickness of his forearms. He had laughed and said, "Yes, my lovely. Have you never heard the saying, 'Devon born, and Devon bred, strong in the arm and thick in the 'ead'?"

The latter was not true of Tom at all, and it certainly wasn't true of Jan. He had always been a bright and inquisitive boy, regularly delighting Aunt Maud by bombarding her with all manner of questions about aircraft, steam trains, motor vehicles, rockets. Now that Felicity thought about it, what had been more surprising was how much Aunt Maud seemed to know about such things.

Later, Jan had gone to university to study for a BSc in Animal Husbandry, but he'd always maintained his interest in general science, particularly physics and engineering. No, there was nothing 'thick in the 'ead' about Jan Gurney.

With a start, Felicity realised she was at the gate of Prior's Cross. As she entered the kitchen with a view to pouring herself a glass of water to take up to bed, she was confronted by the remains of the bacon she had thrown in the bin earlier, scattered around on the floor.

Oh, Oggy! What am I going to do with you?

Her sleep that night was disturbed by vivid and constantly changing dreams. Afterwards she wondered if she hadn't been hallucinating, because the visions seemed to be just as real even when she was lying half-awake.

First, she was running on the moor. But not running as herself—she seemed to be too near the ground—but perhaps as if she were a very small child. She recognised the path by the mire along which she was running. Within the dream, she kept looking towards the mire, then at the path, then back at the mire ... always with a feeling of deep dread.

Fear.

Something was moving in the water. Something big and black.

Now she was running away, pelting across the open moor. She understood that she had to get away from the black thing. Whatever it was.

The next thing she knew, she was hiding in a damp

cave. Cowering in the corner. Afraid. So very, very frightened.

Finally, the dream changed again and she was somewhere she didn't recognise at all. A hill with lots of lush vegetation around, much of it a kind of red-coloured fern. There were strange creatures here. Hideous trolls, strange parrot-like creatures.

Only now, she didn't feel so frightened. That feeling had dissipated. Instead, all her anxiety had been replaced by a feeling of longing ... a deep yearning sensation.

She was sad. Plain and simple.

When Felicity arose the next morning, her head pounded and her limbs were stiff. She was so tired it felt as though she had never been to bed.

What the hell did I eat last night? Or more to the point, what did I drink?

She clutched at her forehead and downed a couple of painkillers with a pint of water, remembering that in spite of everything, she'd had a fun evening.

Jan Gurney, this headache is all your fault. I am going to kill you!

CHAPTER FOUR

Ted Blackstock staggered out of the Market Inn in Tavistock just before ten in the evening, emitting a loud belch as he did so. Four pints of Devon scrumpy usually had that effect on Ted.

He glanced across the River Tavy. On the other side of the water he could see the headlights of cars coming and going in Bedford car park. He cursed. That was his destination, the place he'd parked his own battered Land Rover. As the crow flies it wasn't far at all, just over the other side of the river. But in order to reach it he had to walk up Whitchurch Road, cross over the Abbey Bridge and then walk back down the river. There were more convenient parking places around the inn, but the police station was just a stone's throw away, and the Devon and Cornwall Police were particularly vigilant at chucking-out time. If they saw him leaving the Market Inn and getting into his car, a quick call over the radio and there would be a squad car waiting for him at the roundabout on the A386.

Grumbling to himself, he set off on what felt like a marathon walk. It was, in fact, less than half a mile, but after four pints of scrumpy, it might as well have been a marathon. Reaching the general vicinity of his car, he stood back from it, sticking to the shadows from where he could scour the area to make sure there were no police observing.

Figuring he was safe, he fumbled with his key fob and collapsed into the car. He eased it out of its parking space, swung out onto the Plymouth Road and turned right at the junction towards Bedford Square. He drove gently, not too slowly—that would arouse suspicion after all—but not too fast because that would get him pulled over. He was particularly careful at the roundabout onto the Okehampton Road; there was often a squad car parked on the verge there.

He drove north for only a few hundred yards before swinging right onto Mount Tavy Road, the B road that led to Princetown, where he lived. He took it steady, as the road here was narrow and windy, but once he'd passed Higher Longford Caravan Park, he was able to gun the engine, rattling across the cattle grid below Cox Tor at 70 mph. From here on, sheep ran free on the moor. There might easily be some on the road.

Ted didn't care. That was the farmer's lookout. If the farmer didn't want his livestock knocked into next week, they shouldn't let them wander free.

The thought had barely escaped Ted's narrow mind

when he spotted two red lights up ahead. He hit the brakes, violently bringing the car down to a crawl, and narrowed his eyes.

It could be a police car.

Moving more sedately, he approached the lights before braking again.

How could this be? He was virtually on top of the lights now, but these weren't car tail lights. They were much too close together for that. He ambled on a little further, then stopped altogether. Grabbing his torch from the glove compartment, he climbed out of his vehicle and walked slowly towards the lights.

Flicking on the torch, he shone it directly in front of him, lighting the way as he went. He slowed down, not quite sure what he was seeing. Crept a little closer ... and stopped dead.

It had to be the effects of the cider. He swallowed and blinked hard. In front of him stood the most vicious creature he had ever clapped eyes on.

It had to be a dog. That's what his brain told him. About the size of a wolfhound but with the build of a Rottweiler, he could clearly see the muscles in its shoulders rippling under the short grey fur. Its head was huge, supported on a neck the size of a tree trunk. Red eyes—what he'd imagined were tail lights just minutes before—were set back from the beetle brow and glowed like burning embers. The snout and lower lip were pulled back displaying terrifying fangs, several inches long. The creature, whatever it was, snarled and slavered and licked its lips as it regarded the man standing in front of it.

Ted Blackstock suddenly understood what it meant to be terrified. He inched slowly backwards. In turn, the hound took a few steps towards him.

Dropping his torch, Ted sprinted for the car. He leapt in and slammed the door. There was a brief frenzy of panic as he fumbled for his keys, one eye on the ignition and one on the monster outside.

The hound approached slowly and deliberately. Ted whimpered but finally located the correct key. He jammed it into the ignition, his hands shaking violently. "Come on!" he screeched. He turned the key. The car lurched and stalled. He'd left it in gear!

Frantic now, he wiggled the gear stick into neutral and tried again. *Yes!* The old Land Rover coughed and started. At the second it did so, the hound reached the passenger window. It paused there, staring at him calmly through malevolent red eyes. Ted sobbed, let out the clutch and at last the car lurched forward. He floored the accelerator and sped up the road, constantly checking behind him in his rear-view mirror.

A few minutes later, he screeched to a halt outside the Prince of Wales pub in Princetown, ignoring the *No parking* signs, and lurched up to the bar. He slapped a tenner on the counter and ordered a double whisky. A group of his friends sat at a table near the bar, and they regarded him with interest.

"'Ere, what's on, Ted? You look as though you seen a ghost."

Ted wheeled around, angry at the world and still

shaking. "I seen a ghost alright! A demon, t'were! A devil dog!"

"What?" exclaimed another, "I think you've had too much scrumps, me ol' mate."

"Probably just a dog got loose," offered a third. "If 'ee don' find 'is way 'ome the night, the farmer will settle with him in mornin'."

"I tell you this was no ordinary dog," Ted insisted, his voice cracking. "That weren't nobody's pet. It were pure evil. I were never so blimmin' frightened in my life."

"P'raps it were a hyena, escaped from Paignton Zoo?" someone suggested.

"Oh ah?" quipped the first. "And 'ow did he get up 'ere on the moor? Ketched a bus?"

The group gathered around the table roared with laughter. Ted turned away. He didn't laugh. It would be a while before he was able to laugh again.

Ted Blackstock would never *ever* forget what he saw on the moor that night.

CHAPTER FIVE

Felicity had completely forgotten that Wednesday happened to be market day in Tavistock. The car park had been swamped with muddy Range Rovers, battered old Datsuns and oddly-coloured Smart cars, so she struggled to find a space for her own ageing Nissan. As luck would have it, on Felicity's third turn around the perimeter and just as she was giving up all hope, an old lady in a bright yellow Beetle started reversing out of a space. Felicity snuck in before anyone else could beat her to it.

She stepped out of her car and glanced upwards. A typical October day. The sky seemed heavy, ready to set loose a downpour of biblical proportions unless the weather fairy changed its mind and blew the clouds away. You could never tell what sort of day you'd experience out here on the moor.

With written records dating back before the Norman Conquest, Tavistock was an ancient market town numbering fewer than 15,000 inhabitants. Nestled in the valley of the River Tavy on the western edge of Dartmoor and only a few miles from Cornwall, the pretty little town had always been popular with tourists. For centuries, Tavistock had once been at the heart of Devon's lucrative tin mining industry and, while that industry had long since disappeared, the landscape still bore the scars. It continued to be a popular centre for farming though, as witnessed by today's livestock auction.

Popping open the boot of her car, Felicity extracted a little wicker basket. She'd found it in the pantry this morning and had decided that, in the interests of using less plastic, she'd wield this and carry her purchases in style. Now she actually had to carry it in public, however, she couldn't help feeling that it looked a little twee.

Too bad. She didn't have anything else.

Tavistock market had three separate areas. After paying for her parking ticket, Felicity entered the food hall where you could find fish—landed at one of the nearby fishing towns—or dairy products and fruit and vegetables, many grown locally. Beyond that was the pannier market, with an open-air market immediately outside, another area where you could find farmer's produce but with the addition of cheap clothes, unusual jewellery, handmade shoes, bohemian clothes and plastic tat. The final third of the market was a little distance away and consisted of an enormous barn, open on the sides but divided into stalls, with a central viewing gallery and ring. This was where the farmers bought and sold their live produce on the first and third Wednesdays of every month.

As a child, Felicity had loved the auctions. She'd come here with Aunt Maud from time to time. She'd never been able to understand a word the auctioneers said, but Aunt Maud had explained what was happening and interpreted for her, and she'd come to appreciate the rhythm and excitement of the occasion.

Felicity bought what she needed from the food hall: some eggs, butter, cheese and a few mackerel for her dinner. It had been a while since she'd cooked mackerel; in fact, while living in the city she'd mainly settled for convenience foods, but Aunt Maud had loved all kinds of fish, and it seemed a nice thing to do, to eat a fish supper in her house and in her honour.

There remained the problem of cooking it, but in Felicity's experience, most fish could be seasoned, sprinkled with lemon and wrapped in foil before being bunged in the oven for a while.

Oh well. She'd soon find out.

She drifted through and out to the open-air market and browsed the vegetable stalls. What should she have with her fish? New potatoes would be nice, Jersey Royals even better, but this was the wrong season for them. She settled for small red potatoes, grown in good Devon dirt.

Felicity glanced up as heavy drops of rain spotted her head. She had a brolly in her basket, but she wasn't sure she'd be able to carry the basket and manhandle an umbrella at the same time as making her way through the crowd. At that moment, the melodic chanting of the auctioneer drifted out of the barn—that and the lure of being sheltered was enough to entice Felicity inside.

The smell hit her first, and she wrinkled her nose. The pungent odour of animals and farmers combined probably hadn't changed much in several thousand years. Undoubtedly the cattle market was hosed down and disinfected at the close of proceedings every day but, in the meantime, it quite assaulted her senses.

At the same time, the clamouring of bells, the lowing of cattle and baa-ing of sheep and the auctioneer's sing-song narration of all the dealings made her teeth rattle. By contrast, the farmers tended to talk in soft tones with thick Devonshire lilts and it was difficult to understand what they were saying.

"'Ee be a good'n."

"'Ere, Fred, 'ow be ackin' me ol' mate?

"Look at they thews on yon heifer! I be gwin bid on 'er!"

She smiled to hear the soft earnest tones of the farmers and sidled around the gathered throng until she could see the huge reddy-brown bull being paraded around the ring. The massive creature rolled his eyes at the crowd and stamped a little, hesitant to get too close to anyone, fearful of what was happening but still full of bravado. She admired that, while still feeling rather sorry for him.

It sounded like he would fetch a pretty penny.

"Coming through, make way! Coming through!" A young woman in a long brown overall and horse-riding boots led the next animal towards the ring. A beautiful brown cow with soft caramel eyes. Felicity was tempted to reach out and stroke it.

Dutifully, Felicity stepped back, finding herself shoulder to shoulder with a pair of farmers engaged in earnest conversation. She smiled at them politely and turned her gaze away, but while waiting for the woman and the cow to pass, she couldn't help but overhear their conversation.

"No idea what it were, Frankie?" the younger farmer, clad in an expensive fresh-looking Barbour jacket asked.

"None at all," the older farmer replied. "Must have been big. That's all I'm saying."

Felicity pricked her ears up. Writers, by their very nature, are nosy—and Felicity was nosier than most. She enjoyed listening to people's conversation. She would mentally squirrel away what she heard and write the substance down in her notebook later. The shortest of snippets could often provide a mine of inspiration.

"Where'd you find it, then?" the younger farmer was asking.

"Bottom of Bostock's field. You know, at the edge of Foxtor Mire?"

"Ah right, yeah. The grim mire side? Steep isn't it, there?"

"That's the one. Quite marshy at the bottom, but it's not too bad at the top, so I lets my horsies graze there from time to time. But knowing I'd be bringing him here today, I let old Bill, my prize bull, out there the other night."

"You're sure he wadn't stolen? It's been known."

"I thought the same, I'm telling you. He wadn't stole. I'm getting on, but I'm not senile yet. I locked that gate up proper. I walked round and round that cursed field looking for some gap in the fence. But there weren't no gap." The old farmer coughed, shuffling in place. "I did find summat though."

"What? What did you find, Frankie?"

"I found bones. At the bottom of the field, half in and half out of the marsh there."

"Not Bill, surely?" the young farmer sounded horrified. "There's nothing on this moor big enough to kill a bull as feral as that creature was, Frankie!"

"You'd think," Frankie sniffed and dashed at his nose with the sleeve of his filth-encrusted mustard-coloured jumper. "'Cept the bones I'm talking about looked like a rack of ribs and the spinal column of a big bit of beef, I'm telling you."

"Maybe a hunter? Some kids having a lark?" The younger farmer nodded. "Then some wild animals and birds picked the remains clean?"

"Some lark!" Frankie, until now, had remained calm, but now his voice started to rise. "I had a darn good look, and those bones had been sucked clean, not picked clean. There wasn't a morsel of flesh left on them. Whatever did that to my Bill, I ask you? 'Ee was as big as an 'ouse!"

CHAPTER SIX

Felicity, buried under the comfort of a thick duvet, awoke with a start. She gasped and raised herself up on one elbow, trying to shake off a strange dream about a huge side of spare ribs, and foxes from the nearby tor who'd come for tea. She blinked into the darkness, taking a deep breath and waiting for her heartbeat to settle to its normal rate.

What on earth is up with me?

She'd never been one to suffer from nightmares before. Occasional anxiety, perhaps, and this had a tendency to feed into her dreams. Introverted by nature, as most writers are, she supposed, she wasn't averse to spending time in her own company for long periods. But listening to yourself think for days on end can have a detrimental effect on your mental health, and overthinking is a writer's worst enemy. Coupled with an overactive imagination, this did mean she had some mighty peculiar dreams at times.

She snorted. The foxes had been cute at any rate.

Settling back on the pillow, she closed her eyes, taking slow, deep breaths, her limbs heavy, sleep just moments away ...

Rrrrrrrr-rrrrrrr-rrrrrrr-zzzzzzzzzzzz-eeeee.

She started at the sudden intrusion, her heart beginning to speed up again.

Rrrrrrrr-rrrrrrr-rrrrrrr-zzzzzzzzzzzz-eeeee.

Opening her eyes, she sat up and threw her covers aside. The dual-toned sound rattled around her skull. It wasn't that it was particularly loud, more that it had a high-pitched element to it, akin to nails on a blackboard.

Rrrrrrrr-rrrrrrr-rrrrrrr-zzzzzzzzzzzz-eeeee.

"What—?" Felicity shook her head, trying to banish the remnants of sleepiness, and swung sideways, her toes finding the cold bare floor. The wood beneath her feet vibrated, channelling the lower-pitched throbbing sound of the weird noise. "*What* is *that*?

Rrrrrrrr-rrrrrrr-rrrrrrr-zzzzzzzzzzzz-eeeee.

She pushed herself to standing, wobbled a little, then grabbed her robe from the end of the bed. Knotting the cord, she stood at the window and scanned the garden. From her vantage point at the front of the house, there wasn't a lot to look at. In the middle distance she could see the sodium light outside the Gurneys' barn, but it was the only bright spark in an otherwise dark landscape. There were no streetlights between here and there that might have shown up a combine harvester stuck in a hedge on the winding road outside or an overturned tractor in a field close by.

THE CREATURE FROM THE GRIM MIRE

Rrrrrrrr-rrrrrr-rrrrrrr-zzzzzzzzzzzz-eeeee.

Felicity rubbed her throat, increasingly uneasy. Perhaps someone was mowing a lawn somewhere, although who that might be or why they would be doing that at this hour of the night, she had no idea. Or maybe her washing machine had become stuck on a spin cycle? But, thinking about it, she hadn't turned the washing machine on before coming up to bed, so it couldn't be that.

Rrrrrrrr-rrrrrr-rrrrrrr-zzzzzzzzzzzz-eeeee.

On the verge of panic, Felicity made her way to the top of the stairs. She paused and stared down into the dark hallway. Something disturbed the shadows and she squealed, almost missing the first step. She lashed out and grabbed the banister to stop herself from tumbling forwards, painfully wrenching a nail backwards.

Mister Ogilvy trotted up the stairs towards her.

Meow, he yowled.

"Good grief." Felicity let out a shuddering breath, some of her tension ebbing away. "You scared me half to death!"

Meow, Mister Ogilvy replied and slunk past her.

"Where are you off to?" she asked, but he had disappeared into the darkness and she was alone once more.

Rrrrrrrr-rrrrrr-rrrrrrr-zzzzzzzzzzzz-eeeee.

Felicity gritted her teeth and slowly descended the stairs. Halfway down, the whining noise abated in the middle of its strange cycle. *Rrrrrrrr-rrrrrr-rr ...*

She waited on tenterhooks for the hideous noise to

begin again, but when it didn't, she took a moment to bask in the silence of the house.

But that in itself was part of the problem. While she'd been living up in Nottingham, where she'd read for a degree in creative writing, she had never known it to be quiet. Not totally. There had always been the sound of vehicles on a road close by, or revellers tipping out of pubs and clubs, or aeroplanes overhead, or dogs barking, or the general hubbub of city life.

Here in the country the sounds, like the lighting, were much less intrusive. Cows mooing, sheep baa-ing, owls hooting ... but at times, the world was so still and tranquil that you could be forgiven for thinking that you were the last person left alive in some dystopian science fiction story. She occasionally found the silence unnerving, as though the world was holding its breath, watching her, danger lurking in the gloom ...

Smiling at the dramatic turn her thoughts had taken, Felicity, aware that she was more awake than asleep now, decided to fix herself a warm drink. She jogged down the remaining stairs and, yawning, turned right, 180 degrees, into the hall.

And froze.

A man of average height and average build, distinguishable mainly by his bushy moustache and bright clear eyes that brimmed with canny intelligence, gazed over at her from underneath heavy eyebrows. Dark shadows surrounded his eyes, the lower lids of which had started to droop, lending him something of a hangdog expression. Full of character, nonetheless, there was a hint of profound sadness about his face. Dressed in a smart, although slightly dated suit, he stood at the entrance to the kitchen, blocking her way. Felicity opened her mouth to scream, and he looked straight at her, lifting his finger to his lips.

She bit down on her hysterics, fearing he had a weapon, a gun maybe. Instead she let out a whimper, akin to a rapidly deflating balloon.

From behind him, within the kitchen, she could distinctly make out the noise of someone slurping and slobbering noisily.

"Sssh," the man said, "you'll disturb them."

Them? There were more?

Fearing for her life, Felicity made a run for the front door, her fingers fumbling to undo the safety chain and turn the key. It seemed to take an age, but finally everything lined up and she was able to fling the door wide and catapult herself out into the cold night air. She ran down the drive in her bare feet and out into the lane, only then realising she didn't have a way to alert anyone to her plight. Her mobile was inside, there were no phone boxes for miles around. Her nearest neighbour was a long walk for someone clad only in a thin nightshirt and a fuzzy bathrobe with no slippers on their feet.

She skidded to a halt, her feet slipping around in the mud, a light drizzle falling and coating her hair and face with a gentle layer of moisture. She turned about, gazing at Prior's Cross with dread. How had the men entered? Had she left the back door unlocked? She didn't think so.

She'd been a little OCD about security since moving into the property.

Had they come in via a window then? That seemed most likely. But where was their vehicle? Nothing had been parked in the drive. The only possibility was that they'd parked further up the lane, tucked the car out of sight somewhere and proceeded on foot.

Had the whining noise been something to do with them gaining access to her property?

Nobody had followed her out. They didn't seem interested in her at all.

Feeling a little heartened by that thought, Felicity tightened up the cord on her dressing gown and tiptoed back towards the house. She by-passed the open front door and instead hugged the wall and slid along the side. Approaching the kitchen window, she held her breath and, on a count of three, craned her head sideways to peep through. The light had been left on inside, but of the men, there was no sign.

Frowning, Felicity pressed her head against the glass, straining to see around corners, through doors and into the pantry, but of course that was an impossibility.

She tutted. The sound, loud in the quiet night, startled her. She glanced around, her heart beating in fear, expecting someone to rush at her. But nobody did.

Where are they?

She continued around to the back of the house, her bare feet squelching across the lawn. All of the windows were intact. That left the kitchen door. She retraced her steps and approached it carefully. The outdoor broom had been fortuitously abandoned here earlier in the day, left to lean against the wall until Felicity remembered to return it to the shed, and now she grabbed it. An opportunistic weapon.

Hardly able to breathe, she steeled herself, squaring up to the wooden door that separated her from the kitchen. She reached out and clasped the handle, meaning to fling it wide open and surprise anyone inside, but the surprise was all hers.

The door was locked.

She stepped back, eyes wide. With nothing else for it, she continued her circuit of the house, checking on every window, unable to find a different way into the property.

That left only the front door, standing wide open, just as she had left it.

She edged inside, eyes straining as she peered into shadowy corners. She craned her head back, listening for the sound of footsteps on the old floorboards above, but there was nothing. Down here, the living room remained closed up and dark, just as she had left it, the dregs of the fire burned to ash.

The light in the kitchen glowed with warmth. Somewhere, liquid plinked steadily.

Dink. Dink. Dink.

Felicity swallowed. Nothing for it but to check out the kitchen.

Slowly, painfully, still clutching the broom, she inched forwards until she was standing in the spot where she'd seen the man less than ten minutes previously. She tilted her upper body forwards to peer into the kitchen.

Nobody there.

She crept forwards, into the light. The kitchen tap hadn't been turned off properly. Water dripped onto a pile of bowls in the sink. She had not abandoned them there when she went up to bed. The fridge door stood ajar too. She simply would not have left it that way.

She frowned down at the floor in bemusement. Whoever had been in the house had eaten the entire contents of her fridge—all the cheese and vegetables she had bought in the market earlier—*and* raided the bin for the remains of her mackerel supper *and* emptied her cupboards *and* opened the cans of beans and tomatoes and peaches.

They'd had themselves a proper feast and created a mega-mess in the process of it.

What sort of burglars eat you out of house and home?
Hungry ones?
Drug addicts?

Felicity gasped at the thought and backtracked into the hall, picking up the receiver of the large old-fashioned heavy black phone that Aunt Maud had favoured. She half expected the wires to be cut, but as she placed it to her ear she heard the familiar burring sound.

She quickly dialled three nines.

It rang once before connecting. The operator answered. "Emergency. Which service?"

"Police," Felicity said, keeping her voice low, surprised that she had the capacity to speak at all given how tight her throat was. "Please hurry. I think I have a home invasion."

THE CREATURE FROM THE GRIM MIRE

The police were unable to find any trace of a break-in. They had arrived just before daylight and walked the perimeter several times. Felicity was of the opinion they didn't quite believe her tale of a break-in anyway. DS Alderson, a tall and sporty man in his early fifties with a jagged red scar on his neck that suggested its own interesting story, had asked her several times to repeat what had happened.

Never once had he taken notes.

Now he gazed down at the smears of tomato sauce and the clods of drying spaghetti hoops on Felicity's kitchen floor and pursed his lips. "Hmmm," he ventured.

"Hmmm?" Felicity asked. "That's all you can say?" She tightened her dressing gown cord for the umpteenth time and gathered together the material at the neck. Now, with the sun rising in a watery-blue sky and several suited and booted detectives roaming her property, not to mention the man and woman in uniform combing through her flower beds, she felt distinctly underdressed.

He lifted his head and studied her through cool blue eyes.

"I'm in fear of my life," she faltered. "Or I was. Last night, anyway."

"I appreciate that, Ms—Miss—ah, Westmacott. I can assure you the cottage appears secure."

"Appears?" Felicity repeated, her voice little more than a bleat of distress.

DS Alderson nodded, and this time he cracked a

reassuring smile. "You can always improve your home security, of course. Everyone can." He jabbed a finger at the kitchen window. "I see you already have locks on your windows and doors so that's a start. Given that you live here alone—"

"I have a cat," Felicity blurted. "Well, he came with the house. My Aunt left him to me."

"Alright," DS Alderson continued. "Given that you live here alone *with your cat*, it might be worth your while investing in an alarm system."

Do I look like I'm made of money? Felicity wanted to retort.

Perhaps he read her mind because he went on, "You can find one that will suit your specific circumstances, so for example if Tiddles needs to come and go—"

"Mister Ogilvy," Felicity interjected.

"Right. If Mister Ogilvy needs to come and go during the night then you can turn off the sensors in part of the house, or you could set it so that the alarm only comes on if the doors and windows are opened."

"I see," Felicity said. "That's useful information, thank you." *Although the fact remains, Detective, that unless I write another book soon, there'll be no advance, no royalties and no money in the pot for cat biscuits, let alone fancy alarm systems.*

"A good security company will be able to recommend something to suit your budget," DS Alderson added. "I have some leaflets in the car. I'll leave one with you."

He finally drew his notebook and a biro out of his pocket and scribbled down a few notes.

Felicity waited, feeling as forlorn as a schoolgirl outside the headmaster's office. When he'd finished, she walked him to the front door. "It's a strange one, Ms Westmacott, but that doesn't mean we're not taking this seriously." He snapped his notebook closed. "If you have any further cause for concern, you mustn't hesitate to call 999 straight away." He indicated his car. "I'll get you the leaflet about recommended security systems."

"Thank you." Felicity watched him rummage in his boot until her attention was caught by Mister Ogilvy. He sauntered towards the house with a large rat dangling from his mouth.

"Where do you think you're going with that?" Felicity demanded, horrified that he thought he could bring it into her house. Mister Ogilvy gazed up at her, innocent eyes wide. The tail of the rat wiggled and Felicity, recoiling from the sight, shrieked.

Suddenly all five police officers, alerted by her scream, were thundering towards her, intent on arresting her burglar. DS Alderson, returning to the scene first, staggered to a stop directly behind Mister Ogilvy.

He stared at the cat.

Mister Ogilvy turned his head and stared right back at him.

Neither of them blinked.

The rat's tail wiggled again, and DS Alderson shot backwards. "Ewww. Yuck." He grimaced at Felicity. "It looks like you have a little clearing up to do, Ms Westmacott. I'd best leave you to it." He edged a little closer to her and stretched his arm out, unwilling to get too close to Mister Ogilvy and his prize, and handed the leaflet over. "Stand down, guys!" he called to his team, backtracking to his car, the other police officers similarly beating a retreat.

Felicity watched them leave, torn between feeling relieved that she could finally grab a shower and get dressed, and worried about being alone in the house.

Mister Ogilvy dropped the rat at Felicity's feet. It hit the ground with a surprisingly heavy thunk.

"Ick," Felicity gagged. She stepped smartly into the hall. "You can enjoy your catch out there," she informed her cat. "No offence, but I don't want anything quite so alien in here."

And with that, she closed the door in his face.

Felicity turned off the water and stepped out of the shower. In the ensuing silence she heard her mobile phone singing away to itself. *Bat Out of Hell* was her current ringtone of choice. There was something about it that cheered her immensely.

She dashed out of the bathroom and into the bedroom. The display told her that Sasha Bancroft-Hulme wished to speak with her.

Sasha had been Felicity's literary agent for the past five years. She'd been blown away by Felicity's first novel, written partly while Felicity had still been at university, and had managed to negotiate a three-book deal with a modest advance on Felicity's behalf.

The first novel, *Clawing back the Knight*, a historical werewolf horror novel, had sold like hotcakes. The second, *Hungry like the Werewolf*, had sold moderately well on the back of the first. The third, *Weird Wolf*, had barely made a dent in the best-seller charts.

Ever since that release, Felicity had been struggling to come up with something interesting to pique the public's attention once more.

So far, she'd failed.

Felicity groaned. Sasha Bancroft-Hulme? Could this day get any more tiresome? Checking her bedside clock she realised it had only just gone nine. There was an awful lot of day left.

The phone stopped ringing and went to answerphone. Sasha hung up. Seconds later, *Bat Out of Hell* filled the air again.

Felicity grimaced. Sasha was obviously desperate to talk to her.

She picked up the phone and stared at the screen. As much as she liked Sasha, she wasn't sure that she really wanted to engage in a conversation with her. Not right now. But what choice did she have?

She thumbed the screen. "Hi, Sasha!" she sang, hoping she sounded convincingly upbeat.

Sasha's well-modulated tones greeted her. "Hey, Flick! Did I wake you up?"

Felicity pulled her towel tighter. "Not at all. Not at all. I was in the shower."

"How are you liking it down there in the wilds of Cornwall?"

"It's Devon," Felicity reminded her. "I'm on Dartmoor."

"Oh, that's right, of course. I thought it was Exmoor."

Felicity bit her tongue. *Exmoor* was in North Devon. *Bodmin* Moor was in Cornwall, but she supposed it was all the same to Sasha, who had a second home in Brighton and didn't venture to the south-west if she could help it.

"It's ... erm ... fabulous for the most part," Felicity told her.

"You don't sound too sure, hon."

Felicity blew out her cheeks. "I thought I had an intruder last night," she confessed.

"Really? How exciting!" Sasha trilled.

"It scared me half to death," Felicity admitted.

"Oh Flick, my dear girl." Sasha sounded a little more sympathetic, but Felicity decided she was probably laying it on. "Store up that emotion and use it in your next novel."

Felicity rolled her eyes. *Here it comes*, she thought.

"Because as you know, I needed to touch base with you. We've been looking for another deal for you but so far I haven't managed to secure anything."

You're only as hot as your last bestseller, Felicity silently reproached herself.

"Have you come up with anything yet?" Sasha asked.

"I'm playing with a few ideas," Felicity lied. Her creative well appeared to have dried up, but Sasha didn't need to know this. Not yet, anyway.

"Anything I can flog to publishers?"

"I, erm, maybe ... I just need to tweak it."

"Alright. That's marvellous, darling. Can you send me an outline, as soon as?"

"As soon as," Felicity promised.

"Excellent stuff. Great chatting, hon. Bye for now!"

She'd hung up before Felicity could respond. "Bye," she said to thin air.

"Shucks."

She slumped back on the bed, the phone in her hand, her hair drying out beneath the towel. *I just need to tweak it*, she'd told Sasha. *Tweak what?* She had the grand total of zero words in her work-in-progress.

Unless she pulled herself together very soon and found some inspiration from somewhere, she was going to be a horror writer without an agent, without a contract and without an income.

And that was more horrifying than anything she could dream up and put in a story.

Felicity finally made it downstairs just before eleven. She'd planned to spend at least some of the day writing, but heading back into the kitchen to make herself a coffee in lieu of breakfast, she realised that nobody else was going to clear the mess that had been left by her intruders except for her.

Grumbling, she searched for cleaning materials. Aunt Maud had always kept the place spick and span and there was no shortage of bleach and floor cleaner. Her brooms and mops, dustpan and brush were all neatly stored, awaiting a good workout.

With nothing else for it, Felicity had to roll up her sleeves. She started by sweeping up the congealing debris of spaghetti hoops and dollops of tomato into the dustpan and then got down to the nitty-gritty of mopping. When the floor had been given a once-over, she realised it would need a second go, but at least now she could walk around without slipping everywhere.

Taking a breather, she leaned against the sink while the kettle boiled and surveyed what else needed cleaning. The doors of the kitchen cabinets were slick with red and orange stains. Felicity picked up the dishcloth to swab the one nearest her. Whoever had opened this cupboard, fingers covered in sweetcorn and tomato sauce by the look of it, had left some very interesting patterns. A chain of circles, like little suckers, decorated the once-pristine surface.

How peculiar, Felicity thought.

She scrubbed harder. No fingerprints here at all, just these sucker marks. Every cabinet door seemed to be the same. And now when she thought about it, the kitchen floor had been covered in them too. She'd imagined that those circles in the spaghetti juice had belonged to the bottom of someone's expensive shoes.

And obviously the police had thought so too, because they had taken photos.

But who had been walking up the side of her kitchen cupboards in shoes?

More to the point, what sort of burglars broke into

your house in a team, didn't steal anything, practically ate you out of house and home and then disappeared without trace? She would need to go shopping again very soon. All she had left in her cupboards were a couple of tins of pilchards—presumably for Mister Ogilvy because surely no human enjoyed eating pilchards—and some dried pasta.

She drank a mug of instant coffee in between fevered scrubbing of the cabinet doors. Her arms ached with the exertion of it all. Aunt Maud's kitchen was four times the size of her old one in Nottingham. It turned out there was something to be said for minuscule flats and houses after all. She hadn't realised how onerous cleaning Prior's Cross House would be. Maybe remaining here for the long term wouldn't suit Felicity, after all.

Once she'd finished the cabinet doors she gave the floor another going over, and this time restored a little shine to the pale grey slate tiles. She rinsed out the mop and bucket, made herself another cup of ghastly instant and headed into the study.

Pushing the door to, but not closed, she collapsed into the chair at the desk, exhausted by a lack of sleep and the deep cleaning exercise she'd unexpectedly had to undertake.

She pulled her notebook towards her and opened it. The pages, ominously bare, stared back at her in accusation. She flipped open the laptop, as though that would provide some much-needed inspiration, but ended up checking out her social media and reading the latest news.

I should try and do some work, she reminded herself. *Sasha needs me to send her something. Anything will do. I just need to look a little more willing.*

Maybe she should try something a bit different from werewolf stories. Dartmoor was such a wonderfully atmospheric place, she should bathe in its mysterious beauty and come up with something new. Perhaps a horror story with a ghost ...

From the kitchen came a thunk and a rattle. Felicity glanced up and frowned. It sounded as though something had fallen. A broom or a mop, perhaps.

Nothing to worry about.

Prior's Cross House would make an excellent location for a ghost story. Felicity pulled her notebook closer and scribbled that down. She started to list ideas. A writer inherits the house after her aunt has died. Suddenly her ghost haunts—

Clunk.

Felicity raised her head again, listening.

That had sounded very much like a tin of something landing on the kitchen floor. The precious pilchards?

That dratted cat!

"Mister Ogilvy?" Felicity called, forgetting that cats weren't like dogs. They didn't come when they were summoned.

Rolling her eyes, Felicity pushed her chair back. "Just as I was getting somewhere," she murmured.

She pulled open the study door and gasped as a tall, dark shadow flitted across the kitchen door.

"Is there somebody there?" she demanded, her heart

starting to beat harder. What was going on in this house? She was reminded of the notes she'd just written and made the connection instantly.

I have a ghost!

Biting down on a scream, glad of the daylight, she covered her mouth with her fist, fighting the urge to run outside.

"Hello?" she called, her voice trembling. "M-m-mister Ogilvy? Oggy?"

Ssssslurrp. Ssssslurrp.

The oddly wet noises turned Felicity's stomach. She darted a longing glance at the front door, wishing she could dash outside and phone DS Alderson again—after all, he'd told her she could—but the memory of the police finding absolutely no evidence of a break-in was too recent for her to bow to the temptation. It would be humiliating to call him again and then find out Mister Ogilvy had decided to suck the brains out of his latest rat conquest on her clean kitchen floor.

Hair standing on end, she took a few steps forward, willing herself to show a little more courage.

Ssssslurrp. Ssssslurrp.

She nudged against her jacket hanging on a peg next to the front door. Something in the pocket jangled. The noise in the kitchen cut off mid-slurp.

Skin crawling, she crept along the hallway all the way to the kitchen before gently leaning forwards and gazing through the doorway.

There was no one, and no cat, in evidence. The back door remained closed. However, a tin of pilchards lay on the floor. It had been opened somehow, and the contents had spilled out creating yet another stinky mess on the tiles.

Mister Ogilvy?

"I'll kill him!" Felicity grumbled.

And yet ... what sort of a cat can open a tin by itself?

Eyes wide, Felicity examined the worktops and the cupboard doors, looking for evidence that anyone else could be to blame.

Nothing. And nobody.

A clunk and a clink from behind startled Felicity. This time she did shriek. Whirling about she lashed out with both arms, although nothing was anywhere near her. Mister Ogilvy, half in and half out of the cat flap with a fresh rat in his mouth, paused and quickly appraised her, unsure whether to proceed or reverse.

Felicity moaned. If Mister Ogilvy had been outside, who or what had been in the kitchen?

She wailed, cold sweat beading on her forehead. How could she live in this house with all the bumps in the night and the strange goings-on? What had seemed like providence when Aunt Maud had bequeathed the old house to her had now turned into one of Dante's circles of hell.

Felicity shook with fear. It seemed impossible that a woman who had once written a horror story that had temporarily outsold Stephen King had turned out to be so scared of ghosts and ghouls that she couldn't countenance being alone in this beautiful house for one more night.

There was nothing for it. Prior's Cross would have to go on the housing market, and she would need to start clearing out all of Aunt Maud's old bits and bobs.

And with that, Felicity raised her eyes to the attic and grimaced.

CHAPTER SEVEN

Having thoroughly searched the main bedroom where Felicity lay asleep, Mister Ogilvy ventured out onto the landing where he stood scenting the air for a while. The door of the second bedroom was slightly ajar, but it was enough for him to slide his lithe little body through. It was dark, but that had never been an impediment for the cat; his green eyes shone as he systematically searched the room.

Nothing. No amount of looking and no amount of sniffing revealed anything, but nonetheless his whiskers twitched. Something else, besides him, was stalking the night.

He decided to check the kitchen next. That's where they usually were.

Creeping down the stairs, his paws hardly making the slightest indent on the carpet, he slunk into the hallway. The moonlight shining through the small window above the door illuminated one side of the hall, so Mister

Ogilvy kept to the dark side, skulking through the gloomy area, a soundless stalker in the shadows. The door to the kitchen had been propped open, and from inside he could hear a pattering sound.

Mice?

That would be nice.

I might even catch one tonight!

Mister Ogilvy leapt into the kitchen, his night vision now fully adjusted. Like most cats, he could see in the dark almost as well as in daylight. He planted himself in the dead centre of the floor, where he could take in the whole room.

No mice?

Nothing at all!

He heard the faintest lapping sound coming from above his head. Swivelling, he stared up at the kitchen sink. Standing on the edge of the basin was the strangest bird he had ever seen. It was huge! As big as the ones that flew in circles over the barn. He had always steered well clear of those.

But this bird was different. It had a large head and, instead of a beak, a pair of strong jaws. The kind of jaws you'd find on a dog, with a row of teeth top and bottom. Instead of wings, the creature had a pair of what could only be described as *arms* extending out from the body. And then, there was the small matter of the tail. Instead of tail feathers, this creature actually had a long tail similar to—although not as handsome as—his own.

So what made it a bird?

Apart from the head, the whole of the body was

covered in feathers: bright blue, sunshine yellow and phone-box red.

As Mister Ogilvy had entered, the creature had turned its head to look at him, but now, as if indifferent to his presence, it returned to lapping the remnants of Felicity's dinner from the plate in the sink.

Mister Ogilvy was more than a little taken aback. Birds tended to fly off when they saw him.

Perhaps this one can't fly?

The thought pleased him. He would make short work of it if that was the case.

With one nimble leap, he sprang onto the draining board, his claws out. Almost simultaneously, the creature gracefully bounded over to the kitchen table. It turned and faced Mister Ogilvy, its mouth open in an almost-smile, its peculiar hands extended.

Perplexed, Mister Ogilvy hopped down to the floor. He circled the table a few times, not quite sure whether to sniff or hiss. The creature kept a careful eye on the cat, adjusting its position so that it could keep an untrusting eye on him. Mister Ogilvy paused, uncertain how to proceed. He glared up at the creature, narrowing his eyes and starting to keen, then dropped his weight onto his rear legs ready to spring. But before he could turn thought to deed, the creature pulled its lips back wide and emitted an ear-piercing hiss.

Mister Ogilvy, alarmed by the sound, turned as if to flee, but curiosity got the better of him. He paused and swung about, circling the table once more. Whatever else Mister Ogilvy—do-er of daring things, fearless night hunter extraordinaire—was, he reminded himself, he was not a coward.

He *would* have that bird.

He paused once more and made ready to spring. Suddenly there was a flash of green, and the multi-tentacled creature, moving like lightning, appeared out of nowhere. It grabbed the bird thing and wrapped it securely in one of its tentacles before dancing up to the store cupboard. It waited there, regarding Mister Ogilvy with enormous eyes.

Mister Ogilvy took this as a challenge and sprang up to the cupboard. The green thing spun away, navigating the shelving with astonishing speed. It slipped out through the small window and disappeared.

Snarling and meowing his frustration and pleased that there had been no one around to witness his humiliation, Mister Ogilvy made his way up the stairs and back to the bedroom. He clambered up next to Felicity, sharing her warmth, but he didn't sleep for some time. He stared out of the window and into the darkness beyond, his green eyes unblinking.

Felicity groaned and rubbed her eyes.

What time is it?

Something had disturbed her. She remained in place, warm under her duvet, ears straining. Was it her imagination, or had she just been awoken by a shrill scream? The sound created when high-pressure steam was vented by one of those wonderful old locomotives on the Dartmouth Steam Railway. She'd always loved to watch those as a kid. But it couldn't be the railway that had made that noise now. It was too far away. There hadn't been trains on the moor for decades.

She shook her head, trying to clear her fuzzy mind. That sound? It had to have been part of her dream. She'd been having another one. The latest in a long line of similar themes. This time she'd been out on the moor, hiding in a cave, shivering. Watchful. Not far away, just a little over to her right on the nearby hillside, she had spotted something ... something black and shiny ... something that shimmered as it moved in the moonlight. She hadn't known what to do. Should she stay here hiding in the darkness of the cave, watching it? Or should she flee across the moor, away from it?

Tense and afraid, she'd opted to remain in place, safe in her cave but horribly confused, her heart aching with loneliness.

Felicity took a deep breath and exhaled her anxiety away. She pondered; should she get up and make a cup of tea? Mister Ogilvy, snuggling next to her, meowed and growled all at once.

"What's up, Oggy? Did a mouse frighten you?" Felicity smiled. He could be a terrible nuisance, but he was a dear little thing most of the time. She gently stroked him as he lay purring beside her until he slipped into sleep.

Felicity remained awake for some time before she finally dozed too, but even then her slumber was not deep and relaxing. She hovered somewhere between sleep and wakefulness, neither one nor the other, and still the dreams or visions came.

Now she was moving among troll-like creatures, half gorilla, half man. She was not afraid. They were friendly, chattering in a language she could not understand. One held his arms outstretched towards her, evidently pleading for something. Others joined him, beckoning for her to come to them, but she couldn't approach them. Every time she tried, they seemed to get further away.

Her heart sank in dismay and she experienced an overwhelming feeling of yearning, longing for something that she didn't quite understand. That not unfamiliar feeling of deep, deep sadness.

She turned onto her back, careful not to disturb Oggy, fully awake now and feeling completely perturbed. It had all seemed so real. She wondered what it all meant. If these dreams or visions, or whatever they were, continued, she might need to seek help. Proper professional help, from a psychiatrist.

For heaven's sake, she thought, *I'm going crazy!*

CHAPTER EIGHT

Felicity was breathing heavily when she reached the gates to the Gurney Farm. It was a hard pull up the lane towards Princetown even if it wasn't far. She was suitably attired, wearing ragged Levi jeans, knee-length wellies and a heavy pullover over a t-shirt. Autumn was on the cusp of handing over to winter and it could be quite chilly up on the moor.

"Hello, Mary!" she called over the gate. Mrs Gurney was busy feeding the chickens.

"Why, Flick, m'dear," answered Mary Gurney. When her face lit up that way, her cheeks formed into the little rosy apples that Felicity remembered so well. "'Tis good to see you, m'lovely. Are you beginning to settle into the old house?"

"Pretty well. It really is nice." Felicity hesitated. "A bit spooky, perhaps. Noises at night, that sort of thing."

"Get on with you, you silly girl!" Mary chastised her, full of mock scorn. "It's just the old house talking to you."

"Talking to me?"

"Aye. Telling you about her day," Mary nodded. "You have to answer her. Tell her about your'n. She'll settle down right enough then."

Felicity laughed at that quaint notion. Mary was full of them, bless her. "I'll do that next time." She nodded in the direction of the house. "How are Tom and the boys?"

"They'm all well. Tom's out back in the winterin' barn, getting it ready. Jan's up on the hill and ... 'ere, listen, you hab'n heard about Dan'l, I don' suppose?"

Felicity raised her eyebrows inquisitively. She wasn't averse to a little gossip.

"Well! The goin's on," continued Mary. "He took up with the eldest Trelawney girl. Kathy. You know the Trelawneys out at White Horse Farm near Moretonhampstead? 'Arry and Clara? They have three daughters and no son."

Felicity had absolutely no idea who Mary was talking about, but she nodded just the same.

"Well, Clara and me, we've known each other a good long while, an' I bumped into her in town the other day. She been clapping 'er hands as you can imagine. She thought she was getting rid o' one of they girls. 'They'm maids be the bane o' my life,' she used to say to me."

Mary threw the last of the corn to the chickens that clucked and pecked busily at her feet. "Well 'Arry, 'ee up and asks Dan'l to come and live at the White Horse with Kathy, with a view to taking over the farm in a couple o' years' time. Well, Flick, I laughed 'til I cried. See, Clara still has her three maids at home but now she has a son-in-law as well!"

Felicity laughed along with Mary, as much at the older woman's mirth as anything else. "Aww. Dan'l will do okay there, I think," she said.

"Course 'ee will. He'll have to get used to cattle, mind. Cos 'Arry's is a mixed farm and Dan'l's only ever tended sheep, but he'll adapt. 'Ee's a born farmer. Chip off the ol' block." Mary nodded proudly.

"Do you mind if I go through and see Tom?"

"He'd be well 'mazed if you didn't, my girl!"

Felicity crossed the yard—as ever feeling thankful that she was wearing her wellies—and slipped around the side of the house into the wintering barn. Tom greeted her with tender affection, the daughter he'd always wanted but never had. They chatted for a while before Tom said, "If yer lookin' fer Jan, 'ee's t'other side o' Ter Hill, checkin' the ewes."

Felicity flushed. "I wasn't looking for him, but I'm sorry I missed him. It's always nice to see him."

"I'll tell 'im you called, 'ee'll be sad 'ee missed yer."

"I'll pop by again soon," Felicity promised. "By the way Tom ... a couple of days ago, Wednesday morning, I think, and very early, I heard a strange noise. Do you have a new machine that makes a high-pitched whining noise?"

Tom frowned, thinking, then shook his head, puzzled. "No, Flick. You know I'm not one for gadgets. The last machine I bought was that four-wheel drive buggy thingie we use to round up the sheep. Could that have been what you heard? Jan tends to go out on it most mornings."

"What time was that, Tom?"

"'Bout 'arf six."

"No, this was more like four in the morning."

Tom burst out laughing. "Lord, no, Flick. Jan would still be in the land of nod. Funny though, I tend to wake at that time. I've not heard nought."

"Did you see the lightning?"

"I did that, that was some flash! But I don't think it were lightning. There wer'n't no thunder."

"I wondered if it was a long way away? Maybe a lightning strike on Yes Tor?"

Tom shook his head. "No, wrong direction, Flick. Our bedroom window faces south, and it lit up the whole room. I reckon it came from your direction. I thought it might be the marsh gas igniting on the mire. I've never seen it myself, but I have heard of it." He paused for a moment, studying the young, preoccupied woman in front of him. "Summat worrying you, Flick?"

Felicity told him about the noises, feeling rather silly as she did so, although she appreciated getting it off her chest. She told him about the police visit too. Tom didn't laugh at her as she'd feared he might. Instead he knitted his brows together in concern. "Listen," he said, "Why don't Jan an me an' the dogs come down an' have a sniff aroun'? If there's anything there we'll sniff 'er out?"

"Oh, no Tom, I'm just being silly," Felicity protested. "You've got enough on your plate. I'll be okay." She could have bitten her tongue off. She would have loved someone to mooch round Prior's Cross on her behalf.

"Well, Flick, if you do need a hand at any time, you know we'll be here for you."

The buzzing high-pitched whine of a motorcycle zooming into the yard interrupted them.

"Is that the sound you heard, Flick?"

"No, it was nothing like that."

"Well that's Jan on our buggy, so Lord knows what it was if it wasn't that."

Two bright-eyed Border collies bounded into the barn behind the bike, mouths open and tongues lolling. They jumped up at Tom, wagging their tails furiously. "Hey boys!" Tom gushed. "Here they are, Flick. The real workers on this farm. You remember 'Ol Jack here, gettin' a bit long in the tooth now. I s'pose I'll have to look for another young 'un soon. And this 'ere is Jed. You remember Ol' Tess? This is her son. He's a good lad. Earns his keep, but not a patch on Tess. She could read my mind, I swear it."

"Oh, dear," Felicity's face fell. "Is Tess ..."

"Lord no, she just retired. The arthritis got her. Not surprising really. She could run all day if you asked her. She'll be out in a minute to sort these boys out. You should see her at night, Flick. She lies in front of the fire and lets Mother massage her legs, a right pair of softies together, those two."

As if on cue, a third Border collie slowly limped into the barn and made her painful way towards Tom. Her coat was a little shaggy and her jowls grey, but the eyes still shone with warm intelligence. As she approached, the two boys moved away. It wasn't that they were frightened of Tess, it was more a kind of canine *respect*, Felicity decided.

The two younger dogs, working as a team, advanced on Felicity, walking around her, sniffing, then both sat directly in front and stared up at her.

"They're waiting for you to run off, Flick, so they can round you up!" laughed Tom.

Jan ambled into the barn, brows knitted together in a deep frown, but as soon as he spotted Felicity, his face lit up in delight. Eyes glowing—as brightly as the dogs'—he bounded over and caught her up in an embrace. Stepping back, he peered down at his clothes, examined his hands and grimaced, realising what he'd done. "Oh, I'm sorry, Flick! I wasn't thinking. I've just got back from the fields."

Felicity laughed. "That's alright, mate. I've got my *go-to-the-farm-and-get-manhandled-by-farmers* clothes on, so no harm done."

"Something wrong, boy?" Tom asked gravely. He had noticed the look of concern on Jan's face when he had first entered.

"We've lost a ewe, Father."

"Oh," Tom grunted, unhappy. "Foxes?"

"I don't think so. There was nothing left on the bones. I've never seen anything like it in my life." Jan ran a filthy hand through his hair. "A fox will eat his fill at the kill, then rip off some flesh to take back for the cubs, leaving the rest behind. I tell you Father, these bones were completely bare. Even the insides were completely gone."

"A dog then?" suggested Felicity.

Tom shook his head. "Dogs that worry sheep tend to kill and move on without eating any of the flesh. They leave more behind than a fox would." He shrugged helplessly. "It must have been the crows that got to it. I saw a couple of buzzards circling Royal Hill the other day, maybe between the buzzards and the crows they picked it clean."

"Possible," said Jan, but his voice was layered with doubt. "But crows and buzzards don't kill sheep, do they? Jackson has lost one of his, too. And I heard that Frankie Bickle's prize bull has been killed as well. What the hell kind of creature would even take on a three-thousand-pound South Devon bull, let alone kill it? Something out there is doing this, and we have to find it."

"And quickly!" Tom glowered.

CHAPTER NINE

*P*adding downstairs the following morning, Felicity was feeling tired, jaded and extremely angry. She shuffled along to the kitchen as best she could, her mules stubbornly refusing to stay on her feet. She kicked them off in frustration and opened the kitchen door. Standing transfixed, she gaped at the sight that awaited her.

The floor was littered with the remains of food, food wrappers, containers and empty foil cartons. She smacked a hand to her forehead.

This cannot be happening. What on earth is going on?!

Mister Ogilvy, who had followed her downstairs, started sniffing busily at the empty cat and dog food tins and foil cartons, cleaning out one or two as he did so and purring happily.

Felicity reacted without thinking. *That dratted cat!*

To his obvious incredulity, she shooed him out of the kitchen door. "Get out of here, you horrible beastie! Go on, get out!" Felicity had had it with him. "And stay out!" she ordered, slamming the door in his surprised little face.

The sudden rush of fury left her shaken. She collapsed onto a kitchen chair and slumped over the table, head in hands, a mixture of emotions overwhelming her: anger, frustration and perhaps a little fear. Add to that a little held-over grief from losing her beloved Aunt Maud and the fact that she was desperately tired, and she had the perfect recipe for self-pity and despair.

I can't go on like this, she told herself. *I'll have to sell up. Maybe I need proper help for my dreams.* She glared at the closed door. *And as for that horrible little brute of a cat, he'll never set foot in this house again. I'll take his food out to the barn. He can live in there!*

Sighing, Felicity pulled herself together and started to clean up the mess. After throwing a couple of dog food cartons in the bin, she stopped and, with a frown, fished one back out again to examine it more closely.

How on earth did Oggy open this?

The cartons were of the foil type with a foil pull lid. The lid had a tab on one side which you pulled to remove it. They were supposed to be 'easy open'. If anything had ever been so badly named, Felicity wasn't sure what that might be! She could never open the rotten things.

But that was by the by. How on earth had Oggy done it?

Realisation dawned and she smiled at her stupidity.

Of course—he had used his claws to rip through the foil lid and get to the contents that way.

Simple!

To verify her theory, she fished out one of the lids.

It was undamaged.

The three others she retrieved were also pristine. They had been *pulled* away from the foil carton, not torn open.

Now thoroughly confused, Felicity continued her clean-up. Picking up a lettuce leaf, she considered it in confusion. Lettuce! Oggy didn't eat lettuce. No self-respecting cat would! Glancing towards her veggie rack, she did a double take. Not only was the lettuce gone, so were the parsnip, the courgette, the carrots—three of them—and even half a swede she'd wrapped in plastic wrap.

All gone.

She flopped down in the kitchen chair again and tried to marshal her thoughts. The only explanation she could come up with was also the most unlikely to be true, but it was all she had. Oggy must be 'squirreling'. Collecting food he didn't need and storing it in the barn. Or maybe he was burying it. She'd had no previous experience of cats so had no idea whether they did this or not, but what other explanation could there be?

Once the kitchen was tidy and she'd mopped the floor yet again, she made herself a light breakfast then retired to the study, ostensibly to write, but after about ten minutes she gave it up as a bad job. She was too tired and too much of an emotional wreck to produce anything remotely coherent. Felicity slumped into her chair, staring out of the window at the typically stunning view. The moors stretched away from her, a kaleidoscope of gold, yellow and burnished browns and reds, the dusky purple of the heather a glorious highlight.

Fine but chilly, she guessed.

How on earth was she going to give up this place? It was hers now but had probably been Aunt Maud's for sixty or seventy years. This place had been her aunt's whole life.

Sometimes it really felt to Felicity as though Maud was still with her.

She gazed fondly around the room at row upon row of beautiful books. This wasn't just Aunt Maud's library, it was her treasure trove. How many hours had Maud spent in this room, sitting in this very chair poring over one of her volumes?

On impulse, Felicity jumped up and went to the shelves. She walked slowly around the room just taking in the breadth of her library. Romance, fantasy, action, adventure *and* knowledge were assembled here. She glanced through the titles without trying to read them fully. Everyone you might ever want to read: Jack London, Willkie Collins, Bram Stoker and a whole section of Dickens. Aunt Maud had loved her Dickens and had read a couple of those to Felicity as a child. *Oliver Twist*, of course. Even now, Felicity recalled how Quilp from *The Old Curiosity Shop* had given her nightmares.

There was a whole shelf dedicated to the works of

HG Wells. Each volume had been resplendently bound in green leather and embossed in gold. Felicity quickly read through some of the titles: *War of the Worlds, Kipps, The History of Mr Polly, The Shape of Things to Come,* together with collected essays and political commentaries. Aunt Maud must have had everything he'd ever written. They'd all been kept in excellent condition, hardly worn at all, with the exception of one volume, which showed signs of having been well handled. It sat at the beginning of the collection.

The Time Machine.

Curious, Felicity reached for it. Taking it down from the shelf, she walked back to the desk, lay it down and ran her hands gently over the beautiful leather, admiring the gold tooling on the front. Turning the front cover she discovered the title page had been annotated. She read it ... blinked ... and then re-read it.

To my dearest Maud
Hg

Incredulous, Felicity stared at it. Surely not *the* HG! How had her aunt known HG Wells? Through Granny Gannicott? That seemed extremely unlikely. Wells would have moved in much loftier circles than a farm labourer and his wife. Though perhaps not ... wasn't he known to be a sort of Proto Socialist, some would say Marxist? Perhaps he *had* known the Gannicotts, who'd held similar beliefs, however unlikely that was.

And what was with the '*my dearest Maud*'? Why was

Maud his 'dearest'? Was that something he wrote on every book he signed? Simply changing the name for each different recipient? Or had it actually meant something?

Felicity switched on her computer and drummed her fingers on the desk impatiently as she waited for it to power up. Fortunately her laptop was relatively new, and a good model besides. In no time at all she was clicking on the 'google' button which sat permanently on her taskbar. She typed in 'HG Wells' and scanned the responses it produced before clicking on the *Wikipedia* article. While not the best source of information on the web, *Wikipedia* tended to get to the point quicker than many other websites. She skimmed through the article.

Wells had been born in 1866 and died in 1946. Felicity did some mental arithmetic. Aunt Maud was born in 1931, so by the time she was a young girl of say ten, Wells would have been around seventy-five. It was just about feasible the two had met, she supposed.

Felicity knew little of Aunt Maud's life. She'd already been an old woman by the time Felicity had started to visit, and she'd never spoken much at all about her past life.

Felicity turned away from the computer screen and picked up *The Time Machine* once more. She flicked over the pages to the start of chapter one.

THE TIME TRAVELLER (for so it will be convenient to speak of him) was expounding a recondite matter to us. His grey eyes shone and twinkled, and his usually pale face was flushed and animated.

How well she remembered it. Thinking back, Aunt Maud had read it to her twice. They had both loved the story, despite it being a little scary in places. She smiled and stroked the pages.

Good memories. Thank you, Aunt Maud.

Moving back to the bookshelf, she replaced the volume and selected *The Island of Doctor Moreau* in its place. Opening the cover she found:

To dear Maud on your 10th Birthday
Hg

Bizarre. What could it all mean?

She pulled out the next volume, and the next. On further examination, she found that most of the HG Wells volumes did *not,* in fact, have a dedication, but a small number did. In each case, those that had been signed were dedicated to either 'Dear Maud' or 'Dearest Maud'.

Felicity replaced all the books in their correct order and flopped back down in the captain's chair, her mind running through a variety of scenarios. In the end, she gave up trying to put a rational explanation to something that was clearly unfathomable and just stared out of the window at the distant hills, watching the clouds speed past in an ever-changing sky.

Time passed and, with a start, Felicity realised she'd been dozing. This wouldn't do! If she slept now, she'd have no chance of sleeping tonight. She jumped up and snapped down the lid of her laptop. Moving purposefully into the hall, she pulled on some warm outer clothing and slid on her wellies. A brisk walk would wake her up.

First, she decided to pay a visit to Mister Ogilvy. She remained resolute in her decision to banish him, but he was still her responsibility. She regretted her earlier outburst, and she couldn't let him suffer, so she carried his water bowl out to the barn to make sure he had a drink.

She found him lying sphinx-like on an old armchair that had been dumped in there. When she appeared at the door, he sat up, meowing pitifully. Felicity steeled herself. "Oh no! You're not getting round me like that, you little horror."

She tried to be firm, but when she left the barn, she had to acknowledge she was crying inside.

After checking that the back door was locked and bolted, Felicity left by the front door, securing it behind her. She crossed the patio, where she and Jan had played as children under the watchful gaze of Aunt Maud, and trotted down the crazy-paved pathway and out through the wooden gate. The track she followed now had been worn into a deep rut over the years. It had been a favourite walk of Aunt Maud's, right till the end of her life. The red soil, for which Devon was famous, had been tramped down over time until it now felt a little like walking on concrete, but as she approached the mire, the soil gave way to browns and then black peat at the mire's edge.

Continuing down the path that ran alongside the mire, she recalled some of the walks she had taken with

Aunt Maud. Maud carried a stick but rarely used it for its designated purpose. Instead, she would prod the ground either side of the path, exclaiming to Felicity, "You 'aves to be careful round here, my lovely. Treacherous, 'er is."

One of Maud's revelations to the ever-curious Felicity concerned the surface of the 'bog', as she referred to it. It consisted of a thin layer of vegetation—lichens, sphagnum, moss and the like, giving the mire the look of solid ground. However, this thin green crust lay on a layer of water, which in turn covered the peat. Many an unwary traveller had fallen foul of this little trap carefully laid by Mother Nature. Thankfully, there had been only a few fatalities in recent years. Most ablebodied people were able to scramble to safety; wet and frightened perhaps, but a fair bit wiser.

In order to emphasise the danger, on one memorable walk, Maud had taken Felicity to the edge of the mire. Then, holding her firmly under her arms, had instructed Felicity to stamp on the crust. "Give 'im a good 'ard stamp. With just one foot, mind you."

Felicity had been astonished at the outcome. She had done as her aunt suggested. One hard stamp on the earth and the seemingly solid ground appeared to be moving in waves, trembling all across the mire.

On impulse, Felicity decided to repeat the experiment now. There was no Aunt Maud to hold her this time, but by keeping her weight on her standing leg she was able to crash her wellie-booted foot down hard on the surface. The effect was the same as she had seen as a child. She laughed loudly, disturbing a couple of nearby rooks, then glanced around self-consciously, afraid any passing hikers had witnessed her antics.

Fortunately, she was quite alone.

She carried on, keeping to the trail of course, passing the ancient granite cross which gave her house its name before deciding to walk to the hill that had, in turn, lent the mire its name.

Fox Tor.

This particular tor was a medium-sized hill of about 500 yards or so, topped with a massive granite outcrop. Over time the rocks had weathered, cracked and, in parts, broken up. This had produced a scree slope. As a child, Felicity had thought that the huge granite blocks which formed the tor were part of a ruined castle, but Aunt Maud had explained that it was a perfectly natural geological occurrence.

Felicity marched on, but as she approached the tor, she began to feel a little uneasy. In gradual increments she experienced a sensation of dread, something akin to the fear she had been noticing at night. It stole upon her, this feeling, becoming increasingly strong until her breath started to catch in her throat, and what had started as a slight tremble became a violent shaking.

What is wrong with me?

She stopped where she was and zipped her fleece up to her neck. It was chilly, but certainly not freezing. She couldn't blame her shivering on the cold. Unable to bear it any longer, she turned and hurried down the slope and onto the path leading to her home. The further she retreated from the tor, the calmer she became. The trembling began to ease, and she was able to take deeper breaths.

She hurried along the path, but as she did so, she became conscious of movement to her right. She stopped. Gazing out at the mire, she noticed that the ground was moving, in the same way it had earlier when she had stamped on it.

She scanned the edges of the mire. Nothing to see. No sign of anything which might be causing the effect. No people, no sheep, no ponies. The ground stilled. Felicity waited. The movement came again. The mire shivered for a while, as though someone had patted the top of a firm jelly. It wobbled, became still, and finally remained undisturbed.

With nothing and no one to see, Felicity was flummoxed. She scanned her surroundings and then, when she still couldn't locate the cause of the disturbance, she hurried home and charged into the kitchen to make herself some strong tea. Strong tea was Felicity's cure-all, and by the time she had drained her first mug, she felt much better—still a little shaky perhaps, but calm enough to think rationally.

Her concern turned to poor Oggy. She had better make him some dinner. But as she pulled open the cupboard door, she remembered that every tin of cat food had either been devoured already, or perhaps carted off to storage.

And what about her own supper? She hadn't had any lunch so was beginning to feel quite hungry. She needed something substantial. She located a forgotten tin of ham at the back of the storage cupboard alongside several outdated tins of beans. In the fridge she found a couple of eggs.

Excellent!

Ham, eggs and beans. A feast for a queen.

Kind of.

Chips would improve matters, but there were none in the freezer. Knowing that she needed more milk as well as the cat food, she decided to take a trip to the nearest convenience store. It would save time to drive so she jumped into her car and drove the short, but very bumpy, distance into Princetown, parking outside the only shop selling provisions. She was relieved to find they had a plentiful supply of cat food, the same brand that had been in the store cupboard. Clearly this was where Aunt Maud had purchased her supplies.

On returning to Prior's Cross, she parked the car in the yard, then looked in on Mister Ogilvy to make sure he was okay. On seeing her, he jumped down from his chair and padded happily towards her, evidently forgiving her for her earlier misdemeanour towards him.

Felicity was having none of it, though. "You stay there, Oggy!" she called, as she turned and walked out of the barn, swinging her canvas shopping bag. "Waitress service this afternoon. I'll bring your dinner to you."

She unlocked the kitchen door and unsuspectingly pushed it open.

Devastation!

On the floor were the empty eggshells of the four

eggs she had found in the refrigerator, together with the wrapper and remains of a loaf of bread.

Felicity took a deep breath and remained remarkably calm. She swivelled on her heel, walked back outside, locked the kitchen door and walked purposefully around the side of the house to the front door. This was the only other entrance to the house. She examined it.

Locked.

She let herself in and, trotting up the stairs, she systematically checked every window before returning to the ground floor to check those. Every single window had been left secure.

Felicity moved into the living room and plonked herself down on the sofa. She stared into the ashes of the previous night's fire. This wasn't the overwrought, hysterical Felicity from earlier. This Felicity was steely and resolute. She carefully and calmly thought through the issues, rationally enumerating each in her mind.

Firstly, this wasn't Mister Ogilvy's doing. It couldn't be. He'd been left in the barn while this was happening. There was no way he could have entered the house. Felicity conjured up his sweet little face in her mind's eye and grimaced. She'd collect him from the barn in a little while and make it up to him.

Secondly, someone had entered this house while she was out. Someone with a key. She made a mental note to check with the solicitors to find out if there were any other sets of keys currently unaccounted for.

Thirdly … this same someone was trying to scare her out of this house! Perhaps make her so frightened that she would sell up. And cheaply! Well, they wouldn't succeed. The same Felicity that earlier in the day would have let the house go for a song, was now absolutely adamant that no amount of money would tempt her to sell up.

She would not be bullied out of her home! Out of Aunt Maud's home.

Right, Aunt Maud? she said to herself.

Fourthly, what if ... and it was a big what if ... what if there really was something up in the rocks of Fox Tor above the mire? What if something was trying to communicate with her? Is that what she was tapping into? And why did it frighten her so? If it frightened her, did that mean something evil was lurking up there? If her hunch was true, then surely she wasn't going mad after all?

But this was bigger than her. More than she could cope with, and that brought her to her fifth point. She couldn't deal with this alone. She would need help. And not the psychiatric help she had, until moments earlier, been considering. No. The help she really needed was six foot tall with broad shoulders and strong arms.

Felicity rose from her seat and started clearing the fireplace ready to lay a new fire. She and Mister Ogilvy would sit in here together tonight. She would try to make things right with him.

Once the fire was going, she cleaned up in the kitchen—again—before heading out to the barn and collecting the cat. She stroked and fussed him as she carried him in, while he did his level best to remain aloof.

She warmed the oven and heated her chips, then located the tinned ham and a can of beans from the store cupboard. Pouring the beans into a saucepan and simmering them slowly, she sliced the ham into thick chunks. She set aside a generous slice for Mister Ogilvy as a treat. The rest of the ham she placed in a frying pan with a small knob of butter and fried it until she had what might almost pass as ham fritters. After transferring the ham to the plate of chips, she poured the beans from the saucepan into the frying pan, swirling them so that they mixed with the butter and ham juices sizzling in the pan, before finally pouring the lot on top of the ham.

"Eat your heart out, Gordon Ramsey," she said as she sat down to her banquet.

Mister Ogilvy also dined well that night. He polished off the ham mixed with his usual tinned food, with the added bonus of a saucer of milk.

Both totally podged, owner and cat settled on the sofa in front of the fire. Felicity switched on the television and flicked through the channels. She didn't like soaps. The storylines were either naïve and boring, or too far-fetched to be believable. Nor was she a fan of cookery programmes, given that most of the ingredients the chefs used were unobtainable in the supermarket she used, especially here in rural Devon. She also hated the so-called 'reality' television shows with a passion. It amazed her that people were so desperate to be on television that they would volunteer to appear in such things. That left her options severely limited.

Eventually, she settled on a wildlife programme

about polar bears in the Arctic, but when one of the cubs ran into difficulty, she switched it off. She couldn't bear seeing animals in distress. In a moment of inspiration, she decided to retrieve the copy of *The Time Machine* she had found that morning.

"I'm going to read to you, Oggy," she said, gently pulling him closer.

Her little friend gave her a look that shouted total indifference before laying his head between his paws and closing his eyes. Nonetheless, as she read, she kept looking down at him. The occasional twitching of his ears convinced her that Mister Ogilvy was indeed listening.

'Upon that machine,' said the Time Traveller, holding the lamp aloft, 'I intend to explore time. Is that plain? I was never more serious in my life.'

None of us quite knew how to take it.

I caught Filby's eye over the shoulder of the Medical Man, and he winked at me solemnly.

As she concluded the chapter, Felicity inserted the thin yellow ribbon that acted as a place marker between the pages and closed the book. "There, Oggy. That was fun. Tomorrow I'll read chap—"

A bright flash of light illuminated the whole house and cut her off in mid-sentence.

Gasping, she jumped to her feet. Mister Ogilvy scrambled from his place beside her. The flash seemed to have come from the rear of the house, not the front where the mire was. It couldn't have been marsh gas. Hesitantly, Felicity crept through to the dark kitchen to peer out of the window.

She couldn't see or hear anything out of the ordinary. No rain. No thunder.

Feeling a little more confident, she stepped out into the yard and walked around the side of the barn. From this point she could see the Gurney farm, further up the hill. Their lights sparkled in the distance and there was no sign of a fire or any other impending emergency.

Felicity shrugged and returned to her own house. Perhaps this time it really had been lightning.

As she closed and locked the kitchen door, she didn't notice the light which suddenly appeared in a window on the upper floor of the barn.

Felicity returned to her place on the sofa, but within a few seconds she was on her feet again. This time a scraping, shuffling sound was coming from above her head. Probably from one of the bedrooms upstairs.

"I've had enough of this!" Felicity waved her clenched fist at the ceiling. "Right! You want trouble? You're going to get trouble!" She plucked up a poker from the companion set next to the fireplace and stormed up the stairs.

But once at the top, her nerve deserted her. She stood silently, peering all around and listening, her senses on alert.

Scrrrrrrrck. Scrrrrrrrck.

There it was again! That weird scraping, shuffling sound.

Scrrrrrrrck. Scrrrrrrrck.

Not on this floor though. It definitely sounded as though something had found its way into the attic! She dashed into the bedroom to collect her torch and then moved to the end of the landing where a trapdoor had been created in the ceiling. Grabbing the pole which stood in the corner of the landing, she pushed it into the slot three feet or so above her head. She heard the clink as the spring mechanism was released and allowed the trapdoor to swing downwards. The other end of the pole was fitted with a hook which allowed her to pull the ladder towards her. Its three sections clicked into place as she lowered it.

Switching on her torch, Felicity carefully climbed the ladder until her head was level with the ceiling. Then, gathering her courage, she climbed another couple of rungs and leaned her weight against the opening. She shone her torch in a wide arc around the void.

Nothing!

Climbing higher to get a better view, she systematically moved the beam of her torch slowly around the huge space. Lots of boxes—so many boxes—a couple of suitcases and two enormous old-fashioned trunks.

Anything could be hiding up here behind these boxes, she thought, blowing her breath out anxiously.

Scrrrrrrrck. Scrrrrrrrck.

There! What was that?

Heart thumping, she leaned forwards, certain something had moved at the far end of the attic. Shining her torch in that direction, she saw two large eyes staring back at her.

Shrieking, Felicity dropped her torch and lost her

footing. She fell a couple of steps, banging her knee and nearly yanking her arm out of her socket as she hastily grabbed hold. She jumped safely down to the landing and thrust the ladder back into the loft, finally slamming the trapdoor closed.

Crashing down the stairs two at a time, she flew into the living room and threw herself onto the sofa, scattering an indignant Mister Ogilvy in the process.

She remained there for some time, her knees drawn, her arms encircling her legs.

She was afraid, and this time she had cause to be.

There's something living in my attic!

CHAPTER TEN

The following morning, after a restless night curled under her duvet on the sofa, Felicity, feeling a little calmer now, decided she needed to investigate further. As she sat at the kitchen table, willing herself to return to the attic, she tried to rationalize exactly what she had seen.

A pair of eyes?

She'd *assumed* they were eyes.

Hmmm.

Now, in the cold light of day, she wondered if she'd been imagining things. Perhaps what she'd actually seen had been two bright objects in among the junk, simply reflecting the light from her torch.

And even if it *were* eyes, what type of creature would be in an attic? A rat?

She shuddered at the thought. No, it couldn't have been a rat. The eyes had been too big for rats' eyes.

Alright then. What has big eyes? An owl! That's it! It

had been an owl that had somehow managed to get into the attic. Why not? Pigeons did it. And bats …

Sitting on her backside wasn't going to get to the bottom of it. There was nothing for it but to head back into the attic and investigate. Given that it was now broad daylight, there was nothing to be afraid of.

Was there?

Just two very large eyes, she thought and sat down again.

Come on, Flick, get it together.

She stood once more and, this time, determinedly made her way up the stairs and along the landing. Dropping the ladder, she started to ascend.

If I see a pair of eyes, I'm out of here, she told herself.

Popping her head through the hatch, she fumbled around until she located the torch she'd dropped the previous evening. Miracle of miracles, when she switched it on, it still worked. She swung the beam around in a wide arc before quickly ducking her head down again.

Just in case.

Now that was stupid. I'm turning into a coward! What would Aunt Maud say? What would Jan Gurney say?

Taking a deep breath, she climbed to the top and stepped into the attic, deliberately slow, sweeping the length of the space with the torch beam. The light played across junk, packing crates, cardboard boxes and piles of stuff.

No ghosts, gremlins, goblins, ghouls or pixies.

Not even a pair of eyes!

Relaxing slightly, she swept the light around her feet. Nearby were several empty tins. She picked one up and sniffed it, drawing her head back sharply. *Ugh. Yeurk. Fish!*

Completely baffled now, she continued to shine her torch about until she caught sight of an old wooden trunk, quite small, with a metal clasp but no lock. She threw back the lid. It was filled with letters and legal-looking documents and notebooks. She picked out one of the notebooks and skimmed through it. It contained beautiful colour drawings of flowers, weeds and bushes—the sort you'd find on the moorland. Aunt Maud had been quite an artist. Another book was filled with drawings of Dartmoor fauna: stoats, foxes, badgers, rabbits and hares. *I'll treasure these*, she thought as she carefully and lovingly packed them back inside the trunk.

Lifting out a metal biscuit tin, she opened it up and found it packed full of postcards. She shuffled through a few of them. They seemed to be from every conceivable place on earth. USA, Canada and all of Europe seemed to be covered. India, China and exotic places she had only read about in books or seen on wildlife documentaries. She scanned a couple of the messages. They all started with *Dear Maud*, then there would be some predictable message referring to the weather and places visited, and all ended with *Love, HG*.

Who was HG? An admirer?

She was about to replace everything when she noticed that there was a document under the bottom card. She freed it. Maud's birth certificate.

Mother: ***Hannah Isabella GRENDON***
Father: ***Herbert G*** ***WELLS***
Place: ***Tavistock***

She re-read it and frowned as the implications of what she was seeing sank in.

Surely not.

There was no way in this world that Aunt Maud could be the daughter of HG Wells!

Was there?

CHAPTER ELEVEN

Felicity stowed the last tin of pilchards in her store cupboard and pushed the door closed. She had driven across the moor to Tavistock and visited the supermarket there to do a proper shop and now her cupboards, fridge and freezer were full.

At least for the time being.

She wagged a finger at Mister Ogilvy, who had padded in from elsewhere in the house. He scented the air, his nose and tail lifted high, a look of expectation on his cute little face. "Don't you get any ideas, Oggy," Felicity warned. "I'm expecting all this to last for a few weeks." She switched on the kettle and extracted a Jammy Dodger from Aunt Maud's old biscuit tin. "Bar milk and biscuits maybe."

She busied herself with making a cup of tea, while disposing of her biscuit in two bites and pinching another one. Mister Ogilvy threaded his way in and out of her legs until she relented and gave him a saucer of milk. She was washing her hands at the sink when she spotted a figure walking along the side of the house out of the corner of her eye. She craned her neck and realised, with relief, that it was only Jan.

He came to the back door, just as he always had when they were children. Felicity, after doing a quick check for smudges or stains on her t-shirt and wiping her mouth in case she had biscuit crumbs around her lips, opened it and beamed at him. "Hi!"

"Hey!" he smiled back at her.

Mister Ogilvy offered Jan a cursory glance and stalked past him with his tail in the air.

"Come in, come in," she urged. "Ignore him. He's obviously feeling antisocial today."

Jan glanced doubtfully down at his clothes. He was wearing a pair of filthy canvas trousers, a thick jumper with a number of ragged holes, and a pair of dung-encrusted wellies. "I'm not sure I should, really."

"Don't be daft! We don't stand on ceremony at Prior's Cross, you know that." It sounded like something her Aunt Maud would have said, and Felicity felt the familiar stab of loss prick at her heart. She threw the door open as wide as it would go and stood back.

Jan, evidently feeling a little self-conscious, elected to peel his boots off and leave them by the step, before shuffling into Felicity's kitchen in his stockinged feet. He handed his coat and scarf to Felicity and she hung them behind the door into the hallway.

Felicity, looking down, snorted. "You've got a massive 'tatie in them there socks," she said in a broad accent that would have matched his mother's any day of the week. Jan grimaced, mortified to have been caught out.

"Yeah. I could definitely do with some new ones. I do get through them."

"At least I'll know what to get you for Christmas this year," Felicity winked at him. "I was just having a cup of tea. Would you like one?"

"I'd love one." Jan pulled out a chair and sat at the table, carefully tucking his feet out of view. "Will you be here for Christmas?"

Felicity had turned her attention to the kettle again. "I should think so. Not sure where else I'd be, unless I went to a friend's ..."

"Come to ours!" Jan blurted, and Felicity frowned.

"Wouldn't you need to check with your folks?"

Jan flushed. "They're not going to say no, are they? They love having you around."

Felicity added a sugar to Jan's mug, gave the brew a good stir and handed it over to him. "It's hot," she said, and took a seat opposite him. "Well, if you're serious and your parents agree, I'd really like that, thank you." She hesitated and swirled her tea around in her half-empty mug. "If I'm still living here, anyway."

Jan's face fell. "Are you thinking of moving?"

Felicity shrugged, unsure how much she could tell Jan about the nightmares and the noises and the lights. Everything that freaked her out. It all sounded silly in the cold light of day.

"I thought you were hoping to write another one of

your books here," Jan continued. "It's the perfect place to do it. Quiet solitude. Isn't that what writers like?"

Quiet? If only I had some, thought Felicity. "Yes, it's a perfect location for writing my next book." Even she could hear the lack of sincerity in her voice. "I'm struggling to find inspiration, that's all."

Jan cocked his head. "Seems to me there've been some weird things going on around the moor of late. You could use that as your inspiration."

"Like the skeleton of the bull, you mean?"

"Exactly that." Jan's brow furrowed. "I've heard tell that Corey Ruddle lost a couple of sheep the other night, too."

"That's bad news!" Felicity knew how hard farmers worked, and how much it affected them when something attacked their livestock. "You must be worried."

Jan glowered. "Yes. We're keeping a careful watch, believe me."

"I hope someone catches whatever it is soon," Felicity said, taking a swig of her tea. "It does feel quite alien around here at the moment. It's all a little unnerving."

Jan studied her over the top of his steaming mug. "You look a little peaky. Are you getting out enough? A walk in the fresh air will do you the world of good."

"I know." Felicity smiled at his concern. "I'm just a little tired, that's all."

"And you know what else is good for you?"

Felicity looked at Jan expectantly.

"Fun!"

"You're right." Felicity laughed at his expression. "I

probably don't get enough of that. I've only been out once since I arrived here, and that was to the pub with you."

Jan cleared his throat, suddenly self-conscious all over again. "Would you, er ... ah ... like to have dinner with me, maybe?"

Felicity cocked her head. *Was he asking her out?* This time it was her turn to flush. She ducked her head and fiddled with her mug some more.

"I—" A sudden thought struck her. Her cupboards were absolutely full of food. "Hey! Why don't you come over one night and I'll cook for you?"

Jan raised his eyebrows. "You cook?"

"You cheeky oaf! Yes, I cook. Not often, but I'm not bad."

Jan grinned. "If you promise not to poison me, I'm game for anything." He pushed his chair back. "I'd better get going. I want to check on the top fields and get the sheep in before it gets dark. Can't leave it all to the old man, now, can I?"

He drained his drink as Felicity went to retrieve his coat.

She paused in front of the hooks and frowned. "Didn't you give me a scarf?" she asked.

"I did," Jan nodded. "A yellow and black one my Mum knitted. My Rupert the Bear scarf."

"Well, it's not here." Felicity hauled one of her jackets from a hook and riffled through a couple of aprons left hanging there, but there was no place to hide. "That's bizarre."

"It's not in the sleeve, is it?" Jan took his coat and pulled it on. "Nope."

"I didn't go anywhere else. It was right here." Felicity walked around the kitchen, retracing her steps in case she had dropped it somewhere. "Oh. I can't see it anywhere!"

"Not to worry, it will turn up."

"I'm so sorry. Maybe Oggy took it."

Jan opened the kitchen door. Mister Ogilvy sat outside, waiting patiently to come back into the warmth of the kitchen. He didn't have the scarf.

He sloped in and headed for the hallway.

Jan laughed. "He's a weird one, isn't he?" He began pulling on his boots.

"You could say that." Felicity leaned against the door jamb to watch Jan. She found herself wishing he could have stayed longer.

She enjoyed his company.

"Text me," she said, "and we'll sort out dinner."

"Will do!" He gave her a cheery wave and set off along the path.

"I'll keep an eye out for your scarf!" she called, and he turned.

"Yes, do that! Otherwise, Mother will want to know what I've done with it."

CHAPTER TWELVE

Felicity gathered up Mister Ogilvy and settled him beside her on the sofa, stroking his head gently. She opened up *The Time Machine* and flipped away the yellow ribbon page marker. "Chapter two tonight, Oggy," she said.

She read aloud to the cat once more, emphasising some passages where this added colour to the story, remembering how Aunt Maud had always modulated her own voice when reading to her as a child. For his part, Mister Ogilvy exhibited not the slightest bit of interest. His notable indifference, amounting almost to disdain, bothered Felicity not one jot. She was enjoying the experience of reading the book. It reminded her of happy times.

She was well into chapter two when a noise distracted her momentarily. A very faint, high-pitched droning sound. A fly, maybe?

No, not a fly.

She put her book down on the sofa and stood up, cocking her head and listening intently. It was the noise she'd heard on two previous occasions.

What on earth is it? Some kind of machinery?

She had already established that it couldn't be a machine on the Gurney farm, and there were no other farms nearby. The likely alternative was that the sound was travelling over the moor from a little further afield. Princetown, perhaps.

Thinking about the town led to a sudden flash of realisation. "It's the prison!" Of course. She walked over to the window and gazed out. Not that she could see anything at this time of night. "It must be some kind of alarm," she told Mister Ogilvy. "Well, I hope they shut it off soon. It's really invasive. It gets right into your head."

As though reacting to her words, it did shut off. Abruptly. At precisely the same moment a flash of light illuminated the night sky. For the first time, Felicity linked the two events together. First the whining noise, quickly followed by the bright flash of light.

She pursed her lips, thinking. How and why were the two events linked? If the whining was a prison alarm, could the flash of light be some kind of searchlight? She quickly dismissed that notion. What use was a searchlight if it only flashed for a fraction of a second? What would that achieve? It wouldn't light up convicts on the run, would it? She shook her head, mentally assigning the problem to the 'boring and/or too difficult' section of her brain.

She plonked herself back down on the sofa. Feeling

restless, she picked up her book and re-inserted the page marker, closed it and lay it down at her feet. "Sorry, Oggy. That's all for tonight."

She felt too confused to read any further. Suddenly exhausted, she closed her eyes for a few seconds, but the moment she did so she began to sense another vision entering her mind. She fought its invasion, not wanting to behold any more strange creatures. They were horrible. Evil.

Too late.

She found herself in a dark place. Cold, damp walls. She was hiding. She glanced down at the ground. There were two things lying there. Hideously deformed versions of people. But they weren't moving. She rocked backwards, fighting back feelings of desperation and fear, but mostly overwhelming sadness. She heard footsteps. Someone was coming. Perhaps they—or it—would be able to help her ...

"Stop!" Felicity shrieked, coming to with a start.

She caught her breath and smacked her hands against the side of her head as though she could somehow banish the visions by pummelling her brain. "In God's name, stop!"

Fleeing to the kitchen, she frantically searched her first aid shelf for Paracetamol. Pouring a glass of water, she leaned against the kitchen sink and swallowed two of the tablets. She breathed deeply several times, rolling her shoulders back and blinking. But as she stood there, a thin layer of perspiration on her brow, gazing through the kitchen window that looked out over the yard, she realised that something was not right.

She could see a square of light coming from the upper floor of the barn.

Felicity's heart began to skip.

Someone was out there?

Grabbing her coat and torch and slipping on her wellies which lay waiting for her in their customary place by the back door, she walked out into the yard and stared up at the light. It wasn't very bright, and it had a slight red tinge.

What could it be? As far as she was aware it was impossible to get up into the higher area of the barn.

The whining started up again. This time it wasn't continuous. It stopped and started, stuttering. The light flashed blue, then green, then blue again, then back to red. The whining stopped.

Simultaneously afraid and curious, she approached the barn and lifted the sneck on the door handle. The door registered its protest, wheezing grumpily as she slowly pushed it open and peeked inside. She shone her torch haphazardly round the barn. There was nothing to see.

Wait a second ...

A ladder stood upright in the centre of the barn, not leaning against anything, but absolutely vertical. She shone her beam of light that way and followed the line of the ladder up ... up ... up to the ceiling, where it disappeared into the upper floor through a square hole where the trapdoor had been.

Felicity approached the ladder and shone the torch upwards through the trap. She could vaguely discern the underside of the roof of the barn. Nothing else.

She narrowed her eyes and extinguished the torch. Keeping perfectly still she listened carefully. A faint shuffling. Someone was moving around up there. She caught the occasional clicking sound and snippets of a muffled voice. The words were indecipherable.

She had no reason to conclude that the sounds here were in some way connected to the sounds in the house, but Felicity made that link in her mind anyway, and now she was in a quandary. Should she investigate? Or should she retire to the relative safety of her kitchen and phone DS Alderson? If the police came and the intruder had disappeared again, she would look like a complete idiot.

For some reason she didn't want DS Alderson to think she was a hysterical fool.

Steeling herself, she slowly and quietly climbed the ladder until her head was just above the level of the floor. In the dim red light—which emanated from some kind of a panel at the very end of the barn—she could just about see a man. He had something clinging to him like a large leather bag.

Felicity squinted, waiting for her eyes to adjust. Why was the man in her barn? And what was he doing?

He appeared to be using a hand tool on a machine. That's where the droning noise emanated from. Felicity couldn't make out what kind of machine it was; it looked rather like a motorcycle but was probably too big for that.

Curiosity overcame her fear. She climbed the last few

steps of the ladder and walked quietly into the loft. She paused, listening as the man began talking again. He spoke softly, using a calming tone, but she still couldn't make out the words. Taking a deep breath, she levelled her torch at the scene and clicked it on.

There was an instantaneous howl of pain.

"Switch off that light, you blasted fool!" the man shouted in anger.

Gasping in shock, Felicity instinctively did as he commanded. She dropped her hand, afraid of what she'd inadvertently done. She could hear the man speaking quietly again, soothing someone or something. As her eyes re-adjusted to the gloom, she realised he had taken a step towards her. She moved away, inching backwards in the direction of the trapdoor.

"Stop!" he ordered. Then more quietly, he said, "please don't step back any further, my dear. You might fall through the trap." He raised his hands, palms facing her. "And please don't be frightened. I won't harm you. Quite the opposite. I need your help. If you're willing …?"

"My help?" Felicity repeated.

"I'll increase the light," he told her. "Just, whatever you do, don't switch on your torch again. White light will damage his sensitive eyes." He nodded at the thing which clung to him. Felicity decided it had to be a child.

"This is surreal," she muttered. She had found a trespasser in her barn, clutching a child and operating a strange machine, and *he* was telling *her* what to do.

Nevertheless, she followed him as he strolled to the

panel at the end of the barn and slowly turned a knob. The intensity of the red light increased significantly, allowing her to see things more clearly. The machine was like nothing she had ever seen before. The inner part of it did indeed resemble a motorcycle with a seat for the 'rider', but instead of handlebars, there was a control panel full of switches, dials and knobs. Two short levers, carved from something that might well have been quartz, extended from the panel. Both of the levers were emitting a faint green glow. Behind the rider's seat was a bench capable of holding three adults, and behind that, two wooden cages rested on a parcel shelf, strapped securely with leather ties. Right at the back, behind the shelf, was what appeared to be a large multi-bladed fan. Completely encircling the odd machine were three two-inch-thick tubes, equally spaced apart and intersecting at the front and rear. The whole apparatus rested on three cast iron Queen Anne legs.

So engrossed by the machine had she been that Felicity hadn't noticed the man approaching her. Catching his sudden movement she swung about, only to recoil in horror, her legs almost buckling beneath her. Clinging to the left side of the man was the most disgusting and terrifying creature she could ever have imagined.

The thing was about the size of a six-year-old child and was naked except for a loincloth. Its skin, perhaps due in part to the red light, appeared to have the grey pallor of death. Its body had none of the soft lines of a child but instead was heavily muscled. Its neck was thick and supported a small head, the top of which was flat and covered in a mop of white, wiry hair. Thin blue lips were pulled back displaying vicious sharp fangs, with the canine teeth particularly prominent. And its eyes, which stared out from under a beetle brow, were fixed and unblinking. The 'whites' were in fact yellow. They glowed in the semi-darkness. In the centre of each was a small, pin-pointed red pupil.

"What the blazes—" Felicity's hand flew to her mouth.

The man, whom she recognised as the intruder of a few days earlier, shook his head slightly and frowned. "Please, my dear," he begged, "he senses your thoughts. You will hurt him terribly if you think badly of him. He is only a child and has suffered a great deal."

"Well …" stammered Felicity, not sure what to think. "Shouldn't it be in a hospital or something? What's wrong with it?"

"He!" The man emphasised the word. "He is a hellventi. A cousin of the Morlocks."

"The Morlocks?" Felicity emitted a slightly incredulous giggle. The old man in front of her was clearly crazy. Either that, or she was. "As in *The Time Machine*?"

"Exactly!" he beamed broadly.

Bonkers. Obviously as nutty as a fruitcake.

Felicity's terror had abated and was now slowly replaced by rising anger. The creature hadn't moved a muscle. The old man was pulling her leg, surely. He was carrying nothing scarier than a big hairy doll or a ventriloquist's dummy. What she had here was a gentleman who was either a lunatic or a shyster.

Either way, she had no more time for him.

"Would you like to tell me who you are and what this ... this ... contraption is?" she said, indicating the machine.

"Certainly," he replied cheerfully. "My name is Herbert George Wells. I am your great-great-uncle, and this—" he said with a proud flourish of his free arm, "is my time machine!"

CHAPTER THIRTEEN

"Is something wrong, Felicity?" the man asked solicitously, his brow knitted with concern.

That just made things worse. Felicity, who had been standing speechless and open-mouthed since the declaration of his 'identity', exhaled sharply. "Wrong? No! No, nothing wrong," she said, slowly edging back towards the trap door. "It's just that I'm in the presence of a complete and utter lunatic, that's all!"

"I'm not a *complete* madman," he replied, evidently hurt at the suggestion. "Oh, I admit to being a little disturbed by some of the things I've witnessed, but I believe I still have some way to go before complete insanity descends upon me."

"Ha." Felicity gawped at the strange old chap in front of her. Despite herself, she couldn't help but feel intrigued. He didn't look particularly dangerous. Waiting by the top of the ladder to facilitate an escape, should it become necessary, she began to feel a little more sure of herself. She was confident she could get away, given that he had the added burden of his large puppet should he try to come after her.

"Wait a minute!" She narrowed her eyes at him. "You called me Felicity!"

"Oh! I'm sorry, my dear. Have I remembered your name incorrectly?"

"No-oo," she said slowly. "That *is* my name, but how did you know that? Who told you?"

"Why, Maud of course. Who else?" He sounded baffled and quickly looked around as though they might be joined by someone else at any minute.

"Aunt Maud? You knew Aunt Maud?"

"Knew her?" His voice rose. "Of *course* I knew her. Maud was my daughter!"

Felicity had to grip the ladder to prevent herself from falling through the trapdoor. The old gentleman leaned towards her as if to help, but she raised a hand.

"Ah-ah-ah!" she warned him. "Please stay where you are, Mr Crazy Person. I feel safer if you keep your distance."

The man backed away, his shoulders drooping. "Very well. Would you mind if I took a seat on my machine?" he queried. "Only Helly"—he indicated the puppet—"is rather heavy."

"By all means," Felicity nodded. This guy needed help. And not just to carry his puppet. "Why don't you just put 'Hilly' down?"

"Helly." The man emphasised the name. "He doesn't want to be put down. He's very frightened."

"Oh, Hilly is *frightened*. I'm *so* sorry!" Felicity feigned concern. "Please tell Hilly from me, I'm *really* sorry."

The man remained silent for a moment, regarding her from under his large bushy eyebrows. His face had grown stern. Eventually he cleared his throat. "Felicity, please don't patronise me. You could at least have the decency to listen to what I have to say without being so immediately judgemental."

Felicity, a good and obedient human at heart, was instantly contrite. "I'm sorry," she said, and considered that thought. "No, I genuinely am. That was unkind of me. It's just that ... well, to be honest ... you frighten me."

The man, now perched sideways on the rider's seat of his machine, gave her a sad, knowing smile. "I know I do. You're transmitting your fear." He nodded meaningfully at the puppet.

Felicity resisted rolling her eyes.

There was an awkward pause, then the man said, "Maud thought a great deal of you, you know?"

Felicity caught her breath. It pained her to hear him talk of her beloved aunt in this way. Nonetheless, she decided to play along, at least for a while. She had to try hard not to sound too condescending. She didn't want to risk upsetting him again. "I know she did. Did she tell you that?"

If she had sounded supercilious, the man ignored it. He nodded and smiled. "Oh yes, when we met, you were often our main topic of conversation. She doted on you. I remember the first time I saw you—"

"You saw me?" Felicity interrupted.

"Why, yes! I had materialised here in this barn and had entered the house by the back door as was my usual way, and because the living room and her study were empty, I assumed, correctly as it transpired, that Maud was sunning herself on the patio. As I opened the front door, she frantically waved me back inside." He laughed. "She was in a bit of a panic. I heard her say, 'Don't leave the garden, children, I'll be back in a minute!' Then she came into the house and explained who you were, and she told me—in no uncertain terms—to make myself scarce. She didn't want you to know about my comings and goings. She felt it would be too much for your young mind to take in."

He shrugged. "You know, now that I think about it, I have to say that I wish she *had* told you about me while you were still young and impressionable; still able to believe in the unbelievable. If she had, perhaps we wouldn't now be at this impasse."

The man paused as if waiting for Felicity to contribute. When she didn't, he continued, "I peeked out through the side of the curtain and watched you at play. You were with a young boy, possibly one of the Gurney boys from up the lane and playing with—of all things— toy cars. I expect Maud influenced you. She was always enthusiastic about anything to do with engineering and science."

He smiled, shaking his head. "I was struck by how pretty you were. So like your great-grandmother, Bella."

"Hmpf!" Felicity snorted. "Just for a minute there, I

was almost convinced!" She waggled a finger at him. "Almost! But you've made an error in your research, my friend. Maud's mother wasn't called Bella, she was called Hannah. Now, enough! I want you, your stupid puppet and your idiotic contraption off my property. If you have to disassemble that thing, fine. I'll give you time to do that." She thought quickly. "I'll give you until midnight tonight. If you're still here then, I'm calling the police." She folded her arms. "Have I made myself clear?"

Instead of looking angry, hurt or distressed, the man just smiled at her.

"Yes, Felicity. Perfectly clear."

Returning to the relative safety of the house, Felicity ensured that Mister Ogilvy was inside then carefully and deliberately bolted the two external doors and checked that the windows were all secure. She peeked out of the kitchen window and tutted. She could still see the glow of the red light on the upper floor of the barn.

She tried to take her mind off what was happening outside. Free writing produced dismal results. Her attempt to read was not successful. She found she was no longer in the right mood for *The Time Machine* and besides, she had to keep re-reading the same paragraph over and over again. The television failed to distract her. She even tried hoovering the lounge, but the noise of the vacuum sent Mister Ogilvy running for cover. With every new thing she did in an effort to take her mind off the weird man in the barn, she would first glare out of the window to check on the situation.

The result was always the same. The red light was still burning!

In the end, she perched on the edge of the sofa and allowed herself to fret. So much of what he had said had struck a chord. If, as she suspected, he was a fraudster, he was certainly very clever. How long had he been stalking her for?

She glanced at the clock for the umpteenth time. Just gone eleven. She wished she hadn't given him until midnight. But then again, why should she wait? It wasn't necessary to honour your word with people like him. She would just check the barn one more time. If he hadn't vacated the premises, she would phone the police station.

Felicity padded through to the kitchen and glared out of the window once more. Complete darkness. The light in the barn had been switched off. He'd gone.

"Yes!" She punched the air and breathed some of her tension out, but her initial relief quickly turned to scepticism. The light might be out but that didn't mean he'd definitely gone. What if he was circling the house at this very moment, looking for a way to get in?

"This is stupid," Felicity mumbled. "I can't stand here in the kitchen all night."

Should she phone the police? What would DS Alderson say? Did she have a good enough cause?

Exhaustion washed over her.

Felicity decided her only recourse, for now, was to

take herself to bed and wait and see. If the old fellow tried to break in, she would be fully justified in making a 999 call. If he didn't try to break in, then fine, it wasn't a problem.

She washed, changed into pyjamas and brushed her teeth. After checking that the poker was in place at the side of her bed, she climbed in, welcoming Mister Ogilvy with a scruggle of his head when he jumped onto the duvet to join her.

Of late, the act of lying down on a bed and the act of sleeping were, in Felicity's case, two quite unconnected events. She tossed and turned, fully awake, for a good three hours before she started to doze. Whilst in that indeterminate state between sleep and wakefulness, she experienced more dreams—or at least sensations—but these were like none she had endured before. She enjoyed the sensation of feeling great warmth. Her friend had arrived and was showering her with love and kindness. She was having fun ... something was making her feel happy and contented.

She woke with a start. The light—bright for late autumn—poured in through the window, suggesting she'd overslept. She sat up. From downstairs came the faintest noise, a sort of shuffling, scratching noise with just the hint of the murmur of a voice. Slipping on her robe, she picked up the poker. Glancing round, she could see no sign of Mister Ogilvy. She hoped he was alright, wherever he was.

As she advanced down the stairs, the noises increased. Definitely originating in the kitchen. She gripped the poker more tightly and crept along the hallway.

At the kitchen door, she hesitated. Surely, she had grounds to phone the police now? Why risk placing herself in danger? She wavered, half-turned to go in search of her phone, but then pivoted back towards the door and took a breath. Straightening up, she increased her grip on the poker.

Come on, Flick. You can do this. Make Aunt Maud proud!

Felicity swung the door open ... and dropped the poker. She was looking in at something that might have been created during a bad LSD trip. Standing beside the kitchen table and opening a tin of pilchards was the man from the previous evening. Beside him was a kind of green octopus-type creature, frantically waving two of its tentacles while dancing in an agitated way on its remaining three. It was clearly exhibiting signs of impatience, waiting for the can of pilchards to be opened.

Standing *on* the table was what at first looked like a bird. Covered in beautiful plumage, there the resemblance ended. In place of a bird's head, it had a miniature dinosaur head. Felicity realised she had seen a likeness of it before.

At the movies!

This was a tiny version of the Tyrannosaurus Rex in *Jurassic Park*. Instead of wings, small appendages similar to human arms extended from its body. On the ends of the arms were what at first glance might have been human hands, but on closer scrutiny Felicity could only count three or four digits. Nevertheless, the creature was, with great dexterity, scraping out the remains of a carton of dog food and scooping it into its large mouth.

Sitting in the corner was the puppet from last night, incongruously wearing red-tinted sunglasses. Felicity could see that the glasses had been modified by having the sides shielded, presumably to prevent the ingress of white light. Helly rocked gently back and forth, nestling Mister Ogilvy in the crook of his right arm. The cat lay there, content enough, as the hellventi gently stroked him with his left hand.

Felicity started forward, intent on retrieving her cat and removing him from danger.

The man raised a commanding hand. "Stop!" She opened her mouth to protest, and he continued, "I promise you that Mister Ogilvy is in no danger. In fact, as you can see, he is enjoying himself." He pointed at her and raised an eyebrow. "But you really must calm yourself, Felicity. Calm your thoughts. You are frightening the children."

She opened her mouth and closed it again and stared around at his 'children'. The dino-bird had stopped eating and now faced her, its mouth wide open and arms outstretched in a combative posture. The octo-creature had danced a few paces away from the table and its eyes had become very large and impossibly round. The hellventi sat stock still, his face towards her. She couldn't see his eyes for the sunglasses, but she imagined he was staring at her through wide, unblinking, red-rimmed eyes.

"Sorry," Felicity heard herself say.

This is a dream. That's all it is. I'll wake up in a minute.

Ignoring the aggressive posturing of the dino-bird, she pulled a chair out from under the table. She sat down heavily, sighing deeply.

It was as if someone had pressed the play button on a video that had been paused; everything went back to as it had been. The dino-bird settled down and began scooping out the last bits of food from its foil tray, then held the empty carton up to the man.

"In a second, Mr Polly, in a second! You can see I'm busy." He finished opening the can of pilchards and dropped the contents directly onto the kitchen table.

Splat.

Felicity winced. Not a plate, bowl or any other container in sight. The octo-creature danced forwards and, displaying amazing flexibility, picked a single fish up with one tentacle and dropped it into its beak-like mouth. It reached for another with a free tentacle, and so on in a blur of motion. In seconds, all of the fish had been consumed and all that remained was a splash of oil on the kitchen table where they had lain.

The hellventi resumed his rocking, crooning some kind of tune. It sounded pleasant in an 'I-like-alien-music' sort of way. Mister Ogilvy, who had raised his head and meowed during the interval, now rested his head again, his eyes drooping. Felicity could hear him purring from where she was sitting.

Well, at least my cat is happy.

She slumped further into her chair, her head swivelling in wonderment at the creatures. She no longer felt fear. Instead, she was resigned to the implausibility of it all. Raising her head, she shrugged. "Alright," she said quietly, "you *are* HG Wells, and you *are* a time traveller."

The man turned to her with a smile that couldn't have been wider, his eyes glistening with pleasure, the relief and satisfaction clear in his voice. "Yes! Felicity, my dear. Yes!"

CHAPTER FOURTEEN

"So, these are creatures you have brought here from the past?" Felicity asked, her eyes wide with wonder.

"From futurity, my dear, from aeons in our future. Tee-zed-beta, to be precise."

"Tee-zed-beta? Is that a place?"

"Ah, no. Forgive my jargon, I get so used to using it in my own mind and writing it down. Tee-zed-beta refers to Time Zone Beta." He gestured dramatically in the air as though he were giving a lecture. "Time Zone Beta is a time period more than one and a quarter million years in the future ... one and a quarter million years in our future!" he repeated for emphasis.

"These children"—he waved a hand towards them—"are all from that period."

"I see," said Felicity.

She didn't.

"Have you read *The Time Machine?*" he asked.

133

She nodded. "Several times."

"It is an account of my journey, largely true, with some elaboration and invention, into a time period which I have called Time Zone Alpha. Tee-zed-alpha is, in round numbers, 800,000 years into the future. Tee-zed-beta is half a million years further into the future."

Felicity nodded, her eyes glassy.

"Let me introduce you to my charges," HG said, gently smiling at each of the creatures in turn. "Sitting on the table and currently taking in your scent—"

Felicity glanced up at dino-bird, who had moved to within a foot of her head and was sniffing the air with his large snout.

"—is what I have classified as an iguanopteryx, because he looks like a cross between an iguanodon and archaeopteryx, the very first bird. The iguanopterges almost certainly evolved from birds, which in their turn, of course, evolved from dinosaurs. His species appears to be some sort of reversion. I call him Mr Polly, partly because he reminds me of a parrot, and partly after a character in one of my novels."

Felicity tried to smile, watching the bird warily as it gazed at her through shiny, unblinking eyes.

"This," HG continued, placing a hand on the head of the green octopus-type creature—thereby causing it to wave its two free tentacles in the air, while at the same time performing a little dance on the three standing tentacles—"is Penny." He patted her. "She is very excitable," he added as an aside. "She has five arms, as you can see. I have classified her as a pentepus, or more

CHAPTER FOURTEEN

"So, these are creatures you have brought here from the past?" Felicity asked, her eyes wide with wonder.

"From futurity, my dear, from aeons in our future. Tee-zed-beta, to be precise."

"Tee-zed-beta? Is that a place?"

"Ah, no. Forgive my jargon, I get so used to using it in my own mind and writing it down. Tee-zed-beta refers to Time Zone Beta." He gestured dramatically in the air as though he were giving a lecture. "Time Zone Beta is a time period more than one and a quarter million years in the future ... one and a quarter million years in our future!" he repeated for emphasis.

"These children"—he waved a hand towards them —"are all from that period."

"I see," said Felicity.

She didn't.

"Have you read *The Time Machine?*" he asked.

133

She nodded. "Several times."

"It is an account of my journey, largely true, with some elaboration and invention, into a time period which I have called Time Zone Alpha. Tee-zed-alpha is, in round numbers, 800,000 years into the future. Tee-zed-beta is half a million years further into the future."

Felicity nodded, her eyes glassy.

"Let me introduce you to my charges," HG said, gently smiling at each of the creatures in turn. "Sitting on the table and currently taking in your scent—"

Felicity glanced up at dino-bird, who had moved to within a foot of her head and was sniffing the air with his large snout.

"—is what I have classified as an iguanopteryx, because he looks like a cross between an iguanodon and archaeopteryx, the very first bird. The iguanopterges almost certainly evolved from birds, which in their turn, of course, evolved from dinosaurs. His species appears to be some sort of reversion. I call him Mr Polly, partly because he reminds me of a parrot, and partly after a character in one of my novels."

Felicity tried to smile, watching the bird warily as it gazed at her through shiny, unblinking eyes.

"This," HG continued, placing a hand on the head of the green octopus-type creature—thereby causing it to wave its two free tentacles in the air, while at the same time performing a little dance on the three standing tentacles—"is Penny." He patted her. "She is very excitable," he added as an aside. "She has five arms, as you can see. I have classified her as a pentepus, or more correctly *Mollusca cephalopoda pentepus*. That said, I doubt if any of my classifications would stand up to scrutiny by the Royal College of Science. It's just what sprang to mind when I first saw them."

"Yes," said Felicity, her head buzzing.

"You've already met Helly," HG said, half-turning and indicating the hellventi, who immediately stopped rocking and stared up at him. "I will tell you more about Helly later. I can't talk of his loss at this time. It is too distressing for him. But he is a fine young man, don't you think?"

As if in response, the hellventi raised himself up on one buttock and noisily broke wind.

Wells immediately pulled a handkerchief out of his pocket and placed it over his mouth and nose. Felicity remained in place, stupefied, not quite believing what had occurred. Well, not until the smell hit her. Gagging, she pulled her robe up over her mouth and nose. Mister Ogilvy leapt down from the hellventi and dashed down the hallway, heading for the living room. The other two creatures took not the slightest heed. The hellventi, for his part, lowered himself down again and carried on rocking and crooning as if nothing had happened.

"Good gracious!" spluttered Felicity once she could breathe again. "What was that?"

"Sorry!" said Wells, wiping his eyes with his handkerchief. "I should have warned you. Hellventi, despite their rather fearsome teeth, are in fact mainly vegetarian. As a consequence, they do have a tendency to be rather flatulent. Undigested greens, I think."

Felicity couldn't help herself. She threw her head back and roared with laughter. Wells, despite his best efforts, eventually had to succumb and joined in. Helly increased the rate of rocking and held out his arms to the two humans, making a sort of guttural chuckling sound as he did so, while Penny did her dance, waving her 'arms' around frantically. Even Mr Polly performed a little jig.

Once Wells had regained his self-control, he clapped his hands and immediately everyone paid attention to him, including Felicity. "I think it's time for the children to go up to the nursery now, don't you, Felicity?"

The nursery?

Felicity nodded, although she had no idea what he was talking about. Which begged a question. "Can you communicate with them?" she asked.

Wells shrugged his shoulders and scrunched up his face. "With difficulty. However, I can communicate with Helly and he can communicate with the others."

"You speak Helly's language?"

"Goodness no, far too complicated, too many whistles and clicks. Nor does Helly speak English very well. But I have spent the last week at Spade House, my home in London, teaching him, and he's learning very quickly. He's not quite there yet, but he will be. In any case, it doesn't really matter. His ESP powers are highly attuned."

"ESP?" queried Felicity.

"Extra Sensory Perception?" Wells raised his eyebrows. Surely she had heard of it.

"Oh yes, of course."

"Helly, like all hellventi and indeed most of the creatures in TZB, is telepathic. He doesn't need the crudity of language to communicate. Observe!"

Wells waved his arm to attract Helly's attention then knelt on the floor in front of him, widening his eyes and staring at the creature intently. The hellventi became rigid, not moving a muscle. After a few seconds he began to nod his head vigorously. Then, uttering a strangled cry, he half-turned towards the table. Instantly, both Mr Polly and Penny turned towards him and stood motionless, their gazes fixed on him. The communication between the three creatures lasted only a few brief seconds. Penny then gently wrapped a tentacle around Mr Polly, moved to the storage cupboard and, in a blur of green, climbed the wall and disappeared through the window at the top. To Felicity's surprise, this swung freely both ways.

"Well, I'll be—" she frowned. "I didn't know it did that." The realisation that she had called the police out to investigate an intruder had her cringing. It had been HG Wells and his 'children' all along. She wondered what DS Alderson would make of that.

Probably best not to tell him, she decided.

Helly rose and moved towards Wells, who was still kneeling on the floor. The hellventi threw his arms around the old man. Wells reciprocated, hugging him back with genuine affection. As they separated, Wells struggled back to his feet and Helly moved towards the cupboard. When he reached the door, he raised his hand towards Felicity.

"Good-bye!" he articulated as he slipped inside.

Felicity stepped forwards to watch him as he gracefully climbed up the shelving and disappeared through the swinging window, breaking wind as he did so.

Wells and Felicity fled to the living room where she collapsed on the sofa in hysterics again.

Wells stolidly attempted to maintain his dignity. "Really, my dear," he gently scolded.

Drying her eyes, Felicity said, "Oh, come on, Mr Wells, you have to admit, he does seem lacking in the everyday graces."

"But this is entirely normal for the hellventi," Wells explained with a straight face. "I once lived with them for a week. It was like being in the centre of a brass band rehearsal."

This sent Felicity into further paroxysms. Once she had fully recovered, she sat upright on the sofa. Wells had seated himself on an easy chair at the side of the long-extinct fire.

"What should I call you?" Felicity asked. "Mr Wells? Uncle? Herbert? George? Time Traveller or Professor?"

Wells chuckled. "Any of the aforementioned will do, but my preference is for HG, that's what Maud called me."

Felicity smiled. "Then HG it will most certainly be. If it's good enough for Aunt Maud, it's good enough for me." A thought occurred to her. "So ... have you come back here to pick up the ... um ... er ... children so you can return them to the future?" asked Felicity with just a faint trace of hopeful anticipation in her voice.

"That was certainly my intention. Penny and Mr

Polly are both ready to go home, but now I have Helly's welfare to consider. If I left him alone without the type of companions he can relate to, I fear it would seriously retard his rehabilitation. You see, although he clearly has a level of affection for me, he still sees you and me as aliens."

"Us?" Felicity performed a double take. "Aliens?"

"Yes, to him we're strange, rather ugly creatures; no offence intended. So, my intention at the moment, at least, is to leave Penny and Mr Polly with him for a while to help heal his mental scars."

"But you *are* taking them somewhere, right?" Felicity asked, her voice tinged with dread. She had a bad feeling that she already knew the answer.

"Ah, well, Felicity, that's what I need to discuss with you."

Felicity instantly cottoned on to his meaning. "No! No! No! You are not leaving them here. They have nearly driven me mad recently and I didn't even know they were here!"

"Yes, they can be a little unruly. They are children, after all. But—"

"Stop right there! The answer is no!"

HG pulled a pained face. "But Felicity! I appeal to you as your dearest Uncle HG—"

"Don't try to butter me up. I only met you a couple of days ago, and even then you were in the blatant act of breaking and entering!"

"Very well." Wells sounded resigned, a half-smile playing on his face, his soft eyes expressing their sadness.

"Perhaps if I appeal to you as Aunt Maud's father, you will at least hear me out?"

"That is so unfair," Felicity pouted. "Yes HG, I *will* hear you out. And when you have finished I will say, in a very loud and clear voice so there can be no misunderstanding, a resounding no!"

"Thank you, Felicity, for at least listening. You need perhaps to be aware of the social context in which these creatures live in TZB." HG cleared his throat. "Let me explain."

Felicity slumped back in her chair in resignation.

"TZB is a very symbiotic society. It's simple and very interdependent. The pre-eminent species is the hellventi, who are descendants of the mixed blood of Eloi and Morlocks. Sadly, they have inherited much of the physiology of the Morlock, but thankfully they also inherited gentleness and kindness from the Eloi. I mentioned that they are in the main vegetarians, however they do love fish, and I think that combination accounts for some of the unpleasant gases they discharge from time to time."

So absorbed was Felicity that she didn't even snigger.

Wells continued. "Don't be misled by their appearance. They are highly intelligent and very competent engineers and builders. Aeons ago they mastered the technique of cold fusion, a process of combining molecules in order to produce electricity which they use to power their production machines. These machines manufacture the very few artefacts which they and their symbiotic companions need. The electricity is also used to energise tubes of neon which they use for lighting in their subterranean factories and power stations. As a consequence of this, their eyes have become attuned to the red end of the spectrum, while white light causes them physical pain and, if exposed for any length of time, could cause damage."

Now Felicity understood Helly's need for sunglasses.

HG confirmed this. "One of the artefacts they produce is the glasses you saw Helly wearing. Increasingly over the last few centuries they have been coming to the surface, their long-term goal being to leave the subterranean life behind and become surface dwellers. However, they are under no illusion. This process will require many generations. Many now live in specially constructed houses on the surface. During the day automatic blinds, opaque to all but the red end of the spectrum, descend to protect them. At night these blinds raise so that the hellventi can enjoy the moonlight and stars and the fresh air of the surface."

HG Wells paused, his face falling. "It was in one such house that Helly and his parents lived until they were surprised by a raiding party of Morventi. Helly managed to hide, but his parents were brutally slain while he watched helplessly from his hiding place."

Felicity gasped. "Poor Helly. Now I understand why you didn't want to discuss this in front of him."

"Precisely! He might not have fully understood the words I was using, but the mental pictures in my mind would have transmitted to him in horrible clarity."

"And the Morventi? Who or what are they?" asked Felicity, now fully absorbed in HG's story.

"They are the filthy, degenerate direct descendants of the Morlocks, with no Eloi blood to mitigate their vileness. They live entirely underground and are carnivorous. As their main source of food, they breed rats as a farmer might breed cattle, but are not averse to sending out raiding parties to capture other unsuspecting creatures. They are smaller and slighter than the hellventi and are of very limited intelligence. Even the crude ingenuity possessed by their Morlock ancestors has been lost."

"And what of Penny and Mr Polly?" asked Felicity.

"Those two species, the pentepus and the iguanopteryx, both by the way more intelligent than any other animal living on the earth in this present time—other than man himself—are the symbiotic relatives of the hellventi. There is no monetary system in TZB, not even a system of barter. Everything is done *quid pro quo*. I can give many examples, but let's just take a few."

He held up a finger. "The hellventi manufacture, from synthetic materials, the components of very sophisticated and intricate little houses, which they leave at the base of trees. The iguanopteryx, who live in the trees and, despite what you witnessed earlier, are excellent climbers, collect the components and assemble them high in the canopy. These houses are very secure and keep them safe at night. In return, the iguanopteryx harvest the highest branches, where the most luscious fruits grow, and leave them in baskets near the hellventi dwellings.

HG studied Felicity's face to check she was following and held up another finger. "The hellventi, with help from the iguanopteryx, build shelters for the pentepus near the edge of the sea or large lakes. These constructions look basic and crude, which is how the pentepus prefer them, but are skilfully constructed to ensure they do not collapse in on their inhabitants. For their part, the pentepus, who emerged from the sea several hundred thousand years in their past, are nevertheless expert swimmers and fishers. With synthetic nets produced by the hellventi, they go out in pairs, the nets stretched between them. On return to the shore, they share their catch with the hellventi and the iguanopteryx, who incidentally are also partial to a fish supper."

HG paused, aware he was probably overwhelming Felicity with his knowledge. It was a lot to take in at once. "I could give you many more examples."

"Fascinating," breathed Felicity. "Absolutely fascinating. So, how did you come to be looking after Penny and Mr Polly?"

"Penny was found on the seashore by a group of hellventi who were building a pentepus shelter nearby. The fact that she was left alone suggests her mother must have perished. Female pentepus are very protective of their young. One of the hellventi took her back to his dwelling and asked for my help. I was in the time zone at that time and I, in turn, brought her here to Maud's nursery."

Felicity nodded. *Poor Penny.*

But there was that word again. *Nursery.* What did he mean?

"Mr Polly's family contracted a form of avian disease. As is the case in such circumstances, they, of their own accord, moved away from the rest of the flock. Sadly, both parents succumbed to the disease and Mr Polly was left to fend for himself. I rescued him and left him with some of my hellventi friends—who, by the way, are immune to the disease—whilst I travelled back to this time with a sample of his blood. I was reluctant to bring him in person in case he infected our own bird species. You are aware that I am a zoologist, I think?"

"And a chemist, and a physicist, yes," confirmed Felicity.

"I was able to discover the cause of the infection and, knowing it to be readily treatable by antibiotics, was able to return. After a short course of injections, I managed to eradicate the disease. However, Mr Polly was left very weak, so I brought him to Maud, who nursed him back to health."

Felicity blinked. *Aunt Maud had been in on all of this? She'd created a nursery to look after the 'children'?*

Wells concluded his little lecture and leaned forward in his chair, resting his chin on his clenched fists, staring into the empty fireplace. After a moment, he rose.

"Where are you going?" asked Felicity.

"To collect the children. I'll take them to Spade House. I can convert one of the bedroom—"

"Sit down!" Felicity glowered. "I knew you were a conman the second you spoke to me in the barn and now you have swindled me with this." She closed her eyes for a second, hating what she would say next. "Yes, of course they can stay here! How can I say otherwise after what you've told me? I hate you, HG!"

HG sniggered. "No, you don't. You think I'm a cuddly old uncle and you're sorry for me and my children. I love you for that, Felicity."

"Hmmm." Felicity shook her head doubtfully. "And how am I going to cope with those three juvenile delinquents?"

"I can stay for a few days if you have a spare room." He obviously knew she did. "And despite what you think of him, Helly will be a huge help. He can communicate on your behalf, and the other sapient species in TZB respect his primacy. You saw what happened this morning. Once he had intimated his wishes to them, they complied without argument or complaint."

Felicity sank further into the sofa. "Heaven help me. Or more to the point, Helly help me!"

CHAPTER FIFTEEN

*A*fter a quick breakfast, and while Felicity began once again to clean up the kitchen, Wells indicated he would take a stroll.

"Are you seriously going out in that get-up?" Felicity looked him up and down. "You look like a stray from the Victorian era."

"I do not!" HG frowned. "I think you'll find I look like a stray from the Edwardian era."

"Hmm," Felicity shrugged, not entirely sure of the difference. "Do you have any fresh clothes with you?"

"There is a suitcase with some of my clothes in the attic. Maud used to launder it then pack it into bags made from that new-fangled plastic stuff. She kept it ready for me, for my visits. I'll get it down when I come back."

"Don't worry, I'll find it," said Felicity. "I need to go into the attic anyway."

"Well if you do, make sure that as you ascend the steps, you put out your left hand and you will feel a wooden post, part of a rafter. On that post is a switch that will provide illumination."

"Electric light, yes." Felicity rolled her eyes.

HG levelled her with a serious frown. "Please remember that Helly is in the attic."

"Oops." Felicity grimaced. She *had* forgotten about Helly.

"Before you flick that switch, shout, 'Helly, light!' and wait. He'll reply, 'Light, yes!' and that will tell you he has put on his glasses. It is then safe to switch on. I'm sorry if this all sounds terribly pedantic, Felicity, but you—"

"It's fine, HG," she interrupted. "I won't forget."

She smiled as she watched him saunter down the crazy paving clad in his old tweed suit, complete with straw boater and swinging his cane like an extra from a Charlie Chaplin movie. *He really is a dear,* she thought. *He tries to put on the 'loveable old duffer' act but I can tell his mind is as sharp as a knife. You don't fool me, HG.*

Once her kitchen chores were completed, Felicity took herself upstairs. After dropping the ladder from the attic, she climbed halfway up and felt around for the switch.

"Helly, light!" she called, as instructed.

There was a loud grunt, and a second or two later, Felicity heard, "Light, yes!"

She switched it on and climbed into the loft, immediately spotting Jan's scarf. Evidently one of the little aliens had taken a fancy to it and brought it up here.

The three children all slowly and hesitantly made

their way towards her. She felt no apprehension at their approach; instead, a wave of pleasure washed over her. It made her smile. She was sensing them! This was their way of saying '*Hello, welcome*'.

It reminded her of the nicer dreams she had been having and made her wonder whether the less pleasant ones had been from when they had been frightened.

"Hello, gang," she said warmly. Her words were greeted by a jig from Mr Polly and Penny, and something that very nearly passed as a smile from Helly.

"Hello, Fel-iss-i-tee," he said. Felicity broke into spontaneous laughter, causing her charges to take a few hasty steps backwards.

"Oh, I'm sorry," she said, regaining her composure and holding her hands out towards them. "It's alright! Come closer." She gently beckoned them, and they advanced slowly, a little less hesitantly this time.

"Helly," she said, staring into his glasses, rather glad that she couldn't see his eyes. "Not Felicity," shaking her head. "Not Felicity."

Helly looked puzzled. "Not Fel-issi-tee," he repeated, shaking his own head.

Pointing to herself, she said "Flick." Then pointing to him, "Helly". Pointing to herself again, "Flick". She nodded vigorously to reinforce the message.

"Flick," said Helly, pointing at her.

"Yes, Helly! Yes, good!" She patted his arm, grinning happily. "Well done, Helly. Well done."

It was the first time she had touched the hellventi, and she was a little surprised. She had read in *The Time*

Machine that the Morlocks had skin that was cold and clammy. Helly's felt warm and dry, quite ordinary really. Obviously, things had changed in half a million years.

Well, I suppose they will, she thought.

"Right, gang, I need to do some sorting out, so off you go and play." To her immense surprise they did just that, moving back to their special place at the rear of the attic. *They must have sensed what I meant*, thought Felicity. *I might be getting the hang of this!*

She quickly found HG's suitcase full of clothing and set it near the ladder ready to take down. On a whim, she began to look through the trunk containing Aunt Maud's papers. Coming upon a thick, A4-size leather-covered notebook, she opened it up and discovered that it was a journal. Scanning through it, she found a number of passages relating to herself. It was clear from what was written that Aunt Maud had indeed loved her dearly. Before long, her eyes brimmed and tears began to run down her cheeks. Being careful not to allow them to fall onto the precious pages, she swiped at her eyes, allowing her grief to spill out.

She felt rather than saw a presence nearby.

It was Helly, a look of abject sorrow on his face. He had sensed her pain and grief and had come to comfort her. He stretched his arms towards her. Felicity took him into her arms and held him tight, her chest hitching as she sobbed. He keened along with her, a sound filled with the sadness of aeons. One and a quarter million years separated these two beings, yet they still shared their grief and sadness in exactly the same way.

After they had both calmed down and composed themselves, they sat side by side on the floor. Felicity continued to read through the journal, finding references to a number of animals that HG had brought to the 'nursery'. Towards the end of the journal, she found references to Penny and Mr Polly and marvelled at how much time and care, and indeed love, Aunt Maud had bestowed upon these 'children', as she referred to them.

The last few entries in Aunt Maud's journal left her puzzled, however.

Monday 5th Aug

HG visited again last night and brought me a little creature which he has classified as 'Canis metamorphosis'. I shall refer to the poor dear as Meta. It appears she has been bitten by a poisonous leech-like creature, related to the haementeria ghilianii of our own time. HG has done his best for the poor thing, but I do not expect her to survive the night. The other two are making such a fuss of her.

Tuesday 6th Aug

Poor Meta made it through the night, but she is very weak. I will try her with a little boiled chicken. I must encourage her to eat, she is so frail. Penny has been naughty today and made a mess. I scolded her but I might as well talk to myself.

Wednesday 7th Aug

Meta making good progress and she has eaten some proprietary dog food today. I would love to give her a bowl of milk as a treat but am afraid she might be lactose intolerant. So, I will stick to boiled water as per HG's instructions. Mr Polly has been excellent. He stayed with her all day just stroking her with his little hands. She seemed to enjoy that. I must think of a better name, I don't much like 'Meta'.

It was Maud's last entry.

CHAPTER SIXTEEN

Felicity had never really had very much to do with children. One or two of her friends from university had succumbed to the temptation to procreate, but, having produced an heir, they had rapidly disappeared from her social circle, and Felicity had never been called upon to babysit. For her part, she imagined that at some stage she would meet the man of her dreams and perhaps have a child of her own.

When HG had abandoned the aliens to her care, she had thought that looking after them—now that they knew and appreciated who she was—would be a piece of cake. But she'd found that, like children, you needed to keep them occupied. It was fine while they were sleeping, and all of them liked to nap, but when they weren't, Felicity had to find them things to do, otherwise they would head for the kitchen and start ransacking her cupboards and the fridge.

Indeed, they *always* seemed to be hungry.

If Felicity had harboured a maternal bone prior to her encounter with her great-great-uncle, then it had been diminished in the few days since.

To be fair, at the moment she fantasised more about writing a second bestseller than breeding. Her books were her babies. Or they would be, if only she could write a few more. Besides, babies are expensive, and Felicity needed to earn a few more pennies to enable her to live the life she craved here at Prior's Cross, in calm isolation, producing work of depth and imagination worthy of great literary prizes.

Felicity tapped her pen on her notepad, distracted by her thoughts. *So, okay,* she was thinking, *no to children at the moment, but yes to the man of my dreams?*

Could Jan be The One?

Was it right to think of him in that way? They had known each other so long, she practically thought of him as a brother. But seeing him again after a few years, she couldn't help but feel attracted to him. What was not to like? Handsome, tall and strong, a great sense of humour and lots of conversation. And they were friends. Great friends.

Surely that was a good place to start.

She doodled Jan's name on her notepad. When her mobile started ringing, she automatically assumed it was him, and reached for it happily. But it wasn't Jan. It was her literary agent, checking up on her.

Felicity groaned and thumbed the green accept

button on her screen. They hadn't spoken for a few days, so it probably made sense to have a quick catch up. "Hi, Sasha."

"Hey, Felicity! How are you doing down there in the wilds of erm ... Dorset, wasn't it?"

"Devon."

"That's right." Felicity heard the sound of papers rustling at Sasha's end. She could picture the scene quite easily. Sasha's office was chaotic, with books and packages and files everywhere. It had to be a fire hazard. Felicity had met with her several times at the beginning of their partnership, and she'd hardly been able to see the agent across the desk, thanks to the enormous number of submissions she had still to wade through, piled sky-high next to her computer.

"You haven't been in touch about your next project and I wanted to talk through that with you," Sasha continued.

Felicity thought she could hear a slight edge to her agent's voice, one that she'd never heard before. "I'm still working on an idea," Felicity replied, trying to sound both casual and in control but, to her mind, she simply sounded lame.

"I need something to take to the publisher, Felicity. Remember, if you want us to renew your contract—"

"Yes. I'll have something very soon ..." Felicity trailed off. The flash of bright rainbow-coloured plumage out of the corner of her eye had distracted her. "Mr Polly?" she asked.

"Mr Polly?" Sasha asked. "You do realise that's already been done? By some Victorian writer or other."

"Edwardian," Felicity said, following Mr Polly out to the hallway. He perched on the balustrade and pecked at his feathers.

"Oh, that's right. John Wyndham."

"HG Wells." Felicity frowned. How could this woman call herself a literary agent? She didn't know *anything* about literature.

"Really? Well, anyway, we'd prefer it if you weren't derivative."

"Of course." Felicity reached out to stroke Mr Polly's head. He regarded her solemnly and sniffed her fingers. When she didn't appear to have anything worth snacking on, he returned his attention to his chest feathers.

Confident that Mr Polly wasn't about to try and destroy the house, Felicity turned back towards the study. "No, I don't mean that I'm going to write a—" She caught her breath. The octo-creature had climbed up onto the desk and was busily tapping away on her keyboard using most of its tentacles. "Penny!"

"Penny?"

"Sorry, Sasha. Just give me one second!" Felicity dashed over to the desk to shut the lid of her laptop, but Penny was already slipping to the floor and scuttling away.

"I really need to know whether you have a viable idea I can sell or not, darling—"

"I'm sure—" Felicity narrowed her eyes. Penny had paused in the corner of the room. She had a firm grip of something shiny. Felicity glanced at her laptop and sucked in a deep, horrified breath.

Her memory stick! She had backed up all of her most recent work to it!

"Listen, if you think we're going to struggle, we can abandon the contract for now and perhaps revisit it somewhere down the line?"

Penny caressed the shiny pen drive and shoved it in her mouth.

"Don't you dare!" shrieked Felicity.

"I beg your pardon?" Sasha sounded most put out.

Penny started to crunch down on the final draft of Felicity's last completed novel, several short stories she had submitted to women's magazines, and the most recent fragments she had managed to put together in an effort to concoct something new for Sasha. In other words, Penny was snacking on months of Felicity's blood, sweat and tears.

"You absolute horror!" Felicity cried, hot, furious tears springing to her eyes.

Sasha exhaled noisily. "Well!"

Felicity, suddenly remembering she was on the phone to Sasha, clapped a hand to her cheek. "No, no. Not you, Sasha! I have an issue here I'm trying to deal with."

"Is that so?" Sasha did not sound convinced.

"An alien just ate my novel," Felicity explained. "She—"

"An alien ate your novel? I've heard it all now!" Sasha laughed in disbelief.

"Let me sort this out and I'll call you right back," Felicity begged. "Just give me five minutes."

"I tell you what Felicity," Sasha replied icily, "don't call us, we'll call you."

"I promise—" Felicity tried to say, but she was speaking to dead air.

CHAPTER SEVENTEEN

Felicity blew a stray hair from in front of her eyes and scraped at her nose with the back of her left hand while simultaneously stirring her cheese sauce with her right. She felt like one of those one-man-bands she used to see at the seaside. With four rings on the go and the oven on as well, the kitchen was hot, the windows steaming up, the dirty dishes mounting up and, in addition, she was fearful she had all her timings wrong. A side of beef rested on a board next to the sink, and her rich dark onion gravy bubbled away, reducing beautifully.

She had hoped she would look cool, calm, collected and gorgeous by the time Jan arrived. She'd made an effort with her hair and make-up and covered her pretty top and leggings in a large chef's apron, but she hadn't counted on the amount of moisture and heat her menu would create.

She stole a look at the red wine, reminding herself to

open it and let it breathe. Maybe she should pour herself a small glass while she was at it. Just try it out. And calm her nerves at the same time.

What had got into her? She didn't normally get this hot under the collar over entertaining a male friend.

Except, if she was being honest with herself, she didn't want Jan to remain simply a friend, did she?

"Oh, nonsense," she told herself, crossly. "Of course I'm happy with Jan as a friend."

She turned the cheese sauce off and poured it over the waiting cauliflower. After sprinkling a little pepper and parmesan on it, she thrust it into the oven, jiggling for space with the roast potatoes and stuffing balls. She wasn't sure Jan liked stuffing with his beef, but she did, and she hadn't felt confident enough to try out Yorkshire Puddings.

Flat Yorkshires would not look good on a first date.

"It's not a date!" she sang, as she clumped over to the sink and rinsed out her saucepan in an effort to calm herself down. She eyed the pile of washing-up to the side. "Rats."

Deciding she ought to make a start on clearing up at least some of the mess before Jan arrived, she began to load the dishwasher. Once that was full, things looked better. She filled the sink to wash glasses and a few glass bowls and methodically began to wipe down the kitchen table and work surfaces.

By the time Jan turned up at the back door, Felicity had almost restored order to the kitchen.

Taking a deep breath, she opened the door wide. "Hi,

Jan, welcome!" she sang, stepping back. He stood awkwardly in front of her, a carrier bag in one hand and a bunch of pretty flowers in the other. He held them out. "Erm, I thought ..."

Felicity rescued him. "Oh, how beautiful. Thank you so much. Come in!"

She bustled around, finding a vase and filling it with water while he hovered at the door. "Would you like a drink?" she asked, turning back to inspect him. He'd obviously made an effort. He was wearing clean jeans that looked suspiciously as though they might be new, and a pale blue shirt that matched his eyes. Even his shoes were sparkling.

He held up his carrier bag. "I came prepared. I wasn't sure whether you preferred red or white wine, so I bought one of each."

"We'll have plenty to go around, then!" Felicity laughed and indicated the open bottle of red on the table. "I've a bottle of Chardonnay chilling in the fridge already, so I'll save these for later."

He grinned. "What are we having? It smells delicious!"

"Beef roast and rhubarb crumble." Felicity shrugged. "I know it's a weeknight, but, er ... I don't get to eat a roast very often, living on my own."

Jan, who ate a huge roast every Sunday, thanks to Mary Gurney's cooking, gave her a thumbs up. "You can't go wrong with a Sunday Roast on a Thursday, I always say." He indicated the kitchen table. "Can I do anything? Would you like me to lay the table?"

"We're not going to eat in here." Felicity widened her eyes in mock shock. "I've set the table in the living room. It'll be cosier in there." *And hide us from the rest of the washing up*, she thought.

"Posh." Jan winked at her.

"That's the idea." Felicity picked up the bottle of red wine and led him through to the living room. She'd hoovered, dusted and plumped the cushions, lit the fire and subdued the lighting. Aunt Maud's best dining table could seat six to ten people, depending on whether the leaves were extended or not. Tonight, Felicity had placed Jan at the head, and she had opted to sit to the side, next to him.

Mister Ogilvy was lording over proceedings by lying sprawled in front of the fire on the rug.

"If you don't mind"—Felicity indicated the fire which needed stoking—"you could build the fire up a little more and choose some music while I dish up."

"No problem." Jan knelt down next to Mister Ogilvy and stroked his head.

She returned to the kitchen and began to arrange her beef on a serving dish and her vegetables in bowls. She realised she'd made enough to feed an army and set some aside. Never mind. It would keep. She could make a delicious bubble and squeak tomorrow. She made a couple of trips down the hall with her meat and vegetable dishes, then returned to the kitchen one last time to decant her gravy into a sauce dish and place the rhubarb crumble in the oven to cook while she and Jan ate their main course.

Jan had selected a range of chilled music. A little Coldplay, Adele, Bruno Mars, One Republic. Music they had enjoyed listening to when they'd been younger. Cheerful conversation flowed as easily as the wine, and Felicity soon relaxed. Jan seemed to enjoy her dinner and, although he protested that he couldn't eat another thing, once she had cleared away the leftover beef and vegetables and brought out the rhubarb crumble and clotted cream, he found space.

For two helpings.

They lingered over the crumbs of the pudding.

"You'll be eating cold beef sandwiches for days," Jan said, "but unfortunately you won't be able to follow it up with dessert. Sorry about that." He rubbed his belly ruefully.

"Not to worry. There's always apples from the tree out the back. I make a mean Caramel Apple Granny."

"I'll be coming over regularly!" Jan smiled.

Felicity flushed with pleasure. "You're welcome any time, you know that."

She stretched and groaned, pushing her chair back. "Right, I'd better clear up and then we can settle down with more wine, if you like?"

"Sounds good." Jan stood too. "Let me help you."

At that moment, the music ended. From the kitchen came the distinct sound of a baking tray sliding along the tiled floor.

Felicity stiffened. *Uh-oh.*

Jan frowned.

Mister Ogilvy jumped to his feet and ran to the door.

Jan followed him. "What was that?" he asked and opened the door.

"I'm sure it's nothing!" Felicity called after him, but he'd gone to investigate. She followed him down the hall and into the kitchen. "Jan—"

How could she tell him about the aliens in her attic?

He pulled up short. "What the—?"

Together they surveyed the wreckage. Every last piece of the dinner had been polished off—almost. The gravy pan had been licked clean. The cauliflower cheese devoured. The roast beef was history. The dinner plates shone as though they had only just come out of the dishwasher. Only the peas remained, and they had been scattered all over the floor.

"Ha-ha," Felicity said, and Jan looked at her doubtfully. "Nocturnal visitors," she explained, wrinkling her nose. "Saves on washing up."

He didn't look convinced.

After seeing Jan out, she watched him walk up the lane until he disappeared into the gloom. She waited there at the door for a while, listening to the sounds of the moor by night, feeling strangely lonely. Although used to living by herself, Jan had been such good company that his sudden absence affected her more than she'd care to admit.

"Ridiculous!" she scolded herself and yawned widely. "Time to make my security rounds."

She started with the front door, locking and bolting it, checked all of the downstairs windows and made her way to the kitchen. Leaning over the sink to check on the window there, a sudden flash nearly blinded her.

Not as bright as previously, but it could only mean one thing. HG was back!

She unlocked the back door and walked out into the yard, staring up at the barn. Within a few seconds, a red light appeared.

You're becoming predictable, HG.

She made her way into the barn, just in time to see a ladder descending from the trap, so smoothly and quickly that she assumed it must be power-driven. Before Wells could climb down, she quickly clambered up. Her tomboy days of climbing trees, ladders and various orchard walls to scrump apples with Jan had not been wasted.

She met Wells at the top. He was busily untying something strapped to the back of his machine.

"Good evening, HG."

"Why, Felicity, how nice of you to meet me. You really are a sweet girl."

"Don't butter me up, HG," Felicity smiled. "It worries me when you do that. Last time it landed me with the three creatures from the Black Lagoon.

Wells laughed. "Oh, come, come, Felicity. They're charming little children, and they are not from a lagoon. Penny was found on the seashore about three miles inland from where Torquay is currently situated, the sea having risen significantly since the present time, of course."

"Oh," Felicity said. That sounded ominous. "Climate change, eh?"

"I found Mr Polly among some trees, roughly where the wood to the north-east of the Gurney farm is currently located, though you wouldn't recognise the trees that grow there in TZB." HG nodded at her. "And Helly's dwelling is a mere stone's throw from where we're standing now."

Felicity held up a hand. "Fine, HG. I don't need a geography lesson. It was a joke. You know? Creatures from The Black Lagoon?"

"Oh, a joke. I see!" Wells scratched his chin. "I'm afraid that one has passed me by. What am I missing?"

"The Black Lagoon? *The Creature from the Black Lagoon*? It's a classic! It was a film made in the fifties?"

"The nineteen *fifties*?" Wells queried, and Felicity nodded. "Ah!" Wells's eyes twinkled in amusement. "There you have the advantage over me. I assume you are referring to talking pictures? I did see one or two in the nineteen *thirties*, but I wasn't much impressed."

Felicity gave up. "Here," she said, "let me give you a hand with that." Wells was struggling to unload a heavy object from the machine. It turned out to be a suitcase. A second was still strapped to the parcel shelf.

"What on earth have you packed in these?

"Oh, just a selection of shoes and clothes. I was concerned by the remark you made about me looking, how shall we say, 'out of time'?"

A selection of shoes and clothes? Two suitcases? Felicity narrowed her eyes. "How long do you plan on staying, HG?"

"Just a few days, but I thought if I brought a selection, you could advise me on what to wear, so as not to be too conspicuous."

Together they manoeuvred the suitcases out of the barn and struggled across the yard. They were almost at the back door when it was flung open and they were met by the very excited children, who came clambering out to greet them.

"Oh, my goodness!" cried Felicity, looking around in alarm, thankful it was a dark night so there were no random ramblers in the vicinity or farmers on tractors rumbling by. "Go back in, children! If anyone sees you, we'll be in trouble."

Yes," confirmed Wells, nodding at the aliens gravely. "Terrible trouble."

Felicity shepherded everyone inside and closed the back door with a firm snap. She hustled around, issuing orders, until eventually all five of them—plus Mister Ogilvy—were settled in the living room. Penny situated herself a few feet from the fire and slowly rocked her head from side to side as she tried to make sense of the flames. Mr Polly had climbed the standard lamp and was perched on the rim of the lampshade, quietly chirping to himself. Helly had insinuated himself between Felicity and Wells on the sofa and was holding on tightly to their arms, looking up, his head swivelling from one to another. Mister Ogilvy nestled on Helly's lap, perfectly content.

It is questionable whether such a family group had ever congregated together in such a way in the entire history of our galaxy.

"Where did you get the clothes you packed in the suitcases?" Felicity asked.

"From Spade House, my home near London," Wells replied.

"So your machine ... it can travel from place to place?"

HG shook his head. "Not in the sense that a motor vehicle travels or even an aircraft, from point A to point B in a certain length of time, dependent on speed. I can only translate spatially during a temporal translation. If I dematerialise at point A, then it is possible to materialise at point B, but it must be either in the future or in the past, as part of a temporal transformation."

Felicity shook her head. *What was he on about?* "Is there a readily available English translation for that?"

Wells smiled indulgently. "Basically, if I want to move the machine from Spade House to my barn here—"

"My barn!" interrupted Felicity.

"Our barn," conceded Wells. "But as I was saying, if I want to move the machine, I have to make a time jump. I can programme the machine to simultaneously move its spatial coordinates, its position in space if you like, to a new place as part of the jump. It need only be a jump of a few minutes, but there has to be a jump."

"Oh, I get it now. You can't travel to the exact moment of time." Clearly impressed, she raised her eyebrows. "That's very useful."

"It's not that useful." Wells shook his head, his face grave. "The materialisation point, the landing point if you like, has to be calculated relative to the take-off point in exact detail. Any discrepancy could be disastrous! Imagine materialising in the middle of a hill!"

"Ha!" Felicity shuddered. "That's a horrible image. So each time you 'jump' from Spade House to here, you are actually taking a tremendous risk?"

"No. I have calculated the relative position of my—sorry—our barn to my laboratory in Spade House *exactly*. Those coordinates have been programmed into the machine."

"What about when you travel to Time Zone Beta? To pick up or return the children?"

"Not so much of an issue. You will notice that I am on the upper floor of the barn. That is to make up for the difference in height between here and TZB. Spatially, my take-off point and landing point are exactly the same."

"And Time Zone Alpha?" asked Felicity

"I never travel to TZA anymore," Wells answered. "It's far too dangerous!"

"Ooh." Felicity pulled a face.

"Time for bed!" Wells announced.

Wells shepherded the children to the attic nursery while Felicity made them both a hot drink. Once he'd returned, they made small talk before he in turn declared himself ready to retire. Left on her own, Felicity, with the hindrance of Mister Ogilvy, tidied up the kitchen and wiped down the counters near the sink.

But suddenly she froze.

Mister Ogilvy had jumped up on the draining board. He stood in front of the window, gazing out, spitting and hissing in a most ferocious way. Felicity reached for him to attempt to calm him down. She frowned at his visible trembling. She had never seen the cat so distressed. Peering out of the kitchen window herself, she struggled to see what could be causing his panic.

When she finally spotted it, she shot backwards.

Staring up at the window, its red eyes shining in the dark, was the most fearsome dog she had ever seen. Could it even be called a dog? Spawned in the depths of hell, big and muscular, its thick neck supporting the most hideously evil head ever created, it stood squarely on its powerful legs, slavering with hunger.

Or something.

Felicity moved quickly to the door and locked it, slamming the two bolts home simultaneously. Cautiously, she tiptoed back to the window.

I'll call HG, she thought. But when she looked outside again, the hellhound had disappeared.

CHAPTER EIGHTEEN

*B*y the time Felicity awoke the following morning and made her way to the kitchen for a much-needed cup of tea, Wells had already left the house. A brief note on the kitchen table informed her that he had decided to take a walk.

The children were all in the kitchen, but surprisingly, there was no mess! Helly had done a good job of explaining the rules to them, although Penny was clutching a tin of pilchards in one of her tentacles and looked poised to detach the lid.

"Please put it back on the shelf, Penny. There's a good girl," Felicity said. To her total amazement, Penny complied immediately.

I'm getting good at this, she thought. *The trick is to say the words out loud, then the pictures will form and be received by the children. Progress!*

"Bowls, Helly, please."

Helly obediently made his way to the crockery

cupboard and returned with two bowls and a large plate. He arranged them in their respective places on the table. He would sit at the head of the table, while Penny, given that sitting on a chair was impossible for her, stood at the side. Mr Polly was the only one now allowed to stand on the table, and only because of his smaller stature.

Mr Polly's breakfast consisted of a carton of dog food and a dozen or so grapes. Penny's was a tin of pilchards, which she brought from the cupboard herself, fish being her favourite food. Helly took his place at the head of the table behind his large plate which contained a half lettuce, a parsnip, a red beet and his personal favourite, half a mangel-wurzel, all of which were—of course—uncooked. Just looking at his food gave Felicity indigestion. Nonetheless, she sat down with them with just a bowl of cornflakes and realised that she felt, unaccountably, rather content.

As she rose from the table to replenish her mug, she heard the front door open.

"Only me!" Wells called down the hallway. A moment later he clattered into the kitchen. Felicity took one look at him and closed her eyes, her hand on her brow. He had chosen to wear plus fours, knee-length woollen stockings, ankle-high brown leather lace-up boots, a jacket with elbow patches and a soft floppy cap.

When he saw her expression, he looked down at his clothing, then back at Felicity.

"No?" he asked, raising his eyebrows.

Felicity shook her head, her expression pained. "Definitely not, HG!"

"I'll get changed," he said and charged up the stairs.

Felicity finished her cornflakes and began cooking breakfast for him. She tittered, remembering how he'd looked. *It's like he's an alien himself,* she mused, *and all because he comes from a different era.*

By the time she heard his footsteps descending the stairs again, his sausages and bacon were on a plate under a very low grill, and two eggs were spluttering in the frying pan. He had changed into a Harris Tweed suit and was sporting a very fetching red bow tie.

"Better?" he asked.

"Better!" she said, adding "marginally" under her breath.

"Thank you, Flick." Helly stood up from the table and expressed his appreciation in his usual way. A noxious cloud of invisible gas filled the room. Like HG, Felicity now carried a handkerchief as a matter of course, and now they both hurriedly retrieved them and covered their mouths and noses.

When it seemed safe to speak again, Felicity said, "You're welcome, Helly. I'll get some mackerel from town for your supper tonight."

"Helly loves mackerel!" Helly said, dancing around with excitement.

"Yes." Felicity glanced meaningfully at Wells. "That's something we can all look forward to!"

Wells, clearly having difficulty controlling his mirth, asked, "What did Helly call you?"

"Flick. It's my nickname."

"Flick? Flick?" He tried the word several times whilst

making a movement with the forefinger of his right hand. "Sounds like someone switching on a light bulb."

He sat down to his breakfast. As he ate, he lapsed into silence.

Felicity poured herself more tea. "Is something bothering you, HG?"

"Yes." He placed his knife on his plate. "I wouldn't normally dream of burdening you with my problems under ordinary circumstances, but as I recall, you mentioned that you had had a number of strange dreams recently. Is that not so?"

"Yes—"

"I had thought that perhaps Mr Polly and Penny were reaching out to the new occupant of the house, following Maud's death, afraid to show themselves until they could be sure you meant them no harm."

"Really?" Felicity asked, then thinking about it, added, "I suppose that makes sense. Now that I know them better, I do tend to pick up on their feelings."

"Exactly." He hesitated. "But did you ever dream about a dog?"

Puzzled, Felicity considered the question. "No," she said eventually, "but I did dream I was running about on the moor and hiding. Could I have dreamt I *was* a dog?"

Before Wells could reply, Felicity, remembering the incident of the previous evening, gasped. "That being said, I *did* see the scariest dog ever last night! A horrendous, ugly-looking brute, it was!"

"Ugly?"

"Like something put together by Frankenstein."

Wells made her describe the dog in more detail, and then she recounted her dreams of running and hiding on the moor, of her strange sensation when in the area of Fox Tor. "I wake up and I'm so frightened," she finished. "In the dreams I've felt so alone."

Wells slumped back in his chair, his brow creased, deep in thought.

"What happened to Fossy?" he asked suddenly.

"Fossy?" For a second, Felicity had no idea what he was talking about, but then it came to her. "Oh, Fossy! Aunt Maud's dog! Sad. Jan told me she had run off. He tried to find her but never did." She watched the spark of interest in Wells's eyes. "Why the sudden interest in all this, HG?

"Whilst I was walking today, up near Fox Tor, I had the strangest and most inexplicable feelings, similar to those which you have described during your own walk in that area." He puffed out his chest. "I am therefore drawn to the inescapable conclusion that Fossy is still alive and hiding in the region of Fox Tor."

"But it's been so long!" Felicity reminded him. "Surely she must be ..." she faltered, "long gone."

Wells shook his head, adamant. "I think you'll find she's out there somewhere."

"Then we must find her; she is in terrible danger!" Felicity blurted. "That hound I saw is prowling the moor. It has to be the thing that is killing ewes and ponies. Even a bull. HG, we must find Fossy before it's too late!"

"Yes, I agree. But to find Fossy, first we will need to locate the hound you observed last night."

"But—"

Further deliberation on the matter was put on hold by the rumble of a car entering the yard. Felicity made eye contact with Helly and raised her eyes to the ceiling. Immediately, the three children climbed up the inside of the cupboard and disappeared.

She hurried to the window and spotted Jan climbing out of his Land Rover. Strolling to the door, he gave a cursory knock, opened it and walked in, singing out, "Hi, Flick!" as he did so.

Jan stopped in his tracks, studying the elderly man sitting at the table making up and down flicking motions with his forefinger. "Oh, I'm sorry. I didn't realise you had company." He turned to leave.

"Come in here, you big daft Janner!" she said, grabbing his arm and giving him a swift kiss on the cheek. "This is ... um ... er ..."

Wells was already on his feet and across the room in two strides, smiling and extending his hand. "Felicity's uncle," he said, shaking Jan's hand vigorously. "Harold Gibbs. But please call me HG. Everyone does. You must be one of the Gurney boys. Daniel or John?"

"You know my family, Mr Gibbs ... HG?" Jan asked, surprised.

"Of them," said Wells, quickly realising his mistake. "Felicity has told me all about your family. Didn't you, Felicity?"

Felicity offered a wan smile as Jan looked at her askance.

"Ah-ha." Jan nodded. "So, what brings you to Princetown, HG?"

"Oh, the usual. Walking on the moor, you know?" Wells replied. "I've always wanted to explore it and when I wrote to Felicity and told her so, she very kindly invited me to stay here."

"I wish you'd told me, Flick," said Jan, frowning. "I could have arranged some time off. We could have gone out together, the three of us." He nodded at HG. "Flick and I used to love a short trek across the moor when we were younger, didn't we?"

"Yes," said Felicity lamely. "Sorry. I should have told you. It was rather ... erm ... last minute."

"Oh well, never mind," said Wells who, guessing that Jan's idea of a short trek differed from his own by several very arduous miles, wasn't at all enthusiastic about the idea.

"I came to tell you that there's a meeting of the local farmers in the backyard of the Plume this afternoon to discuss the killings up on the moor," Jan told Felicity. "I wondered if you would like to come?"

"Yes, we would!" Wells broke in, his voice sharp, then seeing the look of consternation that crossed Felicity's face, he modified his tone. "If that's alright with you, Jan? I'd love to get the feel of a community in action, so to speak."

"Of course." Jan, notoriously easy-going, shrugged. "I'll pick you both up at half one. The meeting starts at two."

CHAPTER NINETEEN

Once Jan had gone, the children came back down from their hiding place. Felicity made sure to give them all a proper fuss, a thank you for their quick and quiet departure.

"By the way, HG," she said. "I've been meaning to ask. Where does that window in the store cupboard lead? Can they be seen from the outside when they climb through?"

"No, indeed," said Wells, lifting his chin and looking pleased with himself. "It's my own design. It looks like a chimney from the outside but it is, in fact, a vertical shaft leading up to the attic. It has hand and footholds to enable the children to climb up." He pointed upwards. "There is a light which shines on the outside of the window during the day to give it the appearance of an external window. At night the light is automatically extinguished, again making it look like an outside window."

"Genius," said Felicity, although she hated to make HG's head bigger than it already was.

"I thought so."

She changed the subject. "Getting back to what we were talking about ... I didn't quite understand what you meant by your reference to Fossy and the hound."

HG folded his arms. "Would you mind awfully if we left further discussion on the subject until after this afternoon's meeting?" he asked. "It's just that I think that the outcome of the meeting may have some bearing on how we proceed."

Promptly at one thirty, Jan appeared in the yard with his muddy old Land Rover. The three of them crammed themselves onto the front seat and made their slow and bumpy way up the lane into Princetown.

"Is your Dad not coming, Jan?" Felicity asked.

"No. Father won't come to any of these meetings. 'Talking shops', he calls them. He particularly dislikes hearing the Bickles and Ted Blackstock mouthing off, and of course they'll be tanked up on scrumps by the time the meeting starts. Actually, old man Bickle is okay, but his son Billy is a gob—" He darted a quick look at Wells and stopped himself. "I mean, he's a loud-mouthed waste of time, who's been leeching off his old man for years."

Felicity guffawed. "Say what you mean, Jan. Don't hold back."

Jan laughed with her. "Sorry, HG, but as you can tell

I don't much like those two. I wouldn't mind betting you form the same impression when you meet them. You wait and see if I'm right!"

Needless to say, Jan *was* right.

The meeting was attended by about two dozen farmers and farm workers. There was also a stranger among them, a small, weasel-faced man in a grubby wool coat wearing a Dr Who-type scarf that had probably never been washed. He wandered around the group talking to a number of the farmers, scrawling notes on a pad.

"Who's that, Sid?" Jan asked an old farmer standing nearby.

Sid was often referred to by the locals as 'Daft Sid' because of his many eccentricities, but as Tom, Jan's father, had told him once, "Daft Sid? Ha! 'Ee haves one of the largest farms on the moor an' drives a Mercedes. 'Ee baint as daft as them that calls 'im that!"

Sid eyed the man and gave Jan a wink, "'Ee be one o' them there reporters, Jan. Up from Plymouth, to see what us yokals be doin'. Barney or Arnie, I think 'ee said his name were."

Old Frankie Bickle opened proceedings. He gave a graphic account of the condition in which he had found his bull. He was followed by Donny Jackson from Greenbough Farm, who had lost a ewe and discovered the remains of a Dartmoor pony. He, in turn, called on Jan to verify that he had also lost livestock.

Jan did so, confirming that they had found the

carcasses of two ewes, one each on two separate occasions.

Throughout the proceedings, the speakers were constantly interrupted by Billy Bickle. Bickle, a big man, tall and heavy set, stood with Ted Blackstock. The unruly pair shouted obscenities, unhelpfully demanding that the 'beast' be destroyed, put down and so on. Every sentence they uttered was interlaced with a dozen expletives. Both had clearly been drinking for several hours.

Wells noticed that the younger Bickle was carrying a shotgun.

Jan lost patience. "What exactly are you going to kill, Bickle? We don't even know *what* is doing this, let alone where to look."

"Course us do!" roared Bickle. "Why, Ted 'ere, 'ee seen 'im! Din't you, Ted? Tell 'em."

"That I did!" confirmed Blackstock, his eyes half closed, wavering around on the spot and barely able to stand. "I saw 'im alright. I'm tellin' ya, 'ee were a devil dog! That's what 'ee were!"

"I seem to remember you seeing ghosts once before, Ted, when you were full of scrumpy," quipped Jan, to the amusement of those assembled around him and to the discomfiture of Blackstock and Bickle.

The meeting was interrupted by the arrival of Police Sergeant 'Jock' Galloway, a canny Scot who had migrated to the West Country as a young man. He had joined the police many years before, and gradually won the respect of the locals in Princetown. He peered around the assembled throng, slowly and carefully taking everyone in, then, striding over to Billy Bickle, he snatched the shotgun from him and broke it open. Extracting the two cartridges, he rammed them under Bickle's nose.

"Bickle, you ever come into Princetown with a loaded firearm again, and I will run you into Tavvy lockup so fast, your feet won't touch the ground."

Turning to Billy's father, he snapped, "And you, Frankie Bickle, I'm surprised you let him."

"I din' know 'ee 'ad loaded 'im," Frankie replied lamely, his face turning pink.

Jock stood in front of the gathered crowd, facing them, his face as dark as a thunder cloud. "My friends," he said, keeping his voice level, "a word in your shell-like ears if I may. As you all know, I have been patrolling this moor for many a long year, and I have seen the carcasses of quite a few of your ewes, some that have been worried by dogs, some taken by foxes ... but I'm telling you I have *never* seen anything like this." He shook his head, his face grave. "And as for worrying a bull? I don't believe any dog could do that. A pack of bull terriers might frighten a bull and herd it, but a single dog? No. Not even a devil dog." He said this with a furious glance at Ted Blackstock, eliciting a ripple of laughter from the crowd. "Because a dog facing up to a South Devon bull would end up being tossed from here to the other side of Okehampton."

There were mutterings of "Arr" and "Tis right!" among other affirming comments.

"I believe," Sergeant Jock continued, "that this is the work of a person or persons who are intent on taking the meat. Could be that it's for their own consumption, but more than likely it's because they want to sell it on. That's who we need to be looking for." He nodded at the farmers. "Now, I have nothing against you forming search parties; you may very well unearth something of value to the police but"—he threw a stern look at Billy Bickle—"I don't want any cowboy tactics. Otherwise, this little sheriff and his even littler posse will come and round you up."

Jock's message was well received.

But then Sid piped up. "For what it's worth, I believe it be an alien from another planet that landed ' ere on the moor."

Uproarious laughter greeted his suggestion and despite his protestations—having determined to form two separate search parties—the meeting broke up.

As Jan, Wells and Felicity left the meeting, they were confronted by an incensed Billy Bickle in the yard.

"I din' like the way you spoke about me an' my mate Ted," he said in a sentence which actually included an interesting and colourful array of expletives too. "You bedder watch yourself, Gurney."

Jan curled his lip and rolled his shoulders back. Lifting his chin, he said, "Get out of my way, Bickle. If you're trying to frighten me, you're failing miserably."

Taking Felicity's arm, he brushed past Bickle without a second glance.

Neither of them paid any attention to the reporter busily scribbling notes at the rear of the room, his eyes alight with ill-concealed glee.

Once clear of the yard, Jan suggested they drive up to the Warren Inn for a beer. HG politely declined, adding he was keen to walk along the railway line instead.

"What railway line?" asked Jan, scratching his head.

"The Yelverton to Princetown line. I walked it once before—the scenery is quite stunning. I shan't go all the way, just as far as Kings Tor Halt this time."

Jan looked hard at HG for some time before glancing at Felicity and back to HG again. "There hasn't been a railway between Princetown and Yelverton for sixty or seventy years, HG."

Felicity cut in quickly. "He meant the track. The railway *track!* Didn't you, HG? The track where the line was. That's still there, isn't it, Jan? You can walk along that, can't you?"

"Oh, right. Yes. The track is fine. It's a nice walk, HG, but watch the time. It's starting to get dark earlier now. There's a couple of quarries out along that way, you don't want to fall into them. In fact ..." He thought for a moment and continued, "best to go out through Station Cottages, the other side of the car park. That's where the old station was before it was demolished."

"They demolished the station?" HG looked personally aggrieved.

"We'll see you later," Felicity said, widening her eyes and gesturing with her head, indicating that HG should take off. She pulled Jan in the direction of the car park, hustling him away from HG.

After paying for the drinks, Jan carried them outside to where Felicity sat huddled on a bench. They had decided to sit outside to admire the amazing view from the Warren Inn. They were both bundled up in warm clothing, so the definite chill in the air didn't bother them.

Felicity sighed happily. "Mmm. It's so beautiful, isn't it? The way the light changes as the sun travels around the sky." She lifted her glass to Jan. "You work out in all weathers on the moor, don't you ever get tired of this view? Wouldn't you like to look out of your window and see skyscrapers?" She laughed. "Or lots of shops, coffee houses, that kind of thing?"

Turning to her, Jan gave her a smile that was as old as the moor itself. "What do you think?"

Giggling, Felicity buried her head into his chest. "Put your arm around me," she told him, "I'm beginning to feel the cold."

Jan willingly complied. "How can you feel cold wearing that great fleece?"

"I don't really, it was just an excuse." They both laughed and he kissed the top of her head.

Felicity could have remained that way forever, but Jan diverted her attention elsewhere. "You see that flat rock up by the top of the hill there?"

Felicity reluctantly sat up, scouring the hillside until she could see where he meant. "Oh, yes. What about it?"

"That's called a coffin stone. One of a number on the moor. In days gone by, when someone died on one of the outlying farms, four farm labourers would carry the coffin across the moor to Tavistock for burial. They would look out for flat rocks where they could rest the coffin so that they could take a breather. That rock was one such."

"Really?" Felicity asked, her writer's mind suddenly working overtime. "Fascinating! And why are you suddenly telling me this?"

"Because," said Jan, contorting his face into what he supposed was his most fearsome expression, "one night, at midnight, I am going to drag you out here and make you watch a ghost procession. Up the hill they'll go, then rest their coffin on the stone while the four men sit around it drinking scrumpy and singing *Widecombe Fair*."

Groaning, Felicity pushed him away. "Jan Gurney, there are times when you talk utter nonsense."

Jan snorted. "It's not as nonsensical as Daft Sid's idea of aliens landing on the moor and eating our livestock! You didn't laugh at that."

Felicity pulled a face. "No I didn't, did I?" She chewed her lip. "Ummm, I wonder."

Jan took a swig of his pint. "What do you wonder?"

Felicity hesitated. "Maybe there's something in it?"

"Flick, what are you saying?" Jan laughed.

"Did you notice anything ... well ... odd about Uncle Harold?" she asked, emphasising the 'Uncle'.

"To be honest, Flick, I didn't notice anything *normal* about him. 'Odd' may be an understatement. I mean, what was all that about the railway? The old boy really thought there was still a railway there! And while we're on the subject, why did you cover for him?"

Felicity wrinkled her nose. "Well, you see ... last time

he travelled the line, there *was* a railway, *with* a station in Princetown and a halt at Kings Tor."

"Get out of here! He would have had to be a babe in arms! He couldn't possibly remember it."

Felicity wiped the moisture from the side of her pint and avoided looking at him. "There is no way I can tell you this without you laughing at me, but I'm going to say it anyway." She took a deep breath and gazed straight into his eyes. "Because I, that is *we*, need your help. HG is a time traveller!"

Jan didn't laugh. His mouth dropped open and he simply stared at Felicity.

"Either laugh at me or say something," she said quietly.

"You know, sometimes your sense of humour, well it's just—"

"It's not a joke. I'm deadly serious!" She lifted her head, her eyes sharp.

Jan turned away, then back. He crossed and uncrossed his arms several times, looked to the sky, then at the ground, not quite sure where to put himself or what to say. Eventually he said, "Felicity?" He had never used that name, and Felicity's heart sank. "You know how much I care for you, it's just that ... well ... to be honest, you're frightening me. If you're serious ... I don't know ... Maybe if you just went to see, well ..." He grimaced.

"A psychiatrist, right?" she snapped.

"No. Yes. No! A doctor. What if you went to see a doctor? I'd go with you."

Felicity, quietly furious, wrapped her arms over her

chest and glared at him. "Okay, Jan, tomorrow morning, I'll go into Plymouth and see a psychiatrist. On two conditions."

"Name them, Flick, anything."

"One, you go with me."

"Of course!"

"Two, you come back to Prior's Cross now and look at the evidence. If you still don't believe after seeing it for yourself, even if you have a slight doubt, I'll come with you to Plymouth tomorrow. Agreed?"

"Agreed!"

"Right." Felicity picked up her drink and drank it down in one. Slamming the glass on the table she said, "Finish your pint. Let's get going. There is no point in delaying this."

CHAPTER TWENTY

*A*s they entered the house by the back door, Felicity motioned for Jan to take a seat at the kitchen table.

"Listen carefully, Jan. No matter what happens now, no matter what you see, I want you to promise me you will remain in that chair." She waited until he nodded before continuing, "I want you to try to remain completely calm. Do not speak, or you will transmit your thoughts—"

"Transmit—"

"No speaking! Do you understand, Jan? You *must not speak!*"

"Yes, Felicity," he said and slumped in the chair, his mind reeling, his stomach sinking. He covered his face. *Poor Felicity.* His best friend in the world had suffered a total breakdown and he feared there might be no recovery from it. What could he do? He felt totally helpless.

And yet Felicity seemed so in control. She opened the storeroom door and called up, "Can you come down now, Helly? And bring the other children down."

Children? Jan sat up.

The first to appear was the hellventi. On seeing Jan, he fled to Felicity, raising his arms pleadingly. Felicity picked him up and held him to her side. Jan shifted forward in his seat as though he would stand up and take a closer look, but she held out a restraining hand then put her finger to her lips, ordering his silence.

Next came Penny who, having danced into the kitchen in her customary style, suddenly scuttled behind Felicity in alarm, peeking out at Jan, her eyes wide. Finally came Mr Polly. Seeing Jan, he squawked and bounded onto the draining board, taking up a defensive posture. He hissed loudly, his head jutting backwards and forwards.

"Helly," said Felicity softly, attracting his attention so she might look, as best she could, into his goggle-covered eyes. "This is Jan," she said, pointing. "Jan is *my* friend and Jan is *your* friend."

The hellventi turned his head and stared at Jan for some time, then pointed at Jan, who remained stock still in his chair, staring in wonder at the apparition before him. "Jan! Flick's friend. Helly's friend."

"That's right, Helly, well done!" Felicity stroked his arm. "Can you tell the other children about Jan, Helly?"

All three of the children froze for a few brief seconds, before Helly confirmed, "Children understand, Flick."

"Well done, Helly. You're such a help to me. You really are a special boy."

Helly snuggled closer.

"Right, gang, I'm going to give you a snack as a treat and I'll make you a special meal tonight because you've all been so good. For now, I'd like you to take your snacks back up to the nursery."

Clutching their supplies—a small bag of grapes for Mr Polly, an easy-open can of sardines for Penny and the other half of his breakfast mangelwurzel for Helly—the children climbed to the attic, Helly waving at Jan as he disappeared into the store cupboard.

"Goodbye, Jan!" he called.

"Bye!" Jan automatically replied, still completely stunned.

"Well?" Felicity sat down at the table. "Am I mad?"

Jan looked at the ceiling and then back at Felicity, making a half gesture towards the store cupboard.

"No, Flick, but I am. I'm having a nightmare. I'll wake up in a minute."

Felicity took his large, calloused hand between her two smooth ones. "No, mate. It's not a dream of any kind. HG brought them here from the future. It is for real."

"I don't know what to say," he said. "I can't quite get my head around it."

"You might start with sorry?" she suggested.

Jan brushed a hand through his hair and exhaled slowly. "You're right. I'm sorry. I should have known better than to doubt you. Even when we were kids, you were always right. I still hate you for it, you know," he told her, with mock severity. "But be fair, would anyone have believed what you told me up at the Warren Inn?"

"Only a madman," said Felicity, and chuckled. "What you've done is prove that you're not a madman!"

"I'm beginning to wonder," he said, looking at the store cupboard and shaking his head. "I'm really beginning to wonder."

Wells turned up a few minutes later. He came through the back door, startling Jan and Felicity still sitting at the table. He took in the scene at a glance. Walking over to Jan, he extended his hand.

"Let's start again, shall we? My name is Herbert George Wells. But you may still call me HG."

"You let it slip a bit up in Princetown, didn't you, HG?" Jan smiled.

"I fear I did, but what a terrible shame that the railway no longer exists! Imagine what a tourist draw that would be in this day and age. Heritage vandalism! That's what it is. The planners in the nineteen fifties displayed an *abysmal* lack of foresight."

Felicity stood. "Listen, why don't you two go into the living room? I'm going to prepare the children's supper." She began to sort through the store cupboard looking for the items she needed. "I'll call the children down. You can amuse them while I'm busy here."

No sooner had Jan and Wells settled themselves in the living room, each in one of the comfy armchairs beside the fire, than they were invaded by the children. Helly immediately flew to Wells and threw his arms about him, while Penny shuffled hesitantly behind his chair, peeking out shyly at Jan from time to time, her large round eyes filled with wonderment.

Mr Polly, much to Jan's surprise, jumped up onto the arm of his chair and stood for a while looking at him. He cocked his head, first one way, then the other, clearly unsure about this new addition to his little family. Then to Jan's even greater surprise, Mr Polly hopped onto his shoulder and started chirruping in his ear.

"Awww, I like you too, Mr Polly," Jan said.

Mr Polly chomped his jaws down on a lock of Jan's hair and pulled it. Hard.

"Oww!" Jan tried to extricate himself.

"Mr Polly!" said Wells sternly. "That's not nice."

Helly swivelled his head and fixed Mr Polly with a hard stare. Instantly the iguanopteryx jumped down to the floor, sprang to the standard lamp and shimmied up, perching on the rim of the lampshade. He sat there, quietly chirruping to himself.

"Come on gang, supper's ready!" called Felicity from the hallway.

Immediately the children trooped out leaving Jan, ruefully rubbing his scalp, to marvel that such diverse creatures could so happily co-exist.

Felicity came in and sat on the sofa. "I've left them to it, so I might have some cleaning up to do later. Treats tonight. I bought strawberries for Mr Polly and mackerel for Penny and Helly." She looked meaningfully at Wells.

"Helly and mackerel! That could cause fireworks later on."

Wells shook his head and chuckled, and Jan raised his eyebrows.

"You really don't want to know," Felicity told him. "I'll fix us some supper as soon as the kids are finished."

"Not for me," said Jan rising. "I need to get back to put the buggy and the Land Rover away, then tidy the yard before it gets too late."

"John," said Wells, also rising, "If it isn't too much of an imposition, I wonder if you would mind coming back tomorrow morning? There a few things I'd like to discuss with yourself and Felicity regarding the killing of the animals on the moor."

Jan raised his eyebrows and nodded. "It's Jan by the way, not John. John makes me sound like a grockle. If you can throw some light on this, then I wouldn't miss it for anything. See you tomorrow."

"Not too early!" Felicity called as he climbed into his Land Rover.

Promptly at seven the next morning, Jan swung into the yard of Prior's Cross and tooted his horn.

Felicity, awoken from a deep sleep, glanced at the clock, spotted the time and lay down again, pulling her duvet over her head.

The toot came again.

Now fully awake, she groaned. *How is this happening? It's only just gone seven.*

Toot.

"Nobody sounds their horn at this time of the morning, it's probably illegal!" she grumbled and slipped out of bed to drag herself to the bathroom for a quick sluice. Pulling on an old pair of jeans and a tatty jumper she made her way downstairs, rubbing her eyes with the pair of socks she carried.

She found Wells already up and tending to the children in the kitchen. Helly sat in his usual place at the head of the table, while Penny stood beside Wells, one tentacle circling his waist. She danced impatiently, watching carefully as Wells opened a tin of sild and poured it into her dish.

Jan had let himself in. Seated opposite Helly, he was slurping from a mug of tea. Mr Polly, who had evidently taken a shine to Jan, sat on his shoulder, chirruping in his ear and gently running his tiny hands through the strands of hair he could reach.

"There is clearly something about your hair which intrigues our colourful little friend, Jan."

"That's fine. As long as he doesn't pull it again, I can live with that. Oh, here she is," he quipped, smirking at the sight of Felicity dragging herself into the kitchen, looking very dishevelled.

"What the hell time do you call this?" she grumbled. "Coming here in the middle of the night and making enough noise to wake the dead."

Jan put his hand to his mouth and raised his

eyebrows, pretending contrition. "Abject apologies to your majesty, but I would point out that it's gone seven. Father's been up on Naker's Hill for over an hour now."

Felicity curled her lip and lifted the teapot to see if there was enough for her. "All that proves is that he's as mad as you! You're mad. He's mad. Your brother's mad. Your dogs are mad. There's only your mother with a peck of common sense in the whole family."

"Perhaps I shouldn't mention that Mother's been up since half five, then?" Jan enquired.

"Then she's clearly insane." Felicity sunk onto a kitchen chair, accepting a mug of tea from an amused HG.

Felicity shook her hair back and caught it up in a ponytail. She looked from one to the other, then lowered her head. "Sorry! I know. Little Miss Grumpy climbed out of bed this morning." She grunted, "It's just that I was having the most wonderful dream. The children had returned to 'Futureland'—ABZ or DZP or whatever it was—and were living happily ever after, HG had disappeared in a bright flash and a puff of smoke, and you, Jan Gurney, had been conscripted by the Royal Marines and were serving on the darkest shores of Africa." She giggled at the thought. "All that peace and quiet. Oh, it was bliss!"

Jan pulled a face, playfully hurt. "I'm cut to the quick, but I guess I can take it."

After a few more sips of tea, Felicity perked up. She winked at Jan and, grinning, began to pull her socks on, struggling in the confined space between the table and her chair. Helly jumped down from his place and scuttled over to her. He pushed her hands gently out of the way and smoothed the recalcitrant sock onto her foot, before, and with great dexterity, pulling on the other.

Felicity was overcome by his thoughtfulness. She scruggled his wiry hair and held her arms out to him. As he came to her, she held him tight. "Oh, Helly, you are such a treasure."

What followed was a scene of unmitigated chaos as all six of them, plus of course Mister Ogilvy weaving in and out of legs and chairs on the hunt for any dropped morsels, breakfasted together, but once completed and the dishes cleared, the children returned to the attic nursery. The adults adjourned to the living room, carrying fresh cups of steaming tea.

Once everyone was comfortable, Felicity reminded Wells about his remarks from the previous evening. "You said you had something you wanted to discuss with us?"

"That's right." Wells leaned forwards. "The first thing I want to do is try to establish exactly what happened on the moor the night that Fossy ran off. Jan, you spoke to Maud ... Aunt Maud, the following day, did you not?"

"Mmm." Jan cast his mind back. "I did. I remember it well. She was quite distressed. In fact, I'd say she was beside herself because Fossy hadn't returned."

"Please try to remember her exact words when she told you about the incident," urged Wells. "Take your time. It's important that we get it as nearly correct as we can."

Jan recounted the incident in as much detail as he could recall, while Wells and Felicity listened in silence.

Once he'd finished, Wells sought further clarification. "You said there was a flash, *then* there was a crash?"

"That's what she told me."

"And she saw the creatures after the crash?"

Jan thought for a moment longer. "Yes, that's right. It was the crash that directed her attention to the wreckage. It was then that she saw the creature ... or creatures, actually. She thought one of them appeared to be dead."

Wells nodded, his face grave. "We need to retrace her steps. Felicity, do you know the route she would have taken?"

"Well, her favourite walk was along the side of the mire to the foot of Fox Tor, then back again by the same route."

"I wonder if you would both kindly come out and search with me. Six eyes are better than two. I would love to take Helly with us—he wouldn't miss a thing even with his glasses on—but we dare not."

They followed the route of Aunt Maud's walk, which was pretty much the same as Felicity had taken a few days earlier. The weather was being kind: dull and a little overcast, and with quite a chilly wind, but no drizzle and no mist. Felicity led, confident and sure-footed, as they made their way along the path. Wells, in the middle, occasionally stumbled on loose stones or tripped on wayward fronds of heather, so Jan brought up the rear, ready to catch Wells before he could fall and also to prevent him wandering off in the direction of the mire.

As they approached the incline up to Fox Tor, the path petered out and they were forced to walk on open moorland, dotted with tussocks of coarse grass and littered with rocky scree. Even on a day like today, the view was quite magnificent. To their front lay Fox Tor, a mere stepping stone up to the grander Crane Hill. To their left, steep and imposing, was Ter Hill and behind them lay the mire, constantly being watered by the myriad of streams flowing down from the high hills into this depression and making it one of the wettest, and indeed most dangerous places on the moor. Here they spread out, walking abreast in an extended line around the southern extremity of the mire, searching on the ground for any evidence that Maud's story had been more than a distraught old woman's flight of fantasy.

It was Jan who found the first clue. He called Wells and Felicity over, holding up what looked like a piece of grey plastic.

Wells rushed forward and plucked the item from Jan. "What have we here, then?" he asked and scrutinised it from every angle.

"It looks like a lump of everyday plastic to me." Felicity studied it over his shoulder. "Like the bumper off a car or something."

"Psh!" Wells faced her. "That's what it *looks* like, yes. Observe." He bent the material and twisted it simultaneously.

"It's much softer than it looks?" Felicity held out her hand and Wells relinquished it.

"It's extremely malleable," he agreed. When Felicity released the pressure on it, the material returned exactly to its former shape. "Memory Plastic," he breathed. "Made by the hellventi. As far as I am aware, nothing like it exists on Earth at this time."

Felicity shuddered, suddenly uneasy. She exchanged a look with Jan. He reached out and squeezed her shoulder.

"Let's keep looking!" ordered Wells, and they set to once more, eyes trained on the ground, searching for anything out of the ordinary. A thorough sweep of the immediate area turned up a number of shards of the material as well as several small panels containing electronic components. They began collecting the pieces together in a pile, with a view to taking them back to Prior's Cross, until Jan, who was conducting the final once-over on the very edge of the mire, called to Wells.

"HG? I've found a large piece of leather here. Would that be part of what you're looking for?"

Wells frowned and shook his head briefly. "No, but let's have a look." He tramped across the rough terrain, Felicity following behind him. She almost ran into his back when he pulled up short. He took one look at the material that Jan was holding and groaned loudly.

"What is it?" Felicity asked in alarm.

Wells dropped his walking stick and raised a hand to his head. "No, no, no!"

Felicity edged past him to get a better view. Jan held

up a long, long strip of material that looked like black leather, although with very thin ribs running its entire length. Both ends were submerged in the mire, making it impossible to gauge exactly how long it was.

Wells walked slowly and purposely to one end, then —oblivious to the fact that he was wearing only ankle boots, grey flannel slacks and a powder-blue blazer— stepped into the mire until he was knee-deep. He thrust his arms deep under the water and, after struggling with something for a short while, splashing both himself and Jan, he slowly raised the end of the material clear of the surface of the mire.

Felicity gasped and stepped backwards. Even Jan, accustomed as he was to a variety of gruesome sights during his farming life, grimaced. "What the—?"

It consisted, unmistakably, of the head of some kind of creature, but nothing Jan had ever seen on the moor before. It had the look of something that had crawled out of a Bram Stoker novel, or something Felicity might have included in one of her horror books. But this wasn't fiction.

The three of them stared down at the item in Wells's hands. There were two empty sockets which had once contained eyes, and two rows of vicious, sharp pointed teeth. Two of the teeth on the top row were longer than the others, ferocious-looking canines.

Indicating these, Wells said, "These are effectively hypodermic needles. When the creature bites, it instantly injects a poison into the victim's wound."

"Ewww," said Felicity and backed further away, her

head swivelling as she looked around the mire uneasily. "That really is the Creature from the Black Lagoon," she said.

"More 'The Creature from the Grim Mire'," Wells pointed out, "if we want to be pedantic about such things."

Wells climbed out of the water and retrieved his walking stick. He used it to lever up the edge of the material. The skin of the creature was doubled over, the insides completely gone. "Eaten out by the creatures of the moor," opined Wells. "I can't say I feel sorry for it."

"It sounds like you know what it is," Jan said. He looked anxiously at the old man, who suddenly seemed to have aged even more; his eyes were at once hollow, red-rimmed and deeply, deeply sad.

"I fear I do," Wells replied, his voice almost inaudible. "Not only what it is, but where it came from and how it arrived here."

"HG?" Felicity asked, taking his arm.

"I'm fine," he said, patting her hand. "Let's get back to the house. Make sure you bring all our artefacts."

After stowing all of the bits and bobs they had retrieved on the ground floor of the barn at Prior's Cross, they returned to the house and assembled in the living room, Wells on the sofa and the other two in the armchairs either side of the fireplace.

Hunched forward, his face grey and his eyes bloodshot with tiredness, he sighed wearily.

"You have both been truly kind and obliging, and I

now feel you are entitled to an explanation. This whole sorry business began in TZB."

"That's the time period that Helly, Penny and Mr Polly came from," Felicity interjected helpfully for Jan's benefit.

"I was working, with the help of a couple of the hellventi and a very obliging iguanopteryx—the hellventi often seek their help to construct very tiny intricate solid-state electronic devices, their little hands being so nimble —on a portable version of my time machine. Felicity can attest to how big and clumsy the current machine is."

"That's true," Felicity nodded. "You need to see it to believe it."

"We had reached the point where trials were needed to ascertain its effectiveness. Foolishly, however, I decided to miss out step one, the transmission of non-organic material through time, and move instead to step two, transmission of a living organism."

Jan shot a quick look at Felicity and she raised her eyebrows.

"Clearly, I did not want to carry out trials using myself or any of the other sentient beings of TZB at this early stage, so I chose a creature that is reviled by most of the inhabitants there." Wells cleared his throat. "The subject I chose was a type of leech found on the edge of the marsh, which in TZB is geographically almost exactly where Foxtor Mire lies today."

Jan's mouth dropped open.

"The creature is almost certainly descended from the Amazonian leech, *haementeria ghilianii* of our own time.

It is a repulsive horror, fully two feet long and about two inches thick. Unlike its Amazonian ancestor, it first paralyses the victim with a poisonous bite after which it can feast on its prey at leisure, draining it of blood, then eating the flesh to the very bone."

"Oh, that's gross," said Felicity.

"Indeed it is, as you say, 'gross', my dear," Wells agreed. "All of the creatures of TZB go in fear of it, with the exception of the pentepus, Penny's relatives. They have developed a very effective two-fold defence. Firstly, they are immune to the leech's poison, to the extent that the leeches have learned over the millennia to rarely bite the pentepus, and then usually only in self-defence."

"Fascinating," Jan said. "And secondly?"

"Their second line of defence is even more effective than the first. If the leech does bite them, and that does happen occasionally, as I've mentioned, the blood of the pentepus—which is green by the way, hence their colouring—is poisonous to the creature. One drop of their blood and the leech, in its turn, becomes paralysed."

"That's—" Felicity struggled to find words, "very useful."

"Incidentally, the pentepus feed on the leeches. It is considered a great delicacy, and that helps to keep the numbers low."

"I'm so glad the numbers are low," Felicity grimaced. "Horrible!"

"It was with two of these obscene creatures, captured for me by one of my multi-tentacled friends, that I decided to conduct my experiment at the side of the marsh," Wells continued. "I placed them in a box and attached it to my portable time machine, set the apparatus to move forward two minutes in time and activated it with my remote device. The apparatus, complete with its leech passengers, disappeared as expected, but on the completion of the allotted time, did not reappear. I waited several hours, but it still did not reappear."

"Uh-oh," said Felicity.

"What went wrong?" Jan wanted to know.

"I was forced to conclude that one of three malfunctions had occurred. That it had gone forward in time further than the two minutes set; that it had gone backwards in time to some unknown period; or that the whole thing had disintegrated, never to be seen again."

"Did you ever figure out which?" Jan asked.

Wells's face dropped. "Not until today." He rubbed at his forehead. "I had not foreseen the fourth possibility, which I am now forced to accept is what actually happened. My portable device was connected wirelessly to the main time machine, that being its main source of power. I believe the settings of the main machine overrode the setting I had programmed into the portable version. As the main machine is set for the present time, this caused the portable device also to materialise in that present time—*our* time—in exactly the same location from which it 'took off' ... just a little to the south of what is at present Foxtor Mire."

"But what about the crash Jan said Aunt Maud heard?" asked Felicity.

Wells nodded. "Remember what I told you previously about ground levels changing? The ground at the point where we found the wreckage this morning, in our day, is twenty feet *lower* than it is in TZB."

"Right—"

"Consequently, my portable machine materialised twenty feet above the ground and crashed to earth, destroying the machine and killing one of the leeches. The other leech, unfortunately, appears to have escaped unharmed. During the transfer, the machine must have malfunctioned, causing the molecules to be scrambled and resulting in the passengers being metamorphosed. The leeches, seemingly, have increased to a size four to five times their original dimensions."

"Oh, Lord." Felicity covered her heart with her hand.

"So, you see, my friends"—Wells dropped his head into his hands—"I am entirely responsible for the disaster that has been visited upon you!"

"And this process can't be reversed?" asked Jan.

"Unfortunately not," confirmed Wells, shaking his head. "It's far too dangerous."

The three of them remained silent for several minutes, each thinking their own thoughts, imagining their own horrors. The first to react was Jan. "Well, what's done is done and can't be undone." He slapped his thighs. "We now need to concentrate on how we are going to kill that ... thing!"

CHAPTER TWENTY-ONE

"Would you like to stay to dinner?" Felicity asked a little later on, extricating herself from Helly's grip. Mister Ogilvy jumped from Helly's lap and stalked to the door of the living room, meowing loudly. They had been talking all afternoon and each of them had a tension headache and had probably drunk a little too much tea.

"Yes, please," said Wells. "I'm famished."

Felicity rolled her eyes in mock exasperation. "I wasn't talking to you, but I suppose seeing as you're here." She winked at Jan. "You?"

"I don't know," Jan hesitated. "I should be getting back. I've let my chores slip today ..."

"I understand," Felicity said, collecting up half a dozen mugs to take through to the kitchen. "It was good of you to come over and help us on the moor."

Jan followed her down the hall and into the kitchen,

worried that he'd hurt her feelings. "It's not that I don't want to—"

"No, really, it's fine!" Felicity grinned at him. "We've kept you from your work, I appreciate that." She started to run the tap to rinse the mugs out.

"What are you having, anyway?" Jan asked, looking around as though the answer would be immediately obvious. Felicity, however, had learned her lesson well. There was no way on God's green earth she would ever have left food out for the children to get their grubby mitts on.

"Pork-in-cider casserole with buttered potatoes and green beans."

"Oh, that sounds good." Jan's mouth began to water at the thought. "I can resist everything except cider ..." He started to dig around in his pocket for his mobile phone. "Let me just give home a ring."

"You don't have to—" Felicity protested.

"I want to," he replied, firmly, and disappeared back into the hall where he could make the call in private.

Felicity washed up and started prepping the children's evening meals. By the time Jan had finished his phone call and been temporarily waylaid by Wells to discuss the relative merits of electric cars over fuel-driven motors, Felicity had her casserole in the oven, her potatoes peeled and ready to cook and the children were sitting round the table, calmly eating their dinners. It was a massive step forward in table manners, although to be fair, there was still plenty of mess everywhere.

Otherwise, it was a picture of domestic serenity.

Jan smiled as he came back into the kitchen, clutching yet another pair of mugs that he'd found in the living room. "Sorry about that," he said. "Your Uncle can certainly talk."

Felicity wiped her hot brow with the back of her hand. "Can you stay?" she asked.

"Yes, that's no problem. I'd love to, and everything is fine at home." He noted her flushed face. "Can I do anything? Peel some vegetable or other? Open the cider?"

Felicity snorted. "Most of it's done now, I just need to prepare the beans." She glanced across at the children. "And clean up after this lot." She paused then narrowed her eyes at Jan. "You know there *is* something you could do, actually …"

"Name it. Anything."

"If you wouldn't mind bathing the children? They keep getting covered in food, and I'm not sure whether any of them has ever seen soap and water before."

"Sure!" Jan said, full of confidence. "I'm an expert at bathing children."

"You are?" Felicity asked, somewhat doubtful.

Jan shrugged. "Well, how hard can it be? I've bathed myself often enough."

"I'm glad to hear it," Felicity said, turning her attention back to her beans. "Use the main bathroom. It's the door to the left at the top of the stairs."

"Who wants bubbles?" Jan asked, squeezing half a bottle of bath foam under the water as it ran into Aunt Maud's huge Victorian claw-footed tub.

"Bub-bles?" Helly asked.

Jan swirled the water around. "Look at these!" he enthused, scooping out a handful of suds and blowing them at Helly. "Don't they smell gorgeous?" He turned the bottle around. "Bergamot and rose. Expensive too, by the look of things. See what luxury Auntie Felicity has ready for you?"

Helly and Mr Polly remained at the door, watching Jan with some trepidation.

Not so Penny, however. Cautious at first, she slipped a tentacle over the rim of the bath and then edged it into the water. Exclaiming in excitement, she almost followed the tentacle in until Jan made a grab for her.

"Hang about, there, hang about," Jan urged. "I need to make sure the water is the right temperature for you young'uns." He pulled off his jumper and rolled up his shirt sleeve. "Don't worry, I've seen this on the television. I know exactly what I'm doing."

Dangling his arm over the side of the bath, he was about to manoeuvre himself into a suitable position to dunk his elbow in and test how hot the water was, when there was a tremendous splash. Penny had been unable to wait any longer and had thrown herself headfirst into the tub.

Jan sat back, spluttering, the soapy water in his eyes, dripping from his hair and all down the front of his shirt. "Careful there, Penny!" He realised he'd lost sight of her beneath the bubbles and reached out to pull her up, but she was as slippery as an eel and he struggled to get a grip. He was about to panic and call for Felicity or Wells when she resurfaced. Judging by the gleam in her eyes, she was as happy as a pig in manure.

Jan blew out a breath. She was alright. "How's that water for you?" he asked, and she swam around happily. "I guess it's okay?"

He stood up and confronted Mr Polly and Helly. "How about you guys? You can see how much Penny loves it. Do you want to go in? You can wear your goggles, Helly."

Helly looked at him and reached up with his arms. "Penny!" he said.

"I take it that's a yes." Jan carefully lifted Helly and deposited him into the bath feet first. "Oooh!" the creature said and splashed down with the flat of his hand, spraying Jan with even more water.

"Fun!" said Jan and made the mistake of splashing Helly back. Within seconds they were in a full-on water-fight, and Jan was coming off worst.

Mr Polly sought refuge on top of the toilet cistern, probably the only dry surface in the room, watching the goings-on below in bemusement. There seemed to be more water on the bathroom floor than in the bath itself.

"Okay, okay! I surrender!" Jan told Helly and held his hands up. He peered down at himself and the floor. "I'd better get this lot mopped up," he said, grabbing the hand towel from the rail, but glancing around he realised he'd neglected to bring any bath towels for the children.

He grimaced. *Drat.*

"Just wait there one sec, while I find some towels," he told Penny and Helly as he opened the bathroom door. He could smell the appetising aroma of pork and apples wafting up from downstairs. There didn't seem to be much point in disturbing Felicity. He opened the nearest door to the bathroom and found an airing cupboard. He pulled out a couple of large bath towels and closed the door but, thinking about it, he quickly reopened it and grabbed another couple.

Just in case.

He'd been gone less than thirty seconds, but in that time Helly had grabbed the bubble bath and was now squeezing the entire bottle into the water. Penny had her tentacles wrapped around the taps filling the tub up to the brim, the resulting mountain of bubbles threatening to overwhelm the small room.

"Eek!" Jan dropped his towels then carefully unlatched Penny's suckers from the taps and turned them off.

"Bub-bles," said Helly, squeezing the final dregs from the bottle. "Bub-bles."

As Jan tried to take the bottle from Helly's grasp, Mr Polly jumped down from the cistern and perched on Jan's head, twisting and turning and trying to make a nest.

"Ow! Mr Polly, do you mind?" Jan asked.

"Bub-bles," said Helly, "bub-bles."

"Yes! Too many bubbles," agreed Jan and, with one hand trying to gently untangle Mr Polly from his hair, he bent over the bath and reached down into the water with his other hand to pull the plug and drain some of the water away.

Helly, who had been building a store of gas since his mackerel dinner, chose that moment to eject some of it.

The water bubbled like a jacuzzi in front of Jan's face.

Bwood bwood bwood bwood bwood.

"What—"

Jan shot backwards, sending Mr Polly flying. The shiny bubbles began to pop at a rate of knots as the water turned a toxic shade of green.

Bwood bwood bwood bwood bwood.

The sweet perfume of bergamot and rose was quickly replaced by—

"Goodness gracious!" Jan gagged. "What's that stench?" He rushed for the window and threw it open, hanging outside and coughing and spluttering, his eyes watering. This explained the knowing look Felicity and Wells had exchanged when they'd discussed Helly's mackerel dinner.

Well thank you very much, Jan thought.

"Bub-bles," said Helly, behind him, "bub-bles."

Jan mopped at his eyes. If this was what having children was like, he was about ready to join a monastery high up on a mountain in Outer Mongolia.

CHAPTER TWENTY-TWO

That evening as they rested following the exertions of their day—with Jan sprawled on the sofa barely able to keep his eyes open—Wells interrupted the welcome serenity that had descended over the house once the children had returned to the nursery.

"I hate to mention this," he said quietly, "but there is another rather pressing issue."

"Oh, thank goodness for that." Felicity stirred herself. "I thought we'd run out of pressing, difficult and dangerous issues to keep us occupied."

Wells ignored her sarcasm and continued, "There is currently a little dog on the moor, somewhere in the region of Fox Tor. A terrified little dog. If she isn't rescued soon, I'm certain she will be shot by the first vigilante patrol that comes upon her."

"Not to mention the fact that poor Fossy—if she's still alive, and that seems a big if to me—could be ripped apart by the devil dog that's loose out there." Felicity shivered, remembering the creature she'd seen outside the window.

"No." Wells was adamant. "That, at least, is not possible."

"How can you be so sure?" asked Felicity.

"Because the devil dog and Fossy are one and the same."

There was a stunned silence. Jan sat up and rubbed his face, looking puzzled.

Felicity shook her head. "HG, I've seen that beast. Aunt Maud would never have a dog like that! It's a monster!"

"I agree. I saw Aunt Maud's dog," confirmed Jan. "It was a little terrier. It looked like a cross between a Westie and a Yorkie."

Wells nodded. "I hear what you say. And in a way, you're both correct, of course. Maud *believed* she had the dog you describe Jan, and indeed she did. She may not, however, have been aware of the remarkable ability of this species to transform itself when faced with danger. We've all seen this in nature in the present day: the octopus and the chameleon changing colour, pufferfish and toads inflating themselves, cobras suddenly producing a large hood. Like those, *Canis metamorphosis*, as I named this creature from TZB, changes quite instinctively when it is very frightened."

Felicity tugged at her ear. "It morphs into a devil dog?"

"Yes, like the one you've seen, Felicity."

"Why?" Jan asked, although he had a feeling he had guessed the answer to that.

"I think Felicity will confirm that only a very brave predator would take on Fossy when she assumes her morphed state. The transition back from the morphed state takes place when the creature is calm once more. It might take a minute. It might be longer. I simply don't know, if I'm honest."

An idea suddenly occurred to Felicity. "Fossy is 'Meta' that Aunt Maud wrote about?"

"Yes, exactly," Wells confirmed. "Maud didn't like the name, so she changed it to Fossy. Poor little Fossy was bitten by a leech similar to the creature in the mire, only of course much smaller. A pentepus, out hunting leeches, came across her just after she had been bitten but before the leech had had a chance to start its meal. The pentepus dispatched the offending leech and brought the poor dear to me. Initially I took her home to Spade House, where I was able to isolate some of the poison and clean up the wound. After analysing the venom, I found it to have remarkably similar chemical properties to atropine, a toxin extracted from the berry of the deadly nightshade."

Wells nodded in satisfaction. "Also, Fossy's symptoms did appear very similar to those induced by atropine, particularly paralysis. I knew that without help she was going to die, so I took a terrible gamble and injected her with physostigmine, an antidote to atropine. It probably saved her life. Even so, she was terribly weak. I brought her here for Maud to nurse. Neither of us thought that she would survive the night, but thankfully she did, and she went on to make a full recovery."

"And now she's out there and we have to find her!" said Felicity firmly. "Poor thing. We owe it to Aunt Maud."

Jan had his doubts. "Could Fossy be the one that's worrying the sheep?"

"Definitely not." Wells folded his arms. "Oh, don't misunderstand me, she *is* a predator. In TZB there is no concept of 'pet' as we understand the term. The sentient species do not train or domesticate other lower-order species. The *Canis metamorphosis*, the 'morph-dogs' if you like, run wild and fend for themselves. Unlike wolves and wild dogs of our time, they do not live in packs but as individuals, until it is time to breed. When a male and a female find each other and produce a limited litter, this small family group lives together until the pups are old enough to fend for themselves. After that, they split up and thereafter run alone."

Jan, thinking back to bath time with the children, grunted his approval. Running alone sounded good to him.

"They live on the TZB equivalent of rabbits, voles and particularly rats," Wells continued. "They only morph when threatened with danger. They use their hideous disguise as a defence mechanism, never to attack. Even in the morphed state, the largest creature they would hunt and kill would be a rabbit."

"So Fossy wouldn't kill the sheep?" Jan confirmed.

"No chance. And she most certainly didn't kill Bickle's bull," Wells replied.

"Are you suggesting that the leech is the killer, then?" Jan asked, sounding somewhat dubious.

"Precisely so!" confirmed Wells. "Its *modus operandi* is to slither out of the swamp at night and approach its prey downwind. When close enough it can rear up and strike with alarming speed, rather like a snake. Once it clamps those vicious teeth into its victim, the poor creature is incapacitated in a few seconds. That's how Bickle's bull was dispatched."

"That's horrible!" groaned Felicity. "Poor Fossy. She could be next! But how will we find her?"

"It shouldn't be too difficult," said Jan. "If she's up near the Tor, then there is only one place she could be hiding. In the tinners' girt on the eastern side."

"Tinners' girt?" queried Wells.

"The artificial valleys created by open cast mining of the tin ore. They date back centuries," Jan explained. "Because they contain the spoils from the opencast work, the sides of the girts are quite loose and small caves sometimes form. She'll be in one of those, I reckon. We could search for her first thing tomorrow?"

"We could use a dog," suggested Wells, raising his eyebrows at Jan, "to help us seek her out."

Jan shook his head. "Father will need them tomorrow when he's working with the sheep."

"What about Tess?" Felicity suggested.

Jan laughed. "You've seen Tess, Flick. She'd never make it to the top of the Tor, bless her old heart." He pressed his lips together, pondering for a while. "I don't know. Maybe. Leave it with me. I'll see if I can arrange something." He stretched and slowly pushed himself off the sofa. "Anyway ... I need to get back now. I'll see you here tomorrow morning and we'll go and check out those caves."

"Are you sure your Dad won't mind you being away from the farm so much?" Felicity asked anxiously.

"Father? No! He's as happy as a pig in manure at the moment. He's been itching to get back into the fields with the boys. He's missed it since I more or less took over the field work. As long as I do my bit when I get back at night, he's happy. I told him I was doing some repairs on your barn, Flick, and you know what he's like when it comes to you ... he'd walk to Moretonhampstead to buy you a box of chocolates if you asked him." Jan laughed, kissed Felicity on the cheek, shook hands with Wells and headed off.

CHAPTER TWENTY-THREE

At six the following morning, Felicity was up and dressed, determined not to be the grumpy madam of yesterday. Jan arrived about an hour later, just as Wells was descending the stairs. By that time, Felicity had fed the children, played with them for fifteen minutes, sent them back up to the nursery and cleaned the kitchen.

"What time do you call this?" she directed at Jan as he walked through the door. "I've been waiting here for ages."

Jan, his mouth open, raised his eyebrows and alternated his gaze between Felicity and Wells. "Get her! HG? I ask you, is this the same person who snapped our heads off yesterday morning?"

"There certainly seems to have been a seismic shift since yesterday," Wells agreed.

"Why, what happened yesterday?" Felicity adjusted her halo.

Jan rolled his eyes. "How soon we forget."

Wells simply smiled at them both and poured himself a quick cup of tea.

"I brought someone along," Jan said, and trotted outside to his Land Rover. Felicity watched out of the window as he lifted something from the back and placed it gently on the ground.

Tess!

She was 'wearing' a modified hiker's bergen, complete with carrying straps but with holes cut in strategic places to allow her legs to protrude through. In this ungainly outfit, Tess waddled into the kitchen, looking decidedly uncomfortable.

Felicity, moved to see her favourite canine friend, dropped to her knees and cradled Tess's head in her arms. "Oh, you darling, darling girl, Tess," she said, while the dog wagged her tail furiously.

Mister Ogilvy wasn't quite so enamoured as he sauntered into the kitchen in search of breakfast. On seeing the canine usurper, he arched his back and hissed. Tess responded with a disdainful look and raised her upper lip slightly.

That single gesture was enough to send poor Oggy scurrying into the living room to find cover.

"Breakfast, boys?" Felicity asked breezily.

"Why don't we have brunch, when we get back?" suggested Jan.

"Capital idea!" responded Wells, "I'm all for getting started."

"Great!" Jan started to organise everyone. "I need

something of Fossy's that she used or played with. A blanket or something she slept on maybe? Did she have a favourite blanket or toy?"

Felicity whistled, looking around. "She would have had a bed, I suppose, and Aunt Maud wouldn't have got rid of it. She was expecting Fossy to return ... so ... where would she have put it? Oooh! I know!" She clapped her hands. "The understairs cupboard!"

She skipped out of the kitchen into the hall and flung open the cupboard door to have a rummage. Thirty seconds later she emerged triumphantly, holding a small floppy dog bed and a colourful blanket aloft.

"Just the blanket, Flick," said Jan.

With Tess safely and comfortably secured in her harness on Jan's back, they commenced their expedition to Fox Tor. In truth, Fox Tor is one of Dartmoor's less imposing hills and the climb up to it required no great effort, even for Jan with his additional burden or for Wells with his advanced years. At the summit, Jan lowered his precious cargo to allow Tess to stretch her legs and to do what all dogs must do when they encounter somewhere new with virgin sniffs.

While Felicity looked after Tess, the two men scoured the massive granite rocks which form the summit of Fox Tor. Returning to Felicity they confirmed that, as Jan had predicted, there was nowhere on the summit where Fossy could hide out.

Felicity nodded and gazed around at the glorious landscape, the thick clouds scudding across the heavy sky. Suddenly she experienced an onrush of fear, her heart began to race and a cold sweat broke out on her forehead. She glanced at Wells. "I have that feeling!"

Wells mopped his brow. "I do too!"

Tess struggled into a sitting position and barked once, then lay down and whined softly. Jan looked from one to the other. "What's going on?"

"Fossy is transmitting," Wells told him. "She's frightened. She knows we're here. She thinks we mean to harm her."

Jan accepted Wells's explanation without question. "Then she has to be in the girt." He hoisted Tess onto his back. "Let's go."

The trek to the base of the girt was no more than five hundred yards down the north-eastern side of the tor. It was exactly as Jan had described it, a man-made ravine with a stream running down the centre, its high steep banks created from the spoil of the opencast mining that had taken place in the past.

Jan released Tess from her harness and let her take her time sniffing the blanket, then, when she was ready, he sent her off. Her arthritis temporarily forgotten, Tess quartered to and fro across the girt, her nose never more than an inch above the ground, her intelligent eyes shining from the excitement of the chase. From time to time Jan called her back and made her rest, massaging her back legs before sending her off again.

They had travelled some three-quarters of the length of the girt, when Tess suddenly stopped dead, staring at the ruins of a long-abandoned tinners' hut. She stood stock-still for a moment before sitting and whining softly.

When the others caught up to her they could see that what remained of the side wall of the hut was about two feet from the bank of the girt. A short distance down this natural alley was a hole into the side of the girt.

"There must be something in there," Jan said, his voice hushed.

Confirmation was not long in coming. Out of the hole sprang the devil dog. Snapping, slavering and growling fiercely, it covered the length of the alley in a single bound and stood confronting them at a distance of only a few feet. Its terrifying red eyes shone with defiance, daring the intruders to take just one more step forward.

However, one look at the beast and the intruders didn't have the slightest intention of moving forward. Quite the reverse.

Jan had placed his hand on Tess to prevent her from running off, but Old Tess exhibited no desire to do so. Instead, she lay down, wagged her tail slowly from side to side and continued to whine softly.

"Well, now that we've found her, HG, what do we do?" asked Jan. "I for one have no intention of trying to put a lead on that thing."

"No, I wouldn't advise it. I'm quite certain that if we maintain a distance between us and her, then she won't attack. It is not in the nature of *Canis metamorphosis* to do so. What we're seeing is a bluff, an act of bravado. That said, if we get too close, she may well snap."

Wells attempted to talk to the beast, quietly trying to soothe it, but his words and gentle tone had no effect. He frowned, rapidly running out of ideas.

At that moment Felicity's phone rang, making them all jump.

To say it rang is perhaps misleading. To indicate an incoming call, what it actually did was to play her latest ringtone. She'd substituted *Bat Out of Hell* for a tune entitled *Splodge the Grizzlimp*—a song made popular by the *Covid 19 Tomb Kickers*. As Felicity wrestled with her backpack in an attempt to retrieve her mobile, Wells observed the hound. It ceased its aggressive behaviour, slumped down on its haunches and started licking its forepaws, oblivious to the presence of the intruders.

"Hello?" Felicity fumbled with the phone. "Hello? Drat! I missed it." Felicity stuffed the phone in her back pocket.

The hound jumped to its feet again, snapping and snarling as it had before.

"If your phone rings again, please don't answer it, just let it ring," suggested Wells.

"What?"

"Trust me. Just watch the hound. You too, Jan."

Felicity's phone did ring again. Immediately, the hound slumped down, panting, its tongue hanging out. It observed the intruders, its head swivelling, before slumping down between its paws. After a short interval the phone clicked to answerphone, and the hound was on its feet again.

"Well?" said Wells, "I think we may have hit upon the answer!"

"The music?" Jan exclaimed. "You think it's calming her?"

"Yes," said Wells, "I do. But as a piece of music it's not long enough. We need to get her really calm; then and only then, will she morph back. Also, I think we need to communicate, let her know we mean no harm."

He pointed at Tess, lying patiently at Jan's feet, awaiting further commands. "Tess is receiving, but she can't send."

Felicity's eyes widened as she realised what Wells was insinuating. "We need Helly up here!" she said.

As they turned away from the mire and made their way up the lane leading to Prior's Cross, Jan stopped and turned to the others.

"I'm going on up to the farm to unload Tess. She's been in this harness long enough. Why don't you both come up with me? Mother will cook you some breakfast."

"Yes, please!" said Felicity quickly, before Wells could answer. She felt sure he would have declined.

As Jan released Tess from her harness in the backyard of the farm, Mary Gurney rushed out of the door. "'Ere, you hab'n overdone it with this little maid, have you? You bad bey!"

"No, Mother," Jan told her. "She's had a gentle walk on the moor, that's all. I carried her most of the way."

"You bedder have 'ad, you monster!" Then to the dog, in a soft voice, "There, there my lamb. Mother will rub your legs tonight."

"Mother, I brought Flick and her uncle, HG, home for breakfast. I hope you don't mind?"

"Course I don' mind, you girt daft Janner. The more the merrier, I allus says. Nice to meet you Mr Aidgee." She shook his hand so vigorously that Wells thought his arm would surely come loose from the socket. "I'll 'ave summit cooked for 'ee in the shake of a rat's tail, see if I don'."

The others followed her inside and seated themselves at the dining table while she busily prepared their places.

"Just a child's portion for me, please, Mary," Felicity called after Mrs Gurney as she disappeared into the kitchen.

"What's a child's portion?" asked Wells in surprise. Felicity usually had a hearty appetite.

"One sausage, one egg, two rashers of bacon and a spoonful of beans."

"Good heavens!" said Wells. "And what is, the alternative?"

"A proper breakfast. Two sausages, two eggs, three rashers of bacon, a slice of hog's pudding, two spoonfuls of beans, mushrooms and a slice of fried bread!"

Wells looked horrified and placed his hand onto his stomach. "A child's portion for me as well if you don't mind, Mrs Gurney!" he called loudly, causing both Jan and Felicity to laugh at his expression.

When the food arrived, Wells had exactly the same as Jan, a proper breakfast. "Sorry Mr Aidgee, I din' hear you call out about a chile's portion," she told him, beaming from ear to ear. More seriously, she added, "You godda eat! Keep your strength up me 'andsome."

Wells looked askance at Mary, then at his plate, but he did justice to the meal. He watched as Jan dipped his fried bread into the egg yolk and tried it himself. It was delicious! Why hadn't he discovered this before? And hog's pudding, how good was that? To say that he was stuffed after the meal would have been an understatement, but he looked and felt most content.

"'Ere," said Mary as she collected the plates, "I had a lovely surprise yesterday while you was out, Jan. Your brother called with Bess."

"Dan'l?"

Mary gave him a look which clearly said, 'which hole have you just crawled out of'?

"'Ow many brothers 'ave you got? I bedder 'ave a word with that Tom Gurney when 'ee gets back from the fields. Of course Dan'l, you girt clod!"

"Oh! I'm sorry I missed him." Jan winked at Felicity. "I must cut across to Moretonhampstead one day and see how he's getting on."

"'Ee said 'ee'd heard tell of the monster dog that's killin' the livestock. Said 'ee was minded to join one of they search parties with Bess."

"Oh heavens, no!" said Jan. "Bess would be sure to sniff out the hideaway."

"What?" Mary frowned. "That's what 'ee wants, bain' it?"

"Absolutely!" said Jan, trying to rectify his slip of the

tongue. "It's just that I ... erm ... heard that this hound is really dangerous. I wouldn't want Dan'l getting hurt."

Mary roared with laughter. "Get 'ome to your Mother, you big daft sod! Are we talking about the same Dan'l Gurney? Do you know of a dog that would 'ave the courage to even snarl at Dan'l?"

Still laughing, she bustled out to the kitchen with the empty dishes. Felicity followed her out.

"Let me give you a hand with the dishes, Mary."

"You'll do no such thing, young lady. I'm quite capable of washing a few dishes. I've 'ad a lot of practice, believe it or not. Now off you go and join your friends and leave me in peace!"

Felicity held up her hands in surrender. "Okay. Thank you for a lovely breakfast." Leaning forward, she gave Mary a kiss on the cheek.

Mary flushed and tried, unsuccessfully, to look annoyed. "Oh, go on with you, you bad girl!"

As Felicity joined the others, she overheard Wells saying to Jan, "Your brother sounds like a ferocious character?"

Jan guffawed. "Nothing could be further from the truth, as Felicity knows. He's very quiet and incredibly shy. He's worse even than me, truth be told. That said, he's bigger than me too. And stronger. And, come to think of it, better looking than me! I think deep down I probably hate him!" The latter statement was not borne out by the evident love and pride with which he spoke.

Felicity punched his arm.

"He wouldn't say boo to a goose," Jan continued, "but

it doesn't do to upset him. And that's why Billy Bickle hates the Gurney family."

Now intrigued, Wells leaned forward. "Do tell?"

"Billy and Dan'l were in the same class at primary school in the village. As you can imagine, Billy was the class bully, but one day he went too far. He mistook Dan'l's reticence and his easy-going nature for weakness. Big mistake! Not only did Dan'l give him a good hiding, he grabbed him by the seat of his pants and the scruff of the neck and threw him over the school wall. Needless to say, it was Dan'l that got into trouble with the headmistress. You could tell what she thought of the matter though. Dan'l's 'very harsh punishment' was a ten-minute detention!"

Felicity laughed.

"I say," said Wells, grinning.

"Funny thing was, a couple of days later while Dan'l and I were in the village we spied Frankie Bickle, Billy's father, on the other side of the road. He crossed over to us, and I thought 'uh-oh, we're in for it now'." Jan shrugged. "Instead he patted Dan'l on the back. 'Well done bey,' he said, 'well done!'"

"Wonderful story," said Wells. "And you fear he would find Fossy with 'Bess'. I take it that's another of your wonderful sheepdogs?"

"Bess and our dog, Jed, are from the same litter. Tess's one and only litter. She only had two pups, Jed and Bess. Dan'l loves Tess and he wanted the bitch, thinking she would take after her mother. And boy, she did! He even called her Bess because it sounded like Tess. Father let Dan'l have Bess, but now admits he made the wrong choice! Don't get me wrong, Jed is fine, and he's learning—he'll be a good and willing work dog in time, but Bess is a natural. She reads minds, just like Tess. She would have no problem finding Fossy. That's why I don't want her up on the moor."

After Wells had expressed his appreciation to Mary, he departed alone, explaining that he had urgent matters to attend to at Prior's Cross.

Yes, thought Felicity smiling, *three urgent little matters.*

Mary joined them in the dining room, struggling with her coat. "I'm gwin feed them there chickens," she announced as she finally won the battle with her jacket.

Felicity and Jan moved into the kitchen in search of more tea. Mary, who was outside in the backyard, heard them enter, the kitchen window being open.

Now Mary Gurney wasn't a nosy person, it's just that she was desperate to know when her son was going to pop the question to Felicity. It was obvious that he thought the world of the girl, and she was certain that Flick felt the same way about him. *What's wrong with young people these days? Get on with it!* she thought, as she scattered the feed on the ground.

As Mary moved to the side of the window, hidden from view, she listened in to their conversation, vowing to herself that if the conversation became too intimate, she would move away.

What she heard wasn't at all what she expected.

She leaned against the wall of the house, her mind a whirr. It was obvious from what they were saying that not only did they know exactly whereabouts on the moor the devil dog was hiding out, but they intended to save it!

A livestock killer!

Were they crazy?

And what was it that Jan was talking about now?

Several times he mentioned 'three little aliens' in the attic.

Three lil' aliens? What on earth is going on down at that there Prior's Cross? Mary Gurney wondered, dying to know more and bursting to tell someone all at once.

CHAPTER TWENTY-FOUR

*I*vor Crabbe was a small man in every way.

For reasons that would be only too obvious to any keen observer, he had changed his first name—not by deed poll you understand, but simply by lying—to 'Arnie', after his hero, Arnold Schwarzenegger.

The contrast between Crabbe and the actor could not have been more marked. Hollywood 'Arnie' is a big, imposing, handsome man. Ivor—or Arnie Crabbe—on the other hand, was a slight, rat-faced creature who had only managed to reach the five-foot eight-inch mark at the 'Wellman' clinic at his local GP's surgery by cheating and standing on his tiptoes. And, with no muscle to speak of and a very slight build, he weighed no more than eight stones.

Soaking wet and with rocks in his pockets.

By creatively constructing a résumé which bore little or no relationship to his actual previous employment and by brazenly lying, he had somehow managed to obtain a job as a reporter on the *Plymouth Mail*. Once a reputable newspaper, it had now fallen on hard times, a victim of 'progress' in this age of electronic communication and 24/7-in-your-face news broadcasting that relies heavily on social media for z-list celebrity soundbites and 'stories'.

Of late, he had blotted his copybook on more than one occasion by, in his editor's words, 'twisting the facts to suit the story' and 'an overzealous approach, not built on careful research'. A less charitable person might have called it deceitful.

Ivor, that is, 'Arnie' Crabbe, was effectively on a final warning. He needed a good story and he needed one fast.

A few days previously, an opening had unexpectedly presented itself while Arnie was idling in the newsroom at the *Mail*. A reporter, one Eddie Thomson—Arnie's more successful, talented and honest colleague—had just gone through the door into the editor's office and had left it open. Never one to miss an opportunity, Arnie had sidled up to a filing cabinet near the door in order to ear-wig on what was being said. He quietly opened the cabinet and pretended to rifle through the drawer, pursing his lips as he studied the contents.

Eddie was filling the editor in on rumours he'd heard about problems on Dartmoor. Some dog, or dogs, depending on who was telling the story, were apparently worrying livestock. Quite serious, in his opinion. The editor had sounded interested but asked him to continue with the angle he had on the fire at the Jackson timber yard—much more interesting and important because Mortimer Jackson, the owner, had shares in the newspaper—and suggested he pick the dog story up after he had completed that.

Arnie was still loitering at the filing cabinet when Eddie emerged.

He pulled a file and walked back to his desk with it, the two exchanging cursory greetings as they passed. After collecting a few bits and pieces from his desk, Eddie was gone again, no doubt off to do some in-depth interviews at the timber yard.

Arnie wrinkled his nose. *Why should Eddie get all the best jobs?* He glanced down at the file in his hand—letters to the *Mail's* Agony Aunt—and hastily chucked it back inside the filing cabinet drawer. Then, without a word to anybody, he quietly left the newsroom.

He made his way outside and hung around beside the bins, knowing he couldn't be seen by anyone in the building. After waiting for about ten minutes, he made a spectacle of re-entering the newsroom and slamming the door. He purposely made a show in front of the editor's window that looked out onto the reporters' work area, stripping off his jacket, slinging it over his seat and striding purposefully to the editor's office. After a cursory tap, he walked in.

"Boss, I've just had a tip-off from a contact in Princetown. An eyewitness has seen the creature that is attacking the livestock up there. It might be an animal that's escaped from a zoo or something like that. Want me to take a look?"

The editor was slightly taken aback by this display of enthusiasm, somewhat unusual in Arnie's case.

Nonetheless, it was a pleasant surprise and it did sound like an interesting story. "Okay, Arnie, look into it," he said. "I asked Eddie to investigate this, but he's busy at the moment." He picked his mobile up. "I'll give him a call now to tell him you've taken it on."

All of this had occurred on the day of the meeting at the Plume of Feathers, which he had attended. Unfortunately, despite the tension in the room and the factions within the community that had become evident during the incident with the policeman and the gun, although Arnie had tried to gather more information from the locals in the aftermath, he hadn't had much luck.

Now Arnie, sitting in the only café in Princetown that remained open at this time of year, was desperate to find something substantial to feed back to the editor. Eddie's tip-off had surely been inaccurate. There seemed to be nothing up here that could be construed as particularly newsworthy. Maybe he could write a piece on the bull that had been killed, but even that was tenuous ...

He stared down into his coffee mug. It would not look good to return to Plymouth without a decent story.

"... Arr, an' she said that they aliens is up in someone's attic. That's what she said, I 'eard it plain as day ..."

Arnie's radar immediately fired up on auto. Two women behind him had been chatting at a table over a cup of tea. Now one of them was making preparations to take her leave, pulling on her coat and collecting her bags together.

"Well, Mrs T, I really don' know what to say. The goin's on! A body's not safe these days. I saw those flashes myself, you know. I din' know what to make of it all! You take care now, my lovely!" She bade her friend goodbye and left Mrs T looking thoughtfully into her own teacup.

Arnie swivelled round to smile his most reptilian smile at her.

"Hello! It's Mrs ... em ... er ..."

"Treverick," the old lady replied. "Do I know 'ee, young man?"

Arnie was not a young man, but then again Mrs Treverick *was* quite old and such things are relative.

"I think we were introduced the other day when I was interviewing in the square. I'm with the newspapers, but I'm covering a story for BBC TV," he lied.

"Really?" Mrs T sounded most enthusiastic. Like most Britons, she believed the news began and ended with the BBC. "If you interview me, will I be on the TV?"

"Oh, absolutely!" said Arnie, nodding seriously. "If I could just get your story now, I can get the cameras and everything else ready in a couple of days."

Mrs T was only too pleased to tell her story again. In truth, there wasn't much in it. Arnie scribbled notes in his rather poor shorthand.

It seemed that a Mrs Gurney told her sister Janet, who was married to one of the Thompsons, and had told Brenda Gidley ...

"You knows the Gidleys, from out along Horrabridge way?" prompted Mrs Treverick.

Arnie arranged his face in a semblance of a smile, and she carried on.

"... so, Brenda had told Mrs T that a spaceship had crash-landed on Foxtor Mire ..."

"Wait. A spaceship?" Arnie probed.

"Everyone saw it!"

According to Mrs Gurney, via Janet, the Thompsons and Brenda Gidley, there had been three aliens on board, and they had been rescued and were now living in someone's attic.

"Or was it their cellar?" Mrs Treverick mulled that over for a second. "No, I'm sure it was the attic." According to Mrs T, the spaceship had also carried a devil dog. That was now loose and killing the livestock.

Arnie didn't do what any other self-respecting reporter would have done with a story like this, simply crumple it up and chuck it in the rubbish.

No, no.

Instead, he dutifully wrote it all down, tidied it up, bent it somewhat, provided six unimpeachable eyewitnesses—names he found in the local telephone directory—and hinted that an eminent scientist was currently investigating.

A total fabrication from start to finish.

Then he picked up his mobile and phoned it through.

The next morning, the *Plymouth Mail* carried the story:

Plymouth Mail

Devil Dog Carried by Spacecraft

Reports are emerging of attacks on animals on Dartmoor. Eyewitnesses claim that dozens of sheep, cattle and ponies have been slaughtered on the moor by a devil dog that is running wild. Several of these reliable eyewitnesses allege that the dog escaped from a spacecraft which landed near what locals are now calling the 'grim mire'.

Three dangerous aliens are still said to be at large.

Farmers in the area are now facing certain financial ruin. One source has claimed the dog can kill up to ten or more sheep, ponies or cows every night. In fact, according to one eyewitness, even bulls are not safe.

An eminent scientist from a top British university is currently assisting police and military forces.

A spokesman from the MOD has stated that they are committed to apprehending the animal, and they would not hesitate to use lethal force if required.

A very different Arnie took a seat in the Princetown café the following morning. He purposely chose his 'lucky' chair, the place where he'd been sitting when he'd fortuitously overheard Mrs T's conversation the previous day.

Feeling self-satisfied and overtly smug, he sipped at his coffee, but his self-indulgent mood of euphoria was rudely shattered by his phone as it began playing the theme from *The Terminator*.

"Hello Arnie, Jim Burroughs here ..."

Arnie's editor! He sat up a little straighter.

Burroughs had never used his first name before. As far as Arnie was concerned, it was always 'Boss' and 'Mr Burroughs'.

"Great story," Jim was saying. "Well done. Some good news—"

"Ooh, yes?" Arnie squeaked.

"Yes. A TV company wants to cover your story with a view to syndicating it to the big boys. A crew will be with you at about two-ish. Keep yourself handy and round up a couple of those eyewitnesses you mentioned. The eminent scientist would be useful too. Have them on standby. Okay?"

"O ... kay, Boss," Arnie stammered.

An eminent scientist? Why, oh why had he said such a thing? And where on earth was he going to get his eyewitnesses from? They had been mythical inventions from his devious mind! He thought quickly. Mrs Treverick would do for one, wouldn't she? He could groom her into saying anything. She was desperate to appear on TV. Then there was that loudmouth at the Plume who had claimed he had seen the devil dog. Oh, blast. What had been his name?

He skimmed through his notebook. Blackstock! That was it. Ted Blackstock.

Arnie found Blackstock at his place of work, a delivery warehouse at the local brewery. He quickly explained the reason for his visit and mentioned the importance of having reliable and trustworthy eyewitnesses—just like Ted—for the biggest exposé Devon had ever seen.

Taken aback, Ted listened to Arnie's explanation. He took a beat, but after a heart-stopping moment when Arnie thought he might refuse, Ted agreed to be interviewed.

Yes!

Ted would be very happy to tell his story on TV. It was important that everyone should know about the horrible monstrosity on the loose. A creature from the very bowels of hell!

Perfect, thought Arnie. *No coaching needed there.*

Next up was Mrs Treverick. He had her details, so located her easily enough in her slightly shabby cottage on the edge of town.

He knocked on her door and offered her his oily smile, the one she remembered from the previous day. "Hello, Mrs Treverick," simpered Arnie. "Do you remember me? I've managed to get you an appearance on television as I promised. It cost me a lot of money and effort as you can imagine," he lied, "but I've done it for you. I never let people down, I promise I don't."

Mrs T was so delighted she actually clapped her hands in eager anticipation.

"Now, we just need to go over your story again. You know, television viewers don't like people saying they heard it from this person or that one, they like to hear it *direct,* if you know what I mean?"

Mrs Treverick nodded, but her eyes remained vacant. Clearly she didn't understand.

"So, you need to tell it as if it was *you* who heard and saw everything. Do you get it?"

She still didn't, not really, but she was happy to go along with anything Arnie said. After all, this young man had gone to a lot of expense and trouble to get her on the telly box, and she wasn't about to let him down.

"Now, dear," Arnie continued, "here's how I suggest you tell the story. Of course, it's up to you, you're the star after all, but if it was me then ..."

CHAPTER TWENTY-FIVE

*J*ames Ignatius Pettigrew reached for the remote control to switch the television on. Slouching back on his sofa, he wiped his nose on his sleeve and stretched his legs out, knocking over a pile of pizza cartons and old newspapers. He hardly noticed. He'd become inured to the general level of filth and clutter throughout his house.

A tall man, thin and angular with a baby face which he detested, he wore large, thick spectacles to compensate for his poor eyesight and hoped they gave him an air of intellect. In order to appear more distinguished, he had attempted to grow facial hair but with severely limited success. The 'thing' that now adorned his upper lip could not conceivably match any known definition of the word moustache. Topping off all of this was a mop of prematurely white-grey hair, which grew in profusion in every possible unruly direction.

He settled for the news and flicked idly through the

pile of student marking sitting next to him. It should all have been returned the previous week, but he had a serious case of CBA.

'Professor' Pettigrew—for he insisted that his students addressed him as professor even though he had not, by any stretch of the imagination, earned the right to that title, having yet to complete the copious number of corrections required by his examiners to achieve even his PhD—could barely contain his disdain for the work.

"Dull, dull, dull!" he announced to no one in particular, for he lived alone. He really couldn't abide students at the best of times, but especially when they wanted feedback for their assignments. Furthermore, to his intense chagrin, he was known to his students as 'JIP', an epithet he thoroughly detested. It made him sound like a dog.

Professor James Pettigrew wagged his tail for nobody.

So how had this disagreeable, student-loathing, lazy slouch of a man achieved his lofty academic status?

By employing a mixture of massaging various online model answers, plagiarism and some good old-fashioned down-to-earth cheating, with answers stencilled in biro on his arm and covered by a long-sleeved shirt. Utilising this magic formula, he had achieved an upper second in zoology from a nameless British university. On the day he proudly marched up to receive his degree certificate, there had been a number of raised eyebrows among the university's reputable academics.

Intent on a lectureship in zoology, Pettigrew had drifted in and out of various dead-end jobs after graduating. He had somehow managed to represent these on his curriculum vitae as vital stepping-stones to brilliance. By presenting his largely fabricated CV and falsified references, he had, to his own surprise, secured a post as an Assistant Lecturer (part-time) at a university in the south-west region of England. Using money left to him by his parents, he had bought a large house in Okehampton, the rear of which he converted into a laboratory for his personal use.

All might have been well. He had somewhere decent to live in a beautiful part of the world and a decent job. But things did not go perfectly for James Ignatius Pettigrew. After one and a half semesters, he was suspended from his post following a number of expressions of concern. These were aired by people both in and external to the university and related in the main to, to put it kindly, his failure to 'exercise a duty of care towards the animals in his charge'.

To add to his woes, the RSPCA was keen to follow up on certain allegations with a view to securing a prosecution.

If Pettigrew was to have any hope of being reinstated by the university and cleared by the RSPCA, he desperately needed to salvage his academic reputation and achieve something never before seen.

He tossed the student papers to one side and reached into the nearest pizza box. There were a couple of congealed slices inside and, having plucked off the pineapple, he rammed first one and then the other into his mouth, chewed hard and swallowed. He flushed his supper through with the dregs of some flat beer from a long-opened can.

He used the greasy remote once more, flipping through the channels until he reached the local West Country news.

Some old biddy was being interviewed about some nonsense up on Dartmoor.

Weird place. Weirder people.

He switched to the next channel, but at that moment his brain caught up with what he'd heard, and he hurriedly turned back.

What was that she was saying?

A creature eating livestock up on the moor?

A spaceship that had crash-landed?

Aliens in the attic?

Fascinating.

He hurriedly pulled out his mobile phone to start googling names and places.

If there was an alien on the moor, he wanted to be the one to find it first.

CHAPTER TWENTY-SIX

*C*ollecting his coffee from the counter, Arnie walked to his now-favourite seat in his now-favourite café. His contact was overdue so this was his second cup. He hoped he wouldn't live to regret that. He surreptitiously glanced around, noting the door for the gents, nodding in satisfaction when he spotted it. *Be prepared*, he told himself. It would never do to be get caught short in such a rural part of the world.

He puffed out his cheeks and checked his watch again. The person he had arranged to meet should have been here fifteen minutes ago.

Sipping his coffee slowly, he mused about the—at best—limited success of the TV broadcast the previous night. If he had been an honest man, he would have been forced to admit that *he* had been the weak link in the interview.

Unfortunately, Arnie wasn't an honest man.

He, therefore, blamed the producer for the way it had

been presented, and the cameraman for not getting the lighting right. He also blamed the presenter for not asking the right questions. In fact, he blamed everyone.

Everyone except Arnie Crabbe.

It had started well. Mrs Treverick—she had spelled her name out so that her viewing public wouldn't get it wrong—had presented her well-rehearsed story word perfectly. Yes, she *had* seen the crash site with her own eyes *and* witnessed the capture of the aliens by someone in a big four by four. (Mrs T, by the by, had not the slightest idea what a four by four was, but that was what she had been told to say). She had *definitely* heard the man call to his accomplice that they would 'keep them in the attic' before driving off. After they had gone, she had seen, with *her own eyes* mind you, the devil dog leave the ruined craft and run off onto the moor.

Asked if the dog was killing livestock, she had confirmed that dozens of animals had been slain.

Ted Blackstock was even better. His description of the dog in skin-crawlingly, horrific detail had the television support engineers looking over their shoulders in case the beast was approaching from behind.

The least convincing part of the broadcast had been when Arnie himself was interviewed. The intrepid and canny reporter had, 'after weeks of careful and painstaking research', managed to establish exactly what was causing mayhem on the moor. The government had clearly placed great faith in him by sending out an eminent scientist to assist him in his continuing investigation.

When asked the name of the eminent scientist, he had assumed his best 'I know, and wouldn't you like to?' face and tapped his nose. "I'm not allowed to divulge that information at this stage," he replied.

The interviewer's follow-up question, a simple 'Why?', had flummoxed Arnie, who had been forced to shrug and shake his head.

"Are you and your scientific colleague pursuing further lines of enquiry?" asked the very bright young female interviewer.

"Ah-ah!" said Arnie. "You don't catch out an experienced reporter like me with a question like that! All I will say is that further developments should be expected." He narrowed his eyes enigmatically.

The young interviewer's glance at the camera had said more than a thousand words could ever say.

Later that evening, Arnie propped up the bar in the Plume, buying drinks on the expense account that his editor Jim Burroughs had agreed to extend him. Arnie now called his editor Jim, not Mr Burroughs or Boss. Despite this success, he was feeling somewhat deflated, aware that he had perhaps over-egged it in the interview.

He took a disconsolate slug of his lager. *That's better*, he thought. He had, by invitation of the landlord, tried the local cider. They called it 'scrumpy'. Arnie had quickly decided that only degenerate yokels could possibly stomach it.

His descent into deep gloom was only dispelled when his phone blared out the theme from *The Terminator*. He couldn't believe it! A Professor James

Pettigrew was speaking and declared himself extremely interested in Mr Crabbe's report. Pettigrew was keen to track the aliens and the devil dog with a view to carrying out research in order to produce a paper on them.

Would Mr Crabbe allow him to assist?

Arnie puffed up his chest. Just what he needed! An eminent scientist!

Mr Crabbe would be only too happy for Professor Pettigrew to assist.

After arranging to meet the next day, Arnie ended the call and lifted his eyes towards the ceiling. "Thank you!" he whispered.

Now, waiting impatiently in the Princetown café, Arnie checked his watch once again and tutted. At that moment a tall, ungainly man rattled the door open. His thick glasses and grey-white hair screamed 'boffin'.

Arnie watched him, feeling certain this must be Pettigrew. He waited until the tall man had ordered and paid for his coffee before introducing himself. Arnie had no intention of paying for anyone else's drink, expense account or not!

They sat at 'Arnie's' table, while the journalist recounted the details of his investigation to date. When laid out in this way, it actually amounted to very little.

Pettigrew seized on the testimony of Mrs Treverick. "How reliable was that?" he asked.

"Mrs Treverick is apt to exaggerate and make things up," said Arnie, neatly shifting the blame as he so frequently did. "It was actually hearsay." He recalled Mrs T's gossip trail.

"We need to get back to the source," said Pettigrew decisively. "Why don't I track down this Mrs Gurney?"

"What about me?" Arnie did not want to be sidelined.

"Perhaps you could investigate Mrs Gidley?"

Arnie smiled and slapped his hand down on the table. "Do you know? That's exactly what I was going to suggest!" he lied.

Had these two stalwarts of English society but known it, the son of the aforementioned Mrs Gurney was, at that very moment, walking past the window of the café.

Jan had found a parking place on the main road, not difficult at this time of year, and was making his way to the local store. As he entered, he caught a snatch of conversation that passed between two women standing outside the door.

"... they'm in almos' every attic in the village, I've heard!" one was saying.

"Well I b'aint gwin get 'em out, s'far as I'm concerned, I'll leave that to they scientists!" the second woman responded in alarm.

Must be talking about pigeons? Jan thought. *Although why do they need scientists to get them out? Just say 'boo!' loudly and they'll be gone.* He smiled and shook his head as he entered the shop.

"Mornin', Jan," called Mike, the shop owner, as he walked in. "Where's that young lady of yours today, then?"

Jan coloured slightly. "She's not *my* young lady,

Mike. Nobody owns Flick Westmacott, I can assure you of that. She's just a friend is all."

"Oh, arrr." Mike nodded and smiled. Jan flushed a deeper pink. Sensing his discomfort, Mike quickly said, "How can I rob you, sorry, serve you today, young man?"

"Flour, Mike. Mother's baking and she's run out of flour. Has to be self-raising, apparently?

"To your left, bottom shelf. Still running errands for Mother then?" Mike grinned.

"Nothing changes," said Jan.

"Just seems like yesterday that you used to come in here with a tatty note and with the money wrapped in a hanky. Then on the way home, you used to eat the corners off the loaf!" They both laughed.

"Come to think of it, that probably was yesterday," Jan chuckled. "Here, I'd better take two bags of this flour. If I go home with one and she runs out again, I'll get the blame. 'Why din' you get two begs, you big gormless Janner?'" Jan mimicked Mary's voice. "I can just hear her, can't you, Mike?"

Mike snorted. "I can." He indicated the flour. "Do you want a plastic bag? They're ten pence."

"*How* much?"

"It's not me, Jan." Mike's brow creased in all innocence. "The government takes the money."

"Yer, I'll bet! No thanks! I think I can manage two bags of flour."

"For special customers I provide a paper bag at no charge," said Mike, packing the flour.

"You're all heart."

"I know." Mike shook his head in despair. "It will be the ruin of me."

Jan paid the small-shop-inflated price, took his package and left with a cheery, "Thanks, Mike, take care!"

"And you, Jan. Love to Mother!"

Jan strode up the road and as he passed the café, he thought he recognised one of the two men sitting at a table near the window, but he couldn't quite place him. He didn't think much of it until a moment later, just as he was about to get into his grubby old Land Rover, he was confronted by a young lady carrying a microphone, the top shrouded in a garish orange foam rubber cover. Lagging behind her came a man carrying what looked like heavy recording equipment.

"Hello?" she breezed, "Could you spare a moment? I'm Maggie Adams?" She said her name as though she expected Jan to recognise it, her voice rising at the end of the sentence.

He didn't.

"I'm with Radio West Devon? I'm just doing some interviewing in the village?"

Now it has to be said that there were very few things in this world of ours that disturbed the equanimity of Jan Gurney. One was Billy Bickle's voice and the other was people who chose to end their sentences with a voice inflection, as if every statement was a question.

"What do you want?" asked Jan, surprisingly brusquely for him.

"Have you heard the stories of the aliens? Living in

people's attics?" she asked, thrusting the microphone into his face.

"What? "Jan pushed the microphone back, his sudden shock giving way to a cold grip of fear in the pit of his stomach. "What are you talking about?"

"You mean you haven't seen the TV news?" she asked, pushing the microphone forward again.

Jan gently pushed it away, just a few inches this time, and spoke into it. "You should never believe what you hear on TV and especially local radio. They survive on regurgitating gossip and peddling nonsense." He indicated Maggie should move out of the way and, when she did so, climbed into his Land Rover. As he drove off, he caught a glimpse of her in his rear-view mirror making obscene hand gestures.

Jan drove quickly, one eye on the weather and the condition of the lane, to Prior's Cross.

He needed to speak to Felicity and Wells urgently.

CHAPTER TWENTY-SEVEN

*P*ettigrew frowned across the table at the man sitting opposite him. If brains were made of dynamite, Crabbe wouldn't have had enough to blow his hat off.

Anyone with half a mind would realise that if there was any truth in a piece of gossip, then to get to the kernel of the matter, you had to go back to the earliest source. In this case, that appeared to be someone called Mrs Gurney. Pettigrew would personally track down the Gurney woman and send Crabbe out after Mrs Gidley who had been mentioned somewhere in Mrs Treverick's gossip trail. Mrs Gidley would probably add little to their investigation; however, it would get Crabbe out from under his feet for a while.

He couldn't dispense with Crabbe entirely, unfortunately. At some stage he might need publicity, and Crabbe would be able to provide that.

"It would help if I could examine the crash site," he

said. "Is there any indication as to where the crash occurred?"

"Oh, yes!" confirmed Arnie. "A number of eyewitnesses, reliable ones this time, state that it came from the area of Foxtor Mire."

"Foxes door …?"

"Foxtor Mire. It's a swamp, I think. Somewhere in this region. I'm not sure where."

"You haven't been there?" Pettigrew tried hard to keep the incredulity from his voice.

"Good heavens, no!" Arnie replied indignantly. "It's quite dangerous out there, I believe. And very wet."

Pettigrew couldn't quite believe what he was hearing. *Very wet?* And this was an intrepid reporter, was it? The man was a buffoon! Struggling to control his emotions, he rose from the table.

"Right, I'll go in search of the good Madam Gurney, if you seek out Mrs Gidley, then? Agreed?" Reminding himself Arnie still had his uses, Pettigrew raised a clenched fist and shook it in the air. "Let's get to it, Team Crabbe! What say you?"

"Let's do it!" exclaimed Arnie excitedly, copying the gesture. He gathered up his things and waved goodbye, sauntering off in the direction of the Plume of Feathers, evidently in no hurry to carry out his share of the workload.

Pettigrew sighed as he moved to the counter. "Is there anywhere I can buy an Ordnance Survey map of this area?" he asked the woman serving there.

"Why, yes, my darlin', dreckly opposite. You sees that

big white buildin'? That's the tourist information centre. You'll get one there, my lovely."

The big white building had once been the Duchy Hotel, before it had closed and become the prison officers' mess. It had ceased to provide that service some years earlier and was now utilised as exhibition rooms, incorporating the aforementioned information centre.

As part of his degree course, Pettigrew had taken a map reading module to prepare him for fieldwork. He had failed that module. Now, by a combination of pleading and wheedling, he managed to persuade one of the centre staff to orientate him and point out on the map the location of Foxtor Mire. The obliging man even took him outside and pointed to the very lane he needed to take to bring him to the area of the mire.

As he was about to leave, clutching his precious map, the attendant looked him up and down, "You're not going there now, are you?!" It wasn't so much a question, more a command.

Pettigrew was conscious that the man was looking at his clothes; involuntarily he looked down. He was wearing a light sweater, a pair of jeans with designer rips in strategic places, and cheap trainers. Over his arm, he carried a light 'showerproof' jacket of the type that would get soaking wet if someone so much as breathed on it.

"I ... I had planned to," he stammered.

"I would strongly advise against it. In those clothes, if the mist came down, you'd be soaked through in no time. And it looks as though it will. Foxtor Mire is a very desolate place."

"I had planned to drive as far as the road will take me and observe it from the safety of my car," Pettigrew wheedled.

"It's up to you, sir. But please mind how you go. Once you get off the metalled road, it's easy to get bogged down. Oh, and," the informative man sniffed, "take it easy going down that lane. It's not well-maintained."

Ten yards down the lane and Pettigrew had decided that 'not well-maintained' was a Dartmoor euphemism for 'very nearly impassable'. He swore every time his car lurched over a bump and every time his wheels crashed through a pothole. He was unsure how much of this his precious Citroën 2CV could take.

At a bend in the road, he stopped the car and allowed the engine to idle while he consulted the map.

Yes! There was the bend on the map. From his current location there appeared to be two routes around the mire, one route clockwise and one anti-clockwise route. The question was, which one should he take?

Tracing out the clockwise route with his finger, he found that the metalled road finished abruptly in the next grid square. He guessed that wasn't far. From there it was replaced by a green dotted line, presumably a footpath.

Wait! It seemed to cross a river. The *River Strane*, he read with difficulty. No mention of a bridge?

He smiled smugly. *Well, I shan't go that way! The anti-clockwise route it is!*

According to the map, the path started somewhere close by, so he parked up, climbed out and started searching for the footpath.

Pettigrew had never walked on Dartmoor before. He had expected to find a paved way, with handrails on either side, so he was rather taken aback when what he actually came across was a narrow path, well-trodden but sometimes difficult to see among the tussocks and fern. The trail inclined downwards near the start but levelled off before disappearing to the right. Shrugging his shoulders, Pettigrew pulled his jacket on and started walking, quickly becoming frustrated at the unevenness of the footpath. He decided, after a while, that the ground to his left looked more level and, with only sparse vegetation growing, would be easier to walk on.

He took two steps to his left and immediately plunged up to his waist in icy cold water.

Shrieking and gasping for breath, he scrambled back onto the footpath and lay on his back groaning and shaking, partly with cold, partly with fear. When he'd calmed down a little, he sat up and surveyed the area he had just escaped from. It seemed to move, undulate, quiver like a living thing. He stared at the spot where he had plunged into the mire. The vegetation was now slowly moving back together, covering the gap his body had created. After only a few seconds, there was nothing to show where some foolhardy traveller had transgressed.

He cursed loudly. *When I get back, I'll write a very strongly worded complaint to the authorities. The place should be fenced off! With warning notices!*

The path had now disappeared and been replaced with open moorland rising to a pile of rocks on a hilltop. He consulted his map. The was the mighty Fox Tor, eh? He decided to explore the sloping ground bordering the southern extremity of the mire. It had started to drizzle, and he managed only a few hundred yards before he halted once more and stared disconsolately at his environment. He decided that enough was more than enough.

As he turned to retrace his steps, the drizzle eased and the sun peeked out from behind a cloud. A glint of bright light dazzled him. Something near the edge of the mire had momentarily reflected the sun. Pettigrew squinted.

Something dark and wet.

He approached cautiously, not wishing for another soaking, and examined what at first sight appeared to be a long piece of black, shiny leather.

Pettigrew wasn't in the same league as Wells, but he was a zoologist—after a fashion—and he knew that this was the skin of some animal. Lifting the upper layer confirmed that the innards had all rotted away, or more likely had been eaten by the creatures of the moor.

Digging his hands under the lower layer he managed, with no small difficulty, to partially raise a section of it from the sodden turf into which it had sunk. There was something beneath it. Keeping the carcass raised by using his knee as a prop, he fished underneath and brought out a thin tube of about an inch diameter. He tilted it and a bright, shiny liquid poured out.

Mercury?

He swallowed, his breath catching in his throat. He suddenly felt immensely excited. The Germans had experimented with mercury engines during the Second World War. Had some alien power developed such a thing? His hands trembling, he scrabbled around once more and located another object. He stood up to examine it, allowing the skin to flop down again. This was a piece of plastic—at least, he assumed it was plastic. Attached to one corner was part of an electronic panel, roughly two inches by three, hanging onto the plastic by a single screw.

Wrenching the panel off, he examined it carefully. There were some objects soldered onto it that could conceivably be integrated circuit blocks, but the rest of the components were unfamiliar. Several fine wires were attached to the board in various places, attesting to it being part of an electrical circuit. But what really intrigued him were the small sparkling crystals that were dotted here and there on the panel.

This has to be alien! I have proof of the crash. Now I just need the creatures themselves!

Euphoric now, Pettigrew pocketed the panel and began to retrace his steps. His jaunty mood didn't last long though. The drizzle had begun to fall once more and the mist swirled around him, rolling quickly down the hills and covering the mire. It was with some difficulty that he found the path leading back to the road. He stumbled along it for some time, soaked to the skin and thoroughly miserable, until it occurred to him that he wasn't actually sure he was still on the path. The mist was so thick now that he could barely see a hand in front of his face.

He took a few hesitant steps forward, missed his footing and tumbled headfirst into the mire.

Wriggling and twisting, Pettigrew managed to get his head above the water. He barely had time to scream for help when two strong hands grabbed him and hauled him bodily out of the mire, depositing him, sobbing and shaking, on the path. A tall, thick-set man knelt down beside him.

"You alright, mate?" the man asked, concern etched onto his handsome face. He was dressed in waterproofs and wearing a woollen hat, blond hair attempting to escape from beneath it.

At any other time Pettigrew's answer would have been dripping with sarcasm, but not now. "Yes, I think so," he answered limply, before adding as an afterthought, "thank you!"

There was a momentary pause as Pettigrew struggled to get his emotions under control. He rubbed his eyes then blinked up at Jan and cried, "My glasses! I can't see without them!"

Without a second thought, the big man fell onto his stomach so that his upper body was over the mire and thrust his arm deep underwater. He fished around for a few moments before his hand emerged holding the spectacles. Standing up and taking a handkerchief from his pocket, he cleaned the lenses and handed them to Pettigrew, who was now struggling to his feet with the help of a young woman. She'd startled him. Such was the density of the mist, he hadn't noticed her.

"Are you alright to go on?" she was asking him.

Pettigrew nodded. The handsome man stripped off his waterproof jacket and under-fleece and handed them to Pettigrew.

"Put these on," he commanded. "We'll soon have you under cover."

"How far is it to the road?" asked Pettigrew, anxious for this horrendous adventure to end. "My car is parked there."

"A little 2CV?" asked the man.

Pettigrew nodded.

"No more than about twenty yards," said the man. "You nearly made it." He offered his arm. "Right, hang on to my jumper and don't let go! Lead on, Flick."

The woman went to the front and led the way back along the track.

"Is it wise to allow a woman to lead?" asked Pettigrew anxiously, calling over the man's shoulder.

The man laughed. "If Flick can't find her way back, no one can. She's walked this path more times than you've had hot dinners, and in all weathers!"

Pettigrew, unsure of the veracity of that statement, kept a suspicious eye on the Flick person as she led the way. He was relieved when, after a short time, they emerged onto the road near the 2CV. He leaned against his car, breathing heavily.

"We should be getting back," the man said to the woman. "Hope your little friends in the attic are okay."

She shot him a warning look.

Pettigrew kept his face neutral, not giving any indication that he had even heard the remark.

The woman turned to him. "It's not really my business, but should you be walking on the moor without the right gear?"

"I intended only a five-minute walk," answered Pettigrew, his ire rising when the woman had the audacity to speak to him in such a way, "but the mist came down and I became disoriented."

"The clag can do that," confirmed the man. "I expect you were being pixie led."

The woman gave him a hard dig in the ribs.

"Clag?" asked Pettigrew.

"Mist," the woman explained. "When it's misty the locals say, 'the clag is down'. It happens a lot on the moor. Where are you staying?"

"In Princetown. I'll get back and have a shower and change into some dry clothes," he said, stripping off his outer clothing and handing it back. "By the way, I didn't get your names?"

"Jan and Flick," said the man, smiling, "and in case you're confused, I'm the Jan and she's the Flick."

Pettigrew would have liked to ask their surnames but felt that would be pushing it too far. "Well, thank you, Jan and Flick. My name is Professor James Pettigrew, and I am most grateful to you both."

As he climbed into his little car and slammed the door, Felicity looked sternly at Jan. "That was a bit clumsy, mate!"

Jan hung his head and tugged his forelock, then switching on his Devon accent said, "I be sorry, miss. I be just a girt thick Janner."

"You can say that again." Felicity laughed and embraced him, his slip already forgotten.

But Pettigrew hadn't forgotten it.

Nor had he missed the look that had passed between the two of them.

You're hiding something in your attic, Miss Flick, and I intend to find out what.

They shouldn't be difficult to trace. 'Flick and Jan', he reminded himself as he passed a house on the right of the road. The sign on the gate identified it as 'Prior's Cross House'.

But that can wait. First priority is finding the gossipy woman.

A few hundred yards further up the road, he passed a farm.

Mrs Gurney, he thought as he drove away, *where are you? I need to find you!*

CHAPTER TWENTY-EIGHT

*P*rofessor Pettigrew huddled deeper into his Puffa jacket as he exited the public conveniences located in the corner of the car park. He gazed glumly around at the grey, weathered buildings, shrouded by a glowering sky and watched over by the large Victorian prison that still held inmates to this day.

He sniffed. Why would anyone choose to live up here on the moor, so far from the convenience of civilisation?

It's just so miserable, he thought.

Out of season, less charitable visitors—such as Pettigrew—might well have labelled Princetown a desolate place. Grim. Forbidding even. But the truth was, it always remained a lively and close-knit community, well-loved by the locals who resided within it or close by.

Pettigrew couldn't see that, though. All he saw were the quiet streets, the biting wind racing along Plymouth Hill and the soft west-country drizzle that soaked through every layer of his clothing. He chewed on an ancient boiled sweet he'd discovered in the well of his car and surveyed the shops, the café and the pub through narrowed, scheming eyes.

Who here, in this godforsaken town, was most likely to be able to supply him with the information he needed?

Not much choice, he grumbled to himself.

He elected to try the newsagent. These tended to be the hub of a community, after all. If anyone would know where he could find Mrs Gurney, it would be them.

He crossed the road—not difficult because there weren't many cars around—and pushed open the door of the shop. The bell made a pleasant tinkling sound.

That would drive me batty, Pettigrew thought.

The shop was larger than he'd imagined. More of a General Stores than simply a newsagent. He wound his way around the narrow aisles—the shelves piled high with all manner of essentials—pretending to browse while waiting for the elderly woman already at the counter to finish and leave. She was taking a ridiculously long time, paying for her goods and having a good old chinwag all at once.

What was it with these people on the moor? It was as if they didn't have anything to do all day except stand around and gossip.

Deciding she was never going to leave, Pettigrew grabbed a few bits and bobs that he could take to the till.

He sauntered over, carefully plastering a pleasant countenance over his face. The woman moved aside as he approached. Not fully aside, but enough so that he could squeeze into the space she had vacated and deposit his items.

"But that's as mebbe, baint it, Mike?" the woman was saying to the middle-aged gentleman on the other side of the counter.

"That's the long and the short of it, Mrs Yates, it really is." He winked at her and turned his attention to Pettigrew. "Good morning, sir. How are you doing today?" He lifted up the first item, a Jamaican Ginger Cake, and rang it through.

"Very well, very well!" Pettigrew enthused, flashing a smile at Mrs Yates in what he hoped was a dashing way. "A bracing day to be on the moor, isn't it?"

"Indeed!" Mike agreed, ringing through a jar of baby food.

"Some might say it be daft, to be out in weather like this," Mrs Yates offered. "What with the cloud coming in an' all."

Pettigrew pursed his lips. "Yes, yes, but you can never know what it will do before you set out for the day, can you?"

Mike picked up a bottle of plant feed. "That's true enough," he replied amiably.

"You're up 'ere for the day then? 'Ave you come far?" Mrs Yates evidently liked to know everyone's business.

That gave Pettigrew an idea. "Quite a way, actually." He allowed his face to fall. "I've been driving for four hours already. I had intended to pay a visit to my cousin to let her know that my mother passed away recently."

"Oh, I am sorry to hear that, bless yer heart," Mrs

Yates commiserated. Mike nodded, his face equally grave, as he rang through a bargain pack of Custard Creams.

"Thank you, you're very kind." Pettigrew blinked rapidly, as though trying to bring his emotions under control. "I wanted to do it in person, you know? They were close." He reconsidered this. "Once. The thing is, I've left her address at home and can't remember the way. So silly of me."

Mrs Yates patted his arm. "Oh, dearie me! We've all done things like that from time to time, 'aven't us, Mike?"

"We have, Mrs Yates." Mike turned over the packet of clothes pegs he had in his hands, looking for the price.

Mrs Yates leaned towards Pettigrew, her face kind. "Who is it you be lookin' for, me 'andsome? Mike and I, we knows everyone round these parts ..."

After that, it was easy-peasy.

A few minutes later, Pettigrew had extracted all the information he needed from Mrs Yates, with a little help from Mike who had sketched a map to the Gurney farm. Pettigrew couldn't believe it was the same farm he'd passed only the previous day. He had been so near! He left the shop, a tenner lighter than he'd entered.

That didn't please him, although it was a small price to pay, he supposed.

Who in their right mind likes cheap own-brand Custard Creams, he wondered. He chucked the useless clutter he'd bought into the boot of the 2CV and rooted around on the floor near the accelerator for another sticky, slightly gooey boiled sweet, then floored it out of the car park.

THE CREATURE FROM THE GRIM MIRE

He drove past the farm and parked a little further up, pulling as far into the hedgerow as he could in an effort to disguise his car. He supposed it didn't really matter. People in these parts must be used to ramblers turning up and dumping their cars wherever they chose. He wouldn't look too out of place.

Except that the weather had not improved, and nobody would be walking out on the moor on a day like today. Not if they had a choice.

Or a brain.

He leaned against a stile, the stench of sheep strong in his nostrils, pondering where he'd find the best vantage point to allow him to monitor the comings and goings of the Gurney farm. In the end, he elected to climb the stile, cross the field and huddle in the hedge, creating a peephole through which he could watch all the farm's activity.

He had a long wait.

A very long wait.

The hedge sheltered him in part from the relentless soft rain, but even so, he was soaked through to his underclothes in no time at all.

He waited.

And he waited.

At some stage, he walked back to the car and extracted the Custard Creams, which had suddenly taken on a higher and more desirable status. He trudged back to the hedge, his city-boy boots allowing water, mud and the cold to seep through, and cosied up to the bramble once more, eating biscuit after biscuit and becoming increasingly furious with the lack of activity.

Until, finally, there they were.

A young blonde woman dressed appropriately for the season in waterproofs and wellies, and her huge farming boyfriend, who was probably immune to all the extremes the Devon climate cared to throw at him. The same couple he had met near the mire!

Pettigrew narrowed his eyes, focusing on the young woman.

He was most interested in her.

Or what she kept in her attic, at any rate.

CHAPTER TWENTY-NINE

Pettigrew munched on the last of the Custard Creams and stared miserably through the hole in the hedge to the farmyard. All activity had ceased once the young couple had arrived. They had disappeared inside the large building. He could imagine them in there, warm and dry, and enjoying a nice cup of tea and some fruit cake.

Marvellous.

Come on. Come on. Come back out again.

He jigged around in place, beginning to lose patience until finally, they reappeared. Hand in hand they tramped across the farmyard and set off down the lane. Pettigrew, realising he couldn't crash through the hedge, had to race back up the field and out of the gate to get back on the lane. By the time he'd done that, the couple was out of sight.

Cursing, he shot a look at his car. They couldn't be going far and surely they weren't going for a hike on the moor? If anything, the weather was worse now than it had been. The cloud obscured the tops of the tors. Visibility would be poor even a dozen or so feet higher than where he stood now.

No. Logic suggested they had merely walked down the lane. Pettigrew left his car where it was and trotted after them.

He'd only been walking for a few minutes when he caught sight of them in the distance. He followed them all the way to Prior's Cross House, hanging back as they walked up the drive, and waited for them to go in. Taking a quick look around, noting that the coast was clear, he edged up the drive, treading quietly so as not to disturb the loose gravel.

To the right of the front door was a large bay window. Squinting through the glass, he could tell it was a living room, but nobody was inside. He cut his losses and crossed in front of the main door. He wound his way around the side of the property, carefully ducking below one window until he found himself next to the kitchen window, the back door just beyond that.

Someone pushed open the kitchen window. Pettigrew dropped into a crouch behind a large plant container—not that it would have hidden him had someone decided to venture outside.

"Goodness gracious, Helly!" A man's voice. "I need a gas mask."

"Open the door then, Jan," called the young woman, evidently amused.

"I think he's pleased to see you." An older man's voice.

"That's as maybe, Wells, but he seriously needs to get a grip of that wind problem he has. Dear Lord!"

Pettigrew grimaced as the back door was flung open, expecting Jan to throw himself from the house, given the amount of fuss he was making, but he merely stuck his head out and took a few deep breaths before going back inside.

"That's better," he said.

There was an odd cacophony of squawks and hissing. Pettigrew cocked his head. It sounded like a menagerie in there.

"They're very excited to see you," the older man repeated.

"I know, I know," said Jan. "Come here, Helly, give me a hug."

"Maybe the children want another bath time—" The woman dissolved into giggles.

"They can want," Jan replied gruffly. "As much as I love them."

Children?

Pettigrew risked standing up and edging closer to the window.

"Shall we put the kettle on?" the older man was asking hopefully.

The woman groaned. "I've just drunk a gallon at Jan's Mum's."

"Oh, that's a shame." The old man sounded disappointed.

"Alright, HG," the woman relented, and Pettigrew heard her filling the kettle, just two feet from where he was hiding.

The sound of her feet on tiles told him she'd walked across the kitchen. Pettigrew risked a quick peep through the window, keeping his head low, his eyes level with the windowsill.

His heart skipped a happy beat. He'd been expecting children—isn't that what they'd called them—but here, entirely unexpectedly, were the aliens! The intelligence that Arnie had received had been correct after all.

Pettigrew cooed quietly. *What did they have here?* An octopus-type creature, currently waving its arms around in some sort of dance; some kind of bird, nesting on the young man's head, but with arms instead of wings—mighty peculiar; and a small hairy thing, wearing goggles and being carried around by Jan, who was bravely trying to keep time with the dancing octopus-creature.

Pettigrew wondered about the goggles.

More than an extra-terrestrial fashion accessory, he decided.

"Here, give me Helly." The woman was standing on the opposite side of the room to the window, leaning against the worktop, probably waiting for the kettle to boil. She reached out and took the strange grey creature with a mop of white hair on its head from Jan.

Helly, Pettigrew noted. It had a name.

"Fel-iss-it-ee," said the creature. "Flick!"

Helly could speak!

Pettigrew could have clapped his hands in

excitement. The possibilities with these creatures were endless.

"We need to discuss a plan of action, HG. When are we going to take Helly to the tinners' girt on Fox Tor?"

Pettigrew's eyes grew round. Why would they take the alien named Helly out to somewhere that sounded so forbidding? He fished around in his pocket to find his phone—currently on mute—and quickly googled tinners' girt and Fox Tor.

Aha.

Not so far away. Walkable even.

So, what was up there of interest?

It was worth checking out, for sure.

An orange cat ambled out of the back door. More observant than the humans, it turned its head to look at him. Pettigrew met its eyes. It arched its back and hissed at him.

Blast!

"Mister Ogilvy?" the woman asked.

Time to go.

Pettigrew hurriedly stepped away from the window and, with the cat glaring balefully after him, made a mad dash around the house, down the drive and turned right to head up the lane. By the time Jan had wandered out of the house to investigate what had Mister Ogilvy in a tizz, Pettigrew had melted into the mist.

Stomach growling, Pettigrew tramped wearily up Fox Tor, checking the coordinates on his phone every now and again. The 'tinners' girt' on the eastern side of the Tor appeared to be some kind of sludge pile of rock.

He carefully scanned every potential opening but had no luck.

Increasingly frustrated, his mood becoming blacker by the minute, he considered turning back. He'd almost reached the end of his tether when, finally, he thought he heard a deep growl emanating from somewhere ahead of him.

He dropped onto his front, ignoring the cold, damp rock beneath him, and held his breath. He didn't have to wait long. The growl came again and then an enormous dog slunk out of a cave and looked in his direction. Like some great mythical beast, it looked ugly and twisted, its eyes bright red, its mouth slavering.

Pettigrew swallowed and fumbled for his phone. When Arnie picked up, Pettigrew whispered urgently down the line.

"We're gonna need a bigger dog crate."

CHAPTER THIRTY

*P*ettigrew turned off the headlights of his car as Arnie hunkered down in the passenger seat and coasted quietly past Prior's Cross House for the fourth time in an hour. Everything was exactly as it had been.

"Nope," Arnie confirmed. "It looks like she's still out."

"Perfect. She must have gone to dinner with that big blond lout she's seeing," Pettigrew said. "I saw her and the old fellow walking up the lane earlier." He pulled the 2CV into a passing place and performed a nine-point turn with some difficulty.

"You're really going through with this, then?" Arnie asked. He sounded nervous.

"*We're* going to do it, yes," Pettigrew told him.

"But it's illegal," Arnie whined. "Breaking and entering is a big deal."

Pettigrew shrugged. "You haven't seen these

creatures. I have. Believe me, once we show the world what we've got, they're not going to be bothered about a little trespassing."

"It's not trespassing—"

"We're here," Pettigrew retorted, cutting him off. "Let's strike while the iron's hot."

He drove into the drive of Prior's Cross House and parked up behind Felicity's car. "Let's do this," he said, and popped the car's boot. He handed a head torch to Arnie and pulled on his own, switching it on to better see what they were doing and where they were going. He strapped a large fishing net to his back, and then they retrieved a number of fold-down pet crates before Pettigrew led a reluctant Arnie to the back door of the house.

Breaking into the house itself was surprisingly easy. The back door was old, the glass single-paned, and the lock a simple bolt that needed to be drawn back. Pettigrew used a clay plant pot to break the window, then threaded his hand through the hole and slid back the bolt.

They stepped carefully through into the kitchen. All was still and quiet. Pettigrew wrinkled his nose at the faint tang of fish.

Eww.

"Where now?" Arnie whispered.

Pettigrew pointed towards the hall. "They referred to the creatures as 'children'. I'm guessing they've got them tucked up in bed upstairs."

That made sense. Arnie nodded, his heart beating hard in his chest. He didn't like this one little bit, although he appreciated what Pettigrew was saying about the long-term rewards. He followed Pettigrew through into the hall, struggling with the crates, and then trudged upstairs in his wake. They leaned the crates against a wall on the landing and paused, both of them listening.

Not a sound.

Unbeknownst to them, Mister Ogilvy had followed them indoors, having finished with his hunting foray for the night. Now he stood at the bottom of the stairs, his whiskers twitching in indignation, his eyes glowing with anger.

How very dare they!

Pettigrew turned the handle of the door nearest them. The bathroom.

No aliens in there.

He walked down the hall and opened the next door. Felicity's bedroom. He carefully peered in every corner—using his head torch to illuminate all the shadowy areas—and even went so far as to open the wardrobes and search through those.

Nothing.

In fact, all three bedrooms were empty.

Pettigrew chewed on a filthy fingernail. "They have to be somewhere," he hissed. "She didn't take them with her."

Arnie looked worried. "Where else would they be? Outside maybe?"

Pettigrew shook his head. "They wouldn't risk leaving something so precious out in this accursed weather," he insisted. Then it came to him. The evidence he'd dismissed. The rumours about 'aliens in the attic'. Mrs Treverick on the news ...

He raised his eyes to the ceiling. From above their heads came a slight creak. It might have been the timbers settling. It could have been the wind in the rafters.

Pettigrew knew better.

He made an L shape with the finger and thumb of his right hand and pointed at the attic.

"Bingo," he whispered.

He located the loft pole and gently opened the hatch, quietly pulling the ladder down. Placing his finger over his lips, he winked at Arnie and began to climb up. When he reached the top, he unhooked the fishing net and stepped quietly onto the planking, feeling around for a light switch.

He flicked the switch and all hell broke loose.

At the precise moment Pettigrew was flicking the light switch, Mister Ogilvy chose to launch an attack on Arnie. He had stealthily made his way upstairs and, realising that the two men had bad intentions towards his beloved Helly, he leapt at Arnie's calves, claws unsheathed and teeth bared.

Arnie howled in shock and pain and grabbed the cat by the scruff of its neck. Mister Ogilvy tried to wrench free but Arnie, fearful for his life, held on for grim death and with his free hand opened one of the pet crates and threw the indignant cat inside.

Up in the attic, Pettigrew had switched on the light, illuminating the three aliens at the rear of the space, each in soft little blanket nests. The octopus and the bird blinked at the sudden intrusion, eyes as round as saucers, but the unexpected light caused Helly to shriek with pain and curl into a ball.

The scream jolted Pettigrew and he switched the light off again, relying instead on the beam from his head torch. He panted in the darkness, wondering what to do, then remembered the goggles.

Ah!

"Goggles," he instructed Helly, remembering how the alien creature had seemed to respond to speech in the kitchen with Jan and the woman.

Helly obediently rooted around in his nest and pulled his goggles on.

Pettigrew switched the light back on. The three aliens gawped at him in trepidation.

"It's alright," Pettigrew soothed them. "I'm with Fel-iss-it-ee and Jan. I'm going to take you to them."

After that, it couldn't have been simpler.

CHAPTER THIRTY-ONE

*I*t was late afternoon and the once-grand conference room of the former Duchy Hotel bustled with activity. Reporters and newsmen had gathered from all over the British Isles and beyond. Several television cameras had been set up on tripods and there were radio mikes everywhere. Professor James Pettigrew, peeping out from behind a side door, had to hand it to Crabbe. The journalist had done an excellent job of arranging the press conference at short notice.

Arnie Crabbe was basking in the reflected glory of his friend's big moment. Arnie took a seat at the centre of the presenters' table, smiling and nodding at people he had never met or even seen before. He wanted to give a good impression, convince them that he was a cutting-edge journalist, fully in the know. The gathered news reporters were becoming restless. *Time to make a start*, he thought. He had milked it long enough.

He tapped one of the microphones—there were

dozens lined up in front of him—and leaned forward, blowing into it, something an experienced presenter would never do. As a consequence, it sent out a wail of feedback. He jerked backwards in surprise and tried again, unsure which of the microphones to speak into.

"Ladies and Gentlemen—" he said, then offered a knowing look and a crooked smile for the benefit of the television cameras, imagining it made him look hard-bitten, and added "—and fellow reporters. My name is Arnie Crabbe. I'm the senior reporter for the *Plymouth Mail*, currently working with a number of television companies and in close collaboration with Professor James Pettigrew to research the origins of the aliens that have invaded our world."

"Get on with it!" hissed a voice from the slightly open door behind the presentation desk.

Arnie stood and, in his most theatrical voice, announced, "Ladies and Gentlemen, I give you ... Professor Pettigrew!" He extended a hand towards the partially open door, which now opened fully to reveal the great man himself.

Professor James Ignatius Pettigrew.

Pettigrew, looking his most distinguished in a white shirt and an immaculately pressed suit and wearing a Durham University tie—although the nearest he had ever been to that august establishment had been a day trip to the castle when he was a child—claimed the centre seat, forcing Arnie to take a seat to the side. He cleared his throat and addressed his waiting public.

"Dear friends!"

He paused for effect, his head swivelling to look around the hall like Julius Caesar on the battlefield inspecting his troops.

"Today, I am able to make the most breathtaking and astounding announcement ever made in the history of our planet."

Another lengthy pause.

A few journalists fidgeted. Somebody's phone beeped.

"I have, in a secret location, three aliens from another planet!"

There were gasps and a sudden rush of comments and questions. Arnie held his hands up, while Pettigrew smiled smugly, nodding until the murmuring and chatter had died down.

"I will describe them to you. One is a type of ape-man, a most dangerous-looking brute." He pulled a fierce face. "The second is a type of five-tentacled mollusc." He wiggled his fingers. "And the third is a very interesting specimen. A kind of bird, whose evolution has regressed to its saurian ancestors."

A third pause. Cameras flashed and whirred; television cameras quietly ticked over. The throng began to chatter and throw questions at him again. Pettigrew raised his hand for silence.

"A fourth alien is still at large, but I know its location. Once I have killed that creature—"

"You're going to kill an alien, Professor?" a BBC journalist shouted from the front row. "What does the rest of the scientific community think of that idea?"

Pettigrew glowered at the woman. "I believe it to be too dangerous to capture. I have carried out ... certain research ... on the saurian. I will put my specimens before the public, open to scrutiny by any reputable scientific institution."

"Which reputable—" The journalist attempted to interject again.

Pettigrew decided to ignore the annoying woman. "First, however, we must kill the beast. It poses a threat to the farming community here, therefore action must be taken without delay." He nodded, his face grave. "I suggest we reconvene tomorrow morning at ten, when I will personally lead you to the creature that threatens the people of this county and indeed the country. We will require a cohort of brave and determined men"—he raised a finger—"armed, of course, in order to carry out our duty."

He had intended to close the meeting with that stirring call to arms, but another determined reporter managed to shout above the tumult. "Tom Mohammed with Channel 4 News, Professor. Where do the aliens originate, Professor?"

Pettigrew hadn't even considered the history of the little aliens he held in his care. What did it matter where they came from? Maintaining his composure while faking supreme confidence—he had a long and successful history of lying, after all—he replied with the first thing that came into his head. "I believe them to be from Titan, one of Saturn's moons."

The room exploded and Pettigrew smiled in

satisfaction. Only one man appeared to be underwhelmed. He stood at the back of the hall, not pressing forward towards Pettigrew like everyone else. He looked quaintly out of time, dressed in an old Harris Tweed suit accessorised with a red bow tie. His thick moustache almost covered his pursed lips. Intelligent eyes beamed out from beneath heavy eyebrows, his jaw clenched as he observed the proceedings.

Turning and pushing through the crowd, the man made his way out of the building and was lost from Pettigrew's view.

Wells signalled to a car parked on the main road. It started up and cruised towards him. Felicity was behind the wheel, Jan alongside her.

Wells eased himself into the rear seat, his face grave.

"That man is a monster. We must act tonight if we are to rescue the children. And then again, tomorrow morning, early, if we are to save Fossy." He gripped Felicity's shoulder. "We have no time to lose!"

"We will, don't worry!" Felicity replied, keeping her eyes peeled for a traffic warden and awaiting instructions.

"The man is deranged!" Wells was angry, but Felicity sensed fear as well. Neither she nor Jan spoke; they waited for Wells to continue.

He explained all that had been said, before adding, "If he goes ahead with his threat to reveal the children on television, does he not realise the reaction he will provoke from the Government? He's in a mad little world of his own, doing this for his own self-aggrandisement. Can he really believe that the establishment will allow him to continue without let or hindrance? They will come down on him like a ton of bricks!"

Wells pummelled the back of Jan's seat. "He will be ... what's the euphemism ... *retired*. Permanently. The children will be split up and incarcerated in various secret research institutions. For the rest of their miserable lives they will be poked, prodded and in all likelihood, experimented on until they die."

Wells dropped his head into his hands.

"Then we have to get them away from him." Jan turned in his seat. "When he comes out of the Duchy, Flick, follow him. We have to find where he's keeping the children."

"What did your research on the intro-net reveal on this man, Felicity?" Wells asked.

"Internet," Felicity corrected. "Not a great deal. The profile on his university website states that he is currently 'on leave'. At this time of the academic year, that can only mean that he is suspended, surely? Otherwise they would say he was on sabbatical or research leave or something. Obviously, it doesn't state why. He has never been appointed a professor. His grade is assistant lecturer, five grades below professor. He has a two-one in zoology. It states that he lives in Okehampton but gives no address."

"In other words, the man is a charlatan!" stormed Wells.

"Turn the car round, Flick," said Jan. "If he lives in

Okehampton he will leave Princetown by the Tavistock Road and probably head towards the A386. We daren't lose sight of him."

While Felicity did so, Jan was busy on his mobile phone.

"Hello, Kathy? It's Jan. Is Dan'l there? Is he? Has he got his mobile with him? Will he get a signal there? Alright, my darlin'. I'll speak to you later. I'll tell you what this is all about then."

Jan pumped another number into his mobile and waited. "Dan'l? How are you, man? It's Jan here ..." Jan uncharacteristically swore into the phone. "I'll give you 'Jan who?' When I get hold of you, you big daft Janner! Listen, I need your help. Can you get away?" He listened and smiled. "You're a good man Dan'l Gurney. Can you meet me in Okehampton? Keep your phone handy. I'll contact you with details as soon as I know more. Thanks mate! Oh, and Dan'l, bring Bess!"

Jan hung up and laughed.

"What was that about?" asked Felicity.

"We know Pettigrew is in league with Crabbe, who is obviously no problem, but we don't know if he has other heavies located in Okehampton. I just sent for reinforcements."

"Good thinking," nodded Wells. "He's devious. He might well have others helping him."

"So, what were you laughing about?" asked Felicity.

"When I told him to bring Bess, he said 'Can 'ee think of any way I could persuade 'er to let I come on my own?'" He switched on his Dartmoor accent, imitating his brother.

Felicity chuckled. "But why Bess? Is she aggressive?"

"Not particularly," Jan shook his head. "Sheepdogs aren't bred to be overly aggressive. They need to be a bit sharp with the lambs and ewes if they start to stray, but in the main, they are fairly placid. What Bess is, is fiercely protective of Dan'l, and that could prove useful."

"Look! There's that awful fraud of a man!" cried Wells. They had turned about and were now approaching the Duchy once more. Pettigrew had emerged from the building and immediately turned left.

"He's going into the car park. If he's in his 2CV, he'll be easy to follow," said Felicity.

A few minutes later the little maroon and white French mini emerged, the left indicator flashing.

"North Road!" said Jan. "Stay well behind him, Flick."

"It will be difficult trying to be inconspicuous. We're likely to be the only two cars on the road at this time of year."

They were, until they reached the junction of the Mount Tavy and the Okehampton Road, where another car inserted itself between them.

"Perfect," said Jan. "Let's hope that Ford stays there until we get to Okehampton."

It nearly did. When they turned off onto the slip to drop down into Okehampton, the Ford carried on along the bypass towards Exeter. Once more directly behind the 2CV, Felicity hung as far back as she dared.

As they approached the traffic lights at the crossroads near the centre of town, they turned to red. The little 2CV sped through the red light, narrowly missing an articulated lorry coming the other way, and shot down a lane to the right. Felicity groaned as she hit the brakes hard to avoid the same heavy vehicle.

"He's seen us!" said Jan.

As they waited at the lights, Jan pumped Dan'l's number into his phone. "Where are you? Right, stay there."

The car behind them gently tooted its horn to remind them that the lights had changed. "Turn right!" ordered Jan. "Waitrose car park."

Dan'l was waiting for them, sitting in the dark with Bess alongside him. Wells was struck by the similarity of the two Gurneys as they met and exchanged a bear hug. Both had the same mop of blond hair and the same bronzed clean-cut good looks. However, Dan'l was a good two inches taller than Jan and even broader.

Good heavens, thought Wells, *the man must be as strong as an ox!*

Nor was Felicity left out. Dan'l picked her up as if she were a child and hugged her, giving her a kiss on the cheek. "Alright, Flick, my darlin'? 'Ow be acking, me booty? I hab'n seen 'ee since the las' time!"

Ah, thought Wells. *There the similarity ends. The two brothers speak two entirely different languages.*

After Wells had been introduced and hands had been shaken, he asked, "Do you have an idea, Jan?"

"It's a long shot. That lane Pettigrew drove down

leads to about a dozen or so detached houses. Unless he's driven right through and out of the town again, the chances are he is in one of them." He cocked his head. "Can you contact Helly, with your mind?"

"This is good thinking, Jan. I might be able to, but Felicity will be better, she has built a really strong bond with Helly. But how will that help us?" asked Wells.

"Could you or Flick instruct Helly to communicate with Bess here? You saw how Tess reacted to Fossy, so perhaps Bess could lead us to Helly and the others?"

Wells slapped the palm of his hand against his brow. "John Gurney, you should have been an atomic scientist! Of course! We'll need to drive as close to the houses as we can."

"Then what are we waiting for?" cried Felicity, jumping into her car. Wells climbed into the front, and the two Gurney boys along with Bess took up the entire rear seat with not a hair's breadth to spare. Throughout the conversation that had passed, Dan'l had stood slightly open-mouthed with a look of incredulity on his face, but he had never questioned them once. Now squeezed into Felicity's Nissan, he looked askance at his brother.

"Jan, have I gone mazed?"

"Oh, brother Dan'l, you ain't seen nothin' yet!" said Jan, quoting a 1920s American crooner, a favourite of Mary Gurney's.

They drove up the lane Jan had indicated, their headlights picking out dustbins and a skulking cat but little else, until they came upon the first of a number of quite distinctive detached houses. Stopping the car, they climbed out, not without some difficulty in the case of the two boys in the back.

Wells caught Felicity's arm. "Now, as we walk, Felicity, clear your mind of everything with the exception of a mental picture of Helly. Concentrate hard," he whispered.

With Felicity and Wells leading, the odd group slowly advanced up the lane, passing two houses on the left and a further bungalow on their right. The Gurneys brought up the rear, their heads swivelling watchfully, like border guards on patrol.

Dan'l moved close to his brother and nodded at Felicity. "Be 'em mind readers?" he asked in an awed whisper.

Jan nodded, put his forefinger to his lips. "Trust them."

As they passed the fifth house, Felicity halted abruptly and faced the others, her face creased into a picture of abject grief. "Oh, no!" She shielded her face with her hands, quietly crying.

Jan reached for her but Wells stopped him. "Felicity!" he said, "You have to control the feelings! Their lives depend on it. I take it you have contact with him?"

Felicity nodded, tears rolling down her cheeks. "He's so frightened and so sad! So very, very sad."

Wells spoke again, more kindly. "My dearest, that's why we have to get to him. But we can only do that if you are strong."

"Alright." Felicity nodded and sniffed. "Sorry."

Wells continued, his voice soothing. "Picture Bess. Tell Helly that Bess is his friend, make him contact Bess."

Nodding, Felicity closed her eyes and focussed. She used the technique she had taught herself to communicate with the children. She would speak the words quietly and allow the pictures to form naturally.

"Helly, Bess is with me. Bess is a friend. You need to speak to Bess, Helly." She forced herself to mentally picture Bess, quietly repeating, "Friend." She was sure the word 'friend' was coming into her own mind, as though Helly was repeating it back.

Nothing happened for several minutes, but Felicity continued in her attempts to communicate.

Bess, who was sat leaning against Dan'l's leg, suddenly stood up, turning her head one way then the other and sniffing the air. "He's got her!" said Wells triumphantly.

"Helly," Felicity was saying, her eyes tightly closed, willing herself to remain calm, "bring Bess to you. We will come with her. Bring Bess to you, Helly."

The dog suddenly lurched forward, nearly yanking Dan'l, big as he was, off his feet.

Pulling them on, she ran past two houses and up to the door of a third. She sat smartly, directly in front of the heavy oak door, and barked once, then started whining softly. No lights glowed out of any of the windows of the large Victorian house, and there were no external lights either.

Wells glanced around, considering their next move. To one side of the house, a small modern garage had been added. It had an up and over sliding door which had not been fully closed, leaving a gap of about six inches at the bottom. Pulling a torch from his pocket, Wells was about to get down on his hands and knees when the light was taken from him by Dan'l.

"I be better at this 'ere crawlin' about, I reckon." Stretching full length on the ground with Bess licking at his ear, he shone the torch under the gap. "Citroën 2CV," he said, rising to his feet, "sort of a dark red and white."

Jan nodded, "He's in there, then."

Bold as ever, Dan'l tried the door. It was locked.

"Let's go around the back," suggested Felicity.

They filed along the side of the house to the rear and found a three-foot fence enclosing a small garden. Felicity and the boys climbed it with ease and then hoisted Wells over. Bess took it with a graceful leap. The windows on the ground floor of the rear of the house had been blacked out with opaque paint, however, light gleamed through a transom window above the back door.

"Give me a back," whispered Jan. Dan'l immediately bent over in front of the door, bracing his hands on his knees. Jan climbed onto his back, wobbled a little and gripped at the windowsill.

He steadied himself enough to peer through the window. What he saw froze his heart with terror. Strapped to an old kitchen table was Mr Polly. Hovering over him, scalpel in hand, was Pettigrew!

"In, now! Dan'l!" Jan shouted in alarm, leaping to the ground.

Dan'l didn't hesitate. Taking two steps back, he

hurled himself shoulder first at the door. Not only did the door spring open with a mighty splintering clatter, but one of the hinges was actually ripped from the frame. The force of his onslaught sent Dan'l crashing to the floor, causing a terrified Pettigrew to take a couple of steps back.

Felicity vaulted over the recumbent Dan'l and, rushing to the table, threw her body over Mr Polly to protect him.

Recovering his composure, and now filled with blind rage and sheer hatred, Pettigrew raised the scalpel to strike at Felicity. Wells, with surprising agility, had also scrambled into the room. He leapt at Pettigrew, hitting him with a vicious uppercut on the point of the chin. The scientist's eyes rolled upwards as he stiffened. He fell like a tree without bending, completely poleaxed.

Jan was already releasing Helly and Penny from their cages. Penny threw herself onto him, wrapping all five tentacles around his body. Though severely hampered by the clinging pentepus, he managed to release Helly too. The hellventi instantly dashed to Felicity, flinging his arms around her neck as she hoisted him onto her hip. Felicity held him tightly, while at the same time struggling to undo the final strap holding Mr Polly. Free at last, the little creature bounded off the table and scrambled up Jan's body with amazing alacrity, perched on his shoulder and, after hissing in his ear, pecked his head a few times and pulled his hair as if blaming Jan for all his problems.

"Oww! Do you mind, Mr Polly? I have to see to Oggy."

Poor Mister Ogilvy was meowing pitifully. Jan reached down and scooped up his cage. He started to undo it when he had second thoughts. "Bear with it Oggy, you'll soon be home, I promise."

Dan'l pushed himself to his feet and, with Bess at his side, stood gawking at the strange creatures, his mouth open so wide his chin very nearly hit the floor. Beside him, Wells had begun to rifle through the draws in Pettigrew's desk.

"Felicity, why don't you go and get the car?" the old man suggested. "It will make loading up the children easier."

Felicity nodded, quickly handing Helly over to Jan, who now had Penny wrapped around him, Helly round his neck, Mr Polly on his shoulder, still sounding very unhappy, and Oggy in a cage meowing up at him. Overwhelmed was an understatement. Felicity smiled at the sight and was out of the house and over the fence in a flash.

Wells had found what he needed. He removed all of the scientist's notes as well as the electronic panel he had picked up on the mire, and tucked them into his pockets before slamming the last of Pettigrew's drawers closed.

Jan hugged Helly and handed him over to an astonished, speechless Dan'l. "It's okay," he said addressing both. "Helly? This is Dan'l. Friend. Dan'l this is Helly. Friend."

"Friend," said Helly, ruffling Dan'l's hair. "Like Jan," he said, with his best attempt at a smile.

"Friend," confirmed Dan'l, also with an attempt at a smile—which was even less successful than Helly's.

Jan, struggling with his burdens, said "I'll bring Oggy in his cage. He'll be easier to manage that way."

The sound of a car horn alerted them to Felicity's arrival. They retraced their steps and bundled everything and everyone into the Nissan. Felicity drove, quietly pondering whether the suspension on her little car would ever recover. Wells sat in the front passenger seat holding onto Helly. Jan was in the back with Mister Ogilvy, still in his cage, on his knee, while soothing Penny—who was wrapped around his neck—by stroking one of her tentacles. Dan'l sat next to his brother with Mr Polly on his shoulder gently pulling his hair, while a bewildered Bess sat on his knee, looking about at everyone and sniffing the air.

It is doubtful that Devon had seen anything quite like it.

Not since Tom Cobley and six or seven of his friends had ridden a grey mare to Widecombe Fair.

CHAPTER THIRTY-TWO

Scrambling to his feet, Pettigrew managed to stagger a few paces before slumping down again. He sprawled with his back resting against the wall. Before he could navigate to his desk, he would need the room to stop spinning.

His clamped a hand to his forehead, feeling nauseous, and shook his head to clear the ache. He immediately regretted it. Taking a deep breath, he shuffled along on his bottom until he reached his desk and gingerly eased himself onto his chair. A glance around the room informed him that his nightmare had not gone away. Three of the crates were empty and one was missing completely. Added to that, his back door was swinging precariously on one hinge!

Pettigrew picked up the phone and dialled two nines. Something stopped him from adding a third. He held onto the phone for a few seconds, then put it down again.

He couldn't abide the thought of those brainless people at the call centre laughing at him behind his back.

No. He would go to the police station in Okehampton himself! Someone of his professional standing would have to be taken seriously. In his mind, he rehearsed what he would say to the desk sergeant. Then he thought better of it when he considered what the desk sergeant's response would probably be:

... I see, sir. Someone has stolen your three aliens from another planet ... and do you know why they took them? ... Because they belonged to them? And you had broken into their house and taken them? Yes, yes, I see! ... So, in fact, they weren't stealing them? Just reclaiming their own property, you might say? ... Well look, I'll tell you what, sir. I don't have anyone I can task at the moment, what with us being busy with witches' covens on the moor and sea serpents out along Ilfracombe way, but as soon as I can free up a constable, I'll send him along to see you. In the meantime, there is someone I'd like you to pop along to see at the hospital. Just a second and I'll give him a call ...

No! Involving the police wouldn't work.

He went over the events again. He recognised some of his assailants. The young couple he had seen on the moor and then again at the Gurney farm and Prior's Cross House. Jan and Flick, that was it. The fact that they had been at the Gurney farm did suggest that at least one of them was a Gurney. The thug who had broken his door down? He didn't recognise that one. He felt sure he would have remembered if he had met him before! But, the old man ... hadn't he seen him somewhere recently? He couldn't quite place him. It must have been the bang on the head.

Then it came to him. With a curse, he smashed his clenched fist onto the desk. The old man had been at the press conference! That meant that this gang of bleeding-hearted do-gooders knew of his plans to kill the monster dog tomorrow! They were bound to try to stop him!

He couldn't allow that to happen. It was his last chance to rescue his credibility.

Picking up his phone once more, he dialled, impatiently drumming his fingers as he waited for an answer.

"Arnie? ... It's Professor Pettigrew. Change of plans. We'll have to make an early start tomorrow. I need you to ring around ..."

CHAPTER THIRTY-THREE

*T*he sun hadn't yet emerged from its hiding place when Felicity and Jan started on their trek to Fox Tor.

Felicity's backpack carried all their emergency survival gear: waterproofs, snacks and drinks and most importantly her phone, pre-loaded with the latest *Covid 19 Tomb Kickers* album, and a Bluetooth speaker to amplify the music. Jan's backpack looked just as full but contained only one item: Helly! The hellventi's head, crowned with its mop of white, wiry hair, protruded out of the top, but he was under strict instructions to duck inside and close the cover if anyone came in sight.

Wells had opted to stay behind to look after Penny, Mr Polly and Mister Ogilvy. The Potty Professor, as Jan called Pettigrew, was still on the loose and might well attempt another break-in. Penny and Mr Polly were quite put out by not being included in the expedition, but Mister Ogilvy clearly couldn't have cared less. He had mice to attend to in the barn, and that overrode all other considerations.

Halfway up the Tor, Jan and Felicity stopped climbing and contoured around the hill to pick up the tinners' girt on the other side. They reached it just as the sun took its first peek around Ter Hill.

Helly, now wearing his goggles, announced, "Man coming, Jan," and withdrew into the backpack, pulling the cover down.

Jan was both surprised and somewhat annoyed. They could certainly do without company this morning, considering what they had to do. He scanned the slope. Sure enough, a man was climbing quickly towards them. As he came closer, Jan could hear him wheezing and struggling to catch his breath. Shading his eyes against the rising sun, Jan realised it was Daft Sid. He ran towards him.

"Sid, old mate? What are you doing? You'll kill yourself, man! Take it easy. What's the hurry?"

Sid bent over, noisily gulping in air. When he could finally speak, he straightened up. "Ged 'ome with you, Jan bey. I be tendin' sheep in these hills afore you was a twinkle in yer father's eye. No hill roun' ere' gwin stop Daft Sid."

Before Jan could reply, Sid, sounding anxious, continued, "But I come to warn 'ee, they'm comin', Jan see!" He pointed towards Ter Hill.

He was right. Jan could see dozens of people, several tractors, TV vans and a police Land Rover, all heading towards Fox Tor. Currently making their difficult and hazardous way around the base of Ter Hill, they were still quite some way off and, fortunately, they had a few obstacles to overcome before they could start climbing up Fox Tor. The old leat, a kind of artificial stream, long disused but still difficult for vehicles, should hold them for a while, and the ground at the bottom of Fox Tor was quite boggy too.

Jan puffed out his cheeks. With luck, he and Felicity still had time!

Sid slapped Jan on the shoulder. "I don' know what you'm a hidin' up 'ere in this 'ere girl, Jan. I s'pect 'ee's a dog, but I knows you and I knows your folks, an' I knowed you wudden be up to no good," he said, "so if 'tis a dog in that there cave and he b'aint the one as is worryin' the livestock, then you 'ad better get 'im away from 'ere quick. Those folks comin' up by 'ere is mazed as 'ornets. They'm comin' to kill that dog!"

"I really appreciate your help, Sid. You're a good friend. But there's something I need to do first." Jan hesitated. He really didn't want Sid to see the dog, and he definitely didn't want him to see Helly.

Sid took the hint. "I be gwin walk over to yonder knoll, Jan. I'll try to stop 'em, but I don' think I'll be able to. Too many of 'em!"

Jan and Felicity quickly moved up to the old tinners' hut and released Helly from the backpack. Felicity was digging in hers when, without warning, the devil dog sprang out of its cave and confronted them, snapping and snarling.

Instinctively Jan moved towards Helly to protect

him, but the boy was quite calm and unconcerned. Helly moved slowly towards the dog and sat down only a few paces from it.

Felicity extracted herself from her rucksack, and seeing where Helly was, emitted a strangled cry and made to intercept him.

Helly held up his hand. "Stop, Flick!" he said softly but urgently. "You send bad pictures!"

Felicity understood. Taking a deep, worried breath, she sat behind him a few feet further away, willing herself to remain calm. Jan was doing the same. Felicity, her hands trembling a little, fumbled with her phone and the speaker she'd brought with her. Soon the alien-sounding melodies of the *Covid 19 Tomb Kickers* rang out over the moor. Helly started crooning softly, rocking in rhythm to the music.

The devil dog flopped down on its haunches, its tongue lolling out.

Felicity studied it warily. Was she imagining it or had the fire in its eyes gone out?

"They'm a-comin', Jan! I can't hold 'em," Sid's voice called to them from some way off.

"Helly? Get the dog inside the cave!" Jan said, fighting to remain calm. Time was of the utmost importance.

Helly stopped rocking and stared hard at the beast. The dog sat up, its back rigid, staring right back at the hellventi. Helly stood and walked towards it. The dog didn't blink. As Helly moved past it—seemingly unafraid—it began to whimper softly. It pushed itself to standing and meekly followed Helly into the cave. Felicity, her heart in her mouth, followed behind as closely as she dared, holding out her phone, the music still playing.

Jan watched them go, checking they were safe. He turned just in time to see Pettigrew and a gang of about eight men walking towards him. And what was this he was seeing? Two TV vans had made it all the way up the hill without getting bogged down or breaking an axle. There were a dozen or so reporters, all mud-splattered and soaking wet from the knees down. Many of them had brought along their lackeys, who had been in charge of humping the heavy recording equipment across the uneven ground. Everyone looked utterly exhausted, wet, cold and fed up.

Several tractors had come up too, the going easier for them. They were now stationary, their engines idling. A score or so of farm workers, as well as the usual motley bunch that Jan knew well, faced him. A police Land Rover was parked nearby, two men leaning against it. Jan recognised one as Sgt Jock; the other was in plain clothes. They were not taking any part in the confrontation, probably here to observe.

Dear Lord, Jan thought. *It's like Hollywood on Dartmoor!*

As the leading group approached, Pettigrew moved to the side, clearly not keen on a confrontation with Jan Gurney. Nonetheless, he glared at the young farmer and roared, "There he is!" From his safe distance, he jabbed an accusing finger at Jan. "That is the man intent on shielding the alien devil dog. The dog must be killed, and *he* must be prosecuted!" His head swivelled, checking to see if the cameras were getting this.

A phalanx of eight good men and true had lined up in front of Jan, headed by none other than arch-foe Billy Bickle. Billy carried his shotgun and his friend, Ted Blackstock, stood alongside him, armed with a pitchfork.

The man on the very end of the row spoke up. "You'd best move aside, Jan. We've come to kill the beast. No point in causing an argument between us."

"You know me, Davy Whiddon," replied Jan quietly and calmly. "I'm a sheep farmer, same as you are. Do you seriously think I would protect an animal that was worrying sheep? It's my livelihood, same as it's yours."

Davy raised his eyebrows. He was a fair man, and he knew the Gurneys well. He turned to the other vigilantes. "He's got a point," he said.

"It's just talk!" sneered Bickle.

"Jan," said Davy, pushing his waterproof Tilly hat to the back of his head and scratching the stubble on his chin. "Do you swear that whatever is in that cave has never killed any of the sheep or cattle on this moor?"

"I swear it, Davy," Jan nodded.

"Then that's good enough for me," said Davy Whiddon. He broke from the group. After a beat, a second man joined him, lowering his shotgun and nodding his agreement.

Bickle stared after the retreating men, his face thunderous. He scanned the line, scrutinising the five that remained, satisfied that he still had the upper hand. Drawing himself up to his full height, he said in a badgering tone, "If that's the case, then how come you won't show us what's there? Ha!"

"Yer! Come on, Jan! What's the problem?" asked another of the group.

"Oh, very well!" An exasperated voice drifted out from the cave behind Jan. There was a sudden rush of movement as reporters and cameramen and women dashed closer. Long lenses were aimed expectantly at the cave's entrance, microphones extended, bright lights directed at the gloom.

Jan spun about, half afraid of what he would see, but as Felicity emerged, he had to hold back a relieved laugh. She exited from the shadows, carrying a small terrier in her arms. "I didn't want to bring her out, because I knew you lot would frighten her!"

Felicity lifted the terrier's paw and wiggled it towards the somewhat bemused crowd. "Say hello, Fossy!"

There were a number of 'oohs' and 'aahs' among the reporters.

Felicity lifted the little dog higher so everyone could get a better look. Cameras clicked and whirred. "Fossy got lost on the moor," said Felicity, and moved to stand next to Jan. "Jan Gurney here helped me find her. That's all there is to it." Felicity offered the assembled throng her best smile.

There was a loud guffaw, and another two of Bickle's gang walked off. Bickle glared after them in fury. Turning to the others, he cried, "I still say we kill that dog! It shouldn't be wandering around on the moor on its own."

"No! cried Felicity in alarm, clutching Fossy protectively to her chest.

"I'm not in favour of killing the dog," said one of three remaining men with Bickle. "Not at all. But I do want to see what's in that cave." He took a few purposeful steps towards Felicity.

Jan held a protective arm up. "My gear is in there," he said, "and I'm not having you lot trampling all over it and rifling through it. Once I've left you are welcome to the cave. You could even live in it, Billy, it would suit you!"

Bickle was furious. "You gonna stop us going in there, Gurney?"

"I'm gonna try, Billy. If you want to get at that dog or go in the cave, you'll have to come through me first!"

"Suits me!" said Bickle, and cursing Jan with a variety of colourful metaphors, he took a step forward.

He stopped in his tracks when a voice from above Jan and Felicity called out, "'Ere, wos on? 'Ow be ackin', Jan bey?"

Jan smirked. He didn't need to look behind. He'd know that voice anywhere.

Dan'l! The big fellow scrambled and crashed down the side of the girt, his size elevens scattering gravel in every direction. He stood alongside his brother and folded his massive arms across his impressive chest.

"There be two of us now, Billy bey," said Dan'l, smiling broadly.

"Three!" Daft Sid hove into view and stood by the brothers, lifting his chin defiantly at Billy Bickle.

"Sid, you don't need to get involved with this," Dan'l said, concerned for the wellbeing of the older man.

"If'n you try and stop me, young Dan'l, I'll clip your ear. You're not too big yet!" Sid retorted.

Dan'l laughed. "Sorry, Sid, I should a' knowed better! But why don' us even the odds up? Four agin four? What say ee, Billy bey?" Dan'l gave a low whistle and a black and white head pushed its way between the two Gurney boys.

Bess.

On seeing the four would-be assailants, the border collie lowered her head an inch or two, pulled her ears right back and bared her gleaming white teeth, emitting a long, low growl.

A clearly shaken Billy Bickle appealed to his friends. "There's still only two of em really, plus an old man and a dog. We can still take 'em, right mates? ... Mates? ... Mates?"

Billy turned about. He'd been completely abandoned.

Ted Blackstock was already halfway down Fox Tor, stumbling and falling in his desire to put as much distance as he could between himself and another growling dog. Ted had had enough of growling dogs to last him a lifetime. The two other remaining members of the Bickle gang had moved away to the side. One was staring at the ground and moving tussocks of grass around with his foot, as if looking for something, the other was looking up at the sky and whistling a wistful melody between his teeth.

Bickle remained defiant in the face of abject betrayal. "You're a tough man, Jan Gurney, when you've got your big brother with you," he spat. "It'll be a different matter if 'twas you an' me!"

Dan'l sucked air through his clenched teeth. "You 'old on there, Billy bey." He wrapped an arm around old Sid's shoulders. "Why don' us go over 'ere and sit awhile, Sid?" He whistled for his dog. "Bess, come! You and Jan go right ahead, Billy. Us three won' interfere none, I promise 'ee. That said, you'm a braver man than I be, Billy bey! I wud'n take on Jan Gurney when he be in this mood! Not for nothing!"

Bickle took a step towards Jan, who didn't budge an inch. Bickle stared into cold blue eyes that didn't even flicker. He dropped his head, beaten. There was nothing for it but to walk away. As he did so his father, Frankie, went to him and put an arm around his shoulders.

"It's okay, bey," he said, "let it go. Sometimes that makes you a better man."

Dan'l strode after Bickle. "Billy!" he called, catching up with the father and son. In a low voice, he said, "I'm sorry about what happened to your bull, Billy. I know how much he meant to 'ee. Under the circumstances, I would feel the same, but it weren't no dog as did that, you must know. Let's not part with bad blood atween us, Billy. Your father, Frankie 'ere, and my father, why they bin best mates since they was in school together. B'aint that right, Frankie?"

"Arr, 'tis right 'nuff, Dan'l bey."

Dan'l extended his hand. "What do us say, mate?"

Billy Bickle took the big man's hand and shook it, managing a half-smile. "Thanks, Dan'l," he said quietly, then he and his father walked slowly back down the tor.

When Dan'l returned to the tinners' hut, Sgt Jock and the man in civilian clothes were making a fuss of Fossy, clearly much to her delight. Felicity introduced the man in civilian clothes as DS Alderson, who it seemed to Dan'l was just as interested in the person holding the dog as he was in little Fossy.

Jock was saying, "Well, it seems the circus is packing up and going away."

One of the TV trucks was already out of sight. Another was being towed through the heavy ground by an obliging tractor driver. The press, reporters and others were now spread out across the base of Ter Hill, making their way to the track leading to the old Gobbet tin mine, and from there into Hexworthy.

Jock turned to Jan. "Jan, I'm going to have to take a look in that cave, okay?" Jan knew it wasn't a request.

Jan glanced at Felicity. She met his worried gaze with her own. In resignation, he turned towards the cave and followed the police officer in. Jock, who at that moment was switching on his torch, was sure to find Helly crouched at the rear of the cave. But, to his surprise, Jan noticed that his backpack lay against the side of the cave, near the entrance.

It seemed full!

Well done, Flick.

"I'll just get my backpack, Jock," Jan said, hoisting it

onto his back. "Alright?" Jan gestured around at the empty cave. "All yours."

Jock was in the cave for less than half a minute before he stumbled out, holding his nose, his peaked cap askew and his eyes crossed.

"Dear God!" he blasphemed. "What is that smell in there? It's like rancid mackerel!"

Jan smiled with all innocence. Beside him, Felicity struggled to suppress a fit of the giggles that hovered just below her calm, sanguine exterior.

CHAPTER THIRTY-FOUR

"You mentioned that you had an outline of an idea on how we might kill the fiend, HG?" Jan asked quietly.

Wells and Jan were sitting on either side of the fireplace in the living room at Prior's Cross, with Felicity on the sofa alongside Helly, who was cradling Mister Ogilvy on his knee. Fossy lay curled up in a ball beside him, snoring gently and sleeping the sleep of the exhausted.

Penny, who for now seemed to have formed an uneasy truce with her arch-enemy Mister Ogilvy, was engaged in some sort of game of chase with Mr Polly. Mr Polly would take up a position some distance from Penny and hiss loudly, and she, with amazing speed, would pounce on that spot ... only to find Mr Polly had gracefully bounced to a new location.

They were having great fun.

The adults, not so much.

"It is just that, an outline of an idea." Wells sounded dubious. "There are some fairly major logistical problems to overcome and even then, I'm not sure of success."

"Why not run it by us?" suggested Felicity, stroking Helly's head above his goggles, "then we can all have a good laugh and go to bed."

Wells smiled. "It's not that outrageous, Felicity." He paused momentarily and raised his eyebrows. "Oh, perhaps it is." He shrugged. "It will hinge upon whether there is a narrow pass or valley somewhere on the mire into which we can channel the beast?" He looked at Jan.

Jan thought for a moment. "Somewhere to lure it, you mean? Hmmm. The mire is fed by four or more streams and the River Strane. All that water has to go somewhere. The mire overflows through a narrow gully about three-quarters of a mile due east of the old tin mines at Whiteworks. It goes on to form the River Swincombe. But in that gully is a deep pool, just the place for 'Sluggo' to hide." Jan raised his eyebrows. "But how would you lure it there and for what purpose?"

"Your queries form the basis for my next few questions, Jan. I've seen a number of farms with large portable propane gas bowsers outside. Are these readily obtainable? Could I borrow one from somewhere?" By bowsers, Wells meant cylindrical liquid containers of gas mounted on small trailers.

"There's a place in Okehampton that hires them out. Not just for domestic use but also for fairs and shows where some form of heating is needed."

"Excellent!" Wells slapped his hands against his thighs. "My final question then, and again it's for you Jan ... Would you be able to obtain a half a side of beef, pork or mutton? Ideally, just on the turn?"

"I think I can see where you're going with this," said Jan. "There's an abattoir in Newton Abbot. Whether they would sell to me directly is a moot question. What they do sell directly to many sheep farmers is chickens that have passed the sell-by date and have been classified as unfit for human consumption. The farmers use the chickens as dog food."

"Perfect!" said Wells. "We'll need about a dozen, the smellier the better!"

"Would someone like to let little old me into this conversation?" asked Felicity, "or should I find a rocking chair and do some knitting while the menfolk have their important men-only discussion?"

Wells looked contrite. "Sorry, Felicity, I was just trying to clarify some logistic issues before outlining the plan. Trust me, if this plan is to succeed, it will require all three of us working very hard and exhibiting no small amount of courage and steadfastness. You will certainly not be side-lined, I can assure you."

He smiled at her. "What we would need to do, somehow, is to feed a number of garden hoses—at this stage, I estimate six—under the water at that end of the mire. The ends of the hoses on the surface would be attached to a six-branch manifold that I'm sure Jan and I can fabricate. That would, in turn, be connected to the propane bowser."

"And the chickens?" queried Felicity.

"The creature would be lured to that side of the mire by the smell of the chickens. The leeches are scavengers as well as predators."

Felicity nodded her understanding.

"As it approached, we would turn the gas on. That would bubble to the surface—"

"Because gas is less dense than water." Felicity recalled her science lessons from school.

"Exactly! And being heavier than air, it would lie on the surface and the banks of the gully would help to contain the gas."

"So, if everything went to plan, the creature would climb out of the mire—" Felicity leaned forward.

"—to get to the chickens, and we would ignite the gas." Wells folded his arms in satisfaction.

"Goodbye Sluggo!" said Jan.

"If only." Wells's face fell. He sounded despondent once more. "I foresee three major hurdles and I have to confess that, as yet, I have been unable to find solutions."

"Go on," said Jan, "we're listening."

"Firstly, how do we get the hosepipes underwater in the gully, in exactly the right position and fixed so that they can't move? Positioning will be critical."

Jan pursed his lips.

"Secondly"—Wells held up two fingers—"although the preparation, pipe-laying and so on can be done in daylight, the killing can only be done at night. The leech won't emerge in daylight unless it feels threatened. We need to be able to see the approach of the beast in order to know when to switch on the gas."

"Torches?" Felicity suggested but Jan shook his head.

"We can't use torches. That would give the whole game away, right?" Jan asked Wells.

"That's right," Wells said. "So, thirdly ... even if one and two go perfectly, how can we keep the creature on the surface long enough to be incinerated? At the first hint of fire, it will submerge and swim to safety."

The three humans hadn't noticed that Penny had ceased her game of chase. She was now flopped just below Helly and the two were staring rigidly at each other.

Wells sighed. "I fear unless we can overcome these problems, my plan is doomed to failure."

Helly, to the surprise of everyone, suddenly spoke up. Pointing at Penny, he said, "Penny has answer."

Three heads swivelled in Helly's direction.

"What did you say, Helly?" asked Wells.

Pointing to Penny again, Helly said, "Penny put pipes under water in day. Helly take glasses off at night and watch for leech. Helly see long way at night."

The three stared at Helly for a moment before Felicity broke the silence. "No, absolutely not! I'm not allowing these children to put themselves at risk."

Wells hesitated before reluctantly agreeing with her.

Jan was unsure. He sat for some time, thinking, his hands clenched tightly together, biting on the knuckle of his forefinger. "I'm not sure how much danger we would be putting them in," he said at last. "If Penny laid the pipes in daylight, with Helly nearby, Flick and I could act as lookouts at the entrance to the gully. Any movement on the mire and we would call to Helly. Helly could warn Penny, who would be under strict instruction to get out quickly in the event of Helly's signal. I assume they can communicate if Penny is underwater?"

"Perfectly," said Wells, "water is not a barrier to thought transference."

"I'm really not sure," Felicity protested. "What if Penny ignores Helly? You know what a little rascal she can be!"

Penny moved closer to Felicity and, bending one of her tentacles into a crook, she gently stroked Felicity's arm. "Oh, yes? That's what you're saying now is it, little goody-five-shoes?" Felicity leaned down to gaze into her eyes. "Will you promise to come out immediately if Helly tells you?"

In answer, Penny moved towards Helly and wrapped a tentacle around his shoulders.

"Ummm ... sibling love and devotion ... I don't think!" said Felicity, still unsure. "And what about Helly at night? How dangerous would that be?"

"Helly could be positioned well up on the bank, near the Land Rover. Any trouble and he could get in the car. He'd be safe there," suggested Jan.

"I'm still not sure." Felicity sighed and turned to the children. "Are you two *absolutely sure* you want to do this?"

Penny waved two of her tentacles, while Helly made his best effort at a smile and rocked back and forth until he broke wind. Now fully practised in the manoeuvre, the three adults whipped out handkerchiefs and applied them to their noses and mouths.

"Wod I dode udderstad," said Jan through his handkerchief, "id why Peddy and Midder Poddy are nod affeded by the smell."

Mister Ogilvy and Fossy clearly were. They had made a rapid retreat to the kitchen.

Wells risked speaking without his handkerchief. "In Penny's case, I don't believe the pentepus are equipped with olfactory organs. The iguanopteryx, as well as being fruit eaters and lower-level predators, are scavengers and, in consequence, used to disagreeable smells." Wells choked on the last few words and quickly applied his handkerchief to his face again.

After a suitable pause, Jan carried out a 'sniff test' and declared the all-clear.

"That still leaves hurdle number three," Felicity reminded them, returning to the discussion as if nothing had happened. "How do we stop the beast from submerging?"

Wells grimaced. "I have an idea, but I'm not sure how effective it will be. I think it's worth a try. As you know, I am a zoologist and did work for a short while as a consultant at a zoo. As a consequence of this I have, at my home in Spade House, a tranquilliser gun which I employed to anaesthetise wild animals when surgery was needed." He shook his head, hesitating. "I also keep a supply of pentobarbital, which sadly I was obliged to use to put certain animals out of their misery if their pain could not be alleviated in any other way. I hated doing that, but sometimes there was no alternative."

Memories came flooding back and he took a few moments to compose himself again. "However," he said at last, "I would feel no such compunction in using it on our slimy friend in the mire. That said, I do not think the maximum dose I can get into a tranquilliser dart will kill the beast."

"It might be enough to slow it down and allow us to complete our task, though?" Jan asked.

Wells nodded.

No one spoke for quite some time.

It was Felicity who broke the silence. "That's our plan, then. Let's get to it!"

The next few days were a blur of activity at Prior's Cross. Wells disappeared for a day before returning with his tranquilliser gun, darts and lethal drug, which he kept carefully locked away.

Jan drove to Okehampton and secured a propane bowser, while Felicity scoured the DIY shops and garden centres to procure the necessary lengths of hose and connectors. They drove together to the abattoir in Newton Abbot, where Jan, with his dog Jed beside him, had no trouble convincing the manager that he needed his waste chickens as dog food.

With the manifold and connector for the bowser ready and the chickens 'ripening' in a fox/rat/Fossy-and-Ogilvy-proof box in the barn, Wells called them together.

"Tomorrow is a full moon," he said. "We'll set up in the afternoon, then strike when it gets dark!"

CHAPTER THIRTY-FIVE

With the Land Rover fully loaded, the propane bowser hitched to the tow hook and Helly, Penny and Mr Polly hiding away, huddled together under a tarp on the back seat, they set off from Prior's Cross House just before noon. They travelled down the metalled road which led to the old tin mine. Rounding an escarpment, they crossed a stone clapper bridge over a busy stream and approached a group of derelict buildings, at which point the metalled road ran out and was replaced by a wide footpath.

"This is Whiteworks, the old tin mining complex," Jan said, bringing the vehicle to a halt. "I just want to check the path visibly before we go on." He turned to the children on the back seat, pulling the tarp to cover a stray tentacle. "Stay undercover," he ordered the children and climbed out of the vehicle. Wells and Felicity accompanied him as he walked slowly through the ruined buildings and fenced off mining shafts until he reached a vantage point which allowed him to see into the valley below.

"That little stream down there is the rather grandly named River Strane," he said, pointing it out. "The stream itself isn't a problem. It's quite narrow and has a gravelly base, but the ground around it can sometimes get a bit boggy." He scanned it for a while, his hand shading his eyes from the low sun. "Seems okay today. We should be alright. You can just make out the path leading from the stream and climbing up to the high ground there. That's one of two false summits on Royal Hill. Many's the hiker who has cursed on reaching that false summit, only to discover he's still got a long climb in front of him to reach the top of Royal Hill. Him or her," he added as an afterthought, smiling at Felicity.

"The stream is the only sticky bit. Once through that, we'll climb up to that high ground, then turn down the south slope until we come across the old hut circles. It used to be a Bronze Age settlement. That's as far as we can get with the 'Rover, but we'll be within spitting distance of the gully."

"Bronze Age settlement?" Felicity quipped. "I expect your great-grandad still lives there, Jan!"

Jan decided not to dignify her remark with a response.

Back in the car, they rumbled down to within ten yards of the stream. Jan stopped the vehicle and engaged four-wheel drive and low ratio—there was nothing automatic on the old ex-military Land Rover that he had so lovingly restored. He allowed it to crawl forward and crossed the stream without trouble, but the opposite bank was worse than it had appeared when he surveyed it. The vehicle slithered around as Jan frantically swung the wheel first one way then the other. There was a heart-stopping moment when the Rover nearly turned sideways but Jan regained control and, when the wheels finally bit into firm ground, Wells and Felicity—who had been holding their breath—broke out into spontaneous cheering. Free from the bog, the vehicle crawled steadily up the hill.

After turning down the south slope Jan allowed the vehicle to coast, under control, until they reached a group of hut circles. These circles of stones had once formed the bases of beehive huts, habitation for the Bronze Age settlers who had lived on Dartmoor a long time before. Inching forward, he stopped the vehicle at a point which offered a full view of the gully from end to end.

At the western end, the gully was nothing more than a narrow extension to the mire, covered in vegetation, yet the sound of the overflowing water gurgling out from the mire attested to flowing water underneath. At the eastern end, the vegetation thinned somewhat, and water could be seen flowing onwards to form the River Swincombe. In the middle of the gully lay the deep pool, invisible, covered in vegetation.

Goodness me, thought Felicity, *are we really going to send little Penny into that morass?*

Jan had started unloading the vehicle and allowed Penny, Helly and Mr Polly out. Helly took up his position on the bonnet of the Land Rover, with Mr Polly on his shoulder. Strictly speaking, Mr Polly wasn't required for the operation, but Felicity had been fearful of leaving him alone with the Potty Professor still on the loose.

To ward off the cold, Helly was wearing an old sweater and a pair of corduroy trousers, woollen socks and welly boots, with a fetching pom-pom hat covering his wiry white hair, all bought at knockdown prices in one of Tavistock's charity shops.

He had complained incessantly to Felicity while she was dressing him, "Itch, Flick, itch," but he seemed to be alright with it now, perhaps appreciating his coverings as the cold wind swirled around them.

Wells, in the meantime, was keeping careful watch on the surrounding hills, on the lookout for hostile observers.

Jan laid out the hoses in long loops to ensure they would not be snagged as they were dragged into the water and submerged. One end was weighted so that it would remain in place when lowered. The other end of each hose was connected to the manifold, which in turn was connected to the gas bowser.

Perhaps Jan was having second thoughts. He stared at the gully and then at Penny. "Are you sure you want to do this?" He looked at Helly for an answer.

"Penny good. Penny want swim. Only Helly frightened, Jan!"

Jan knelt and flung an arm around his shoulders. "So am I, Helly!" he soothed. "But we must destroy this monster. Penny is the only one that can lay these pipes.

Will you come to the water's edge? I want to explain to Penny where the end of each hose must rest. I need your help."

Felicity took over watch duties as Wells, Jan, Penny and Helly moved back and forth along the side of the gully. Jan pointed out the eventual resting places for the hose ends. At the end of their reconnoitre, Penny, through Helly, declared that she understood. "Penny ready."

Felicity and Wells moved to positions where they could observe the mire. Any slight disturbance and they would order Penny out.

Jan stayed with Penny, preparing to pay out the hoses while keeping a careful eye out for snags. Helly kept his eyes on the surface of the gully. At a signal, he was ready to transfer a danger warning to Penny.

Wrapping a tentacle around the first hose, Penny slid beneath the water. Jan carefully payed out the hose, and after what seemed like an eternity but was in reality less than a minute, she surfaced, pushing aside the weeds as she did so. Grabbing the next hose, she was gone again.

Less than ten minutes had elapsed when Penny grasped the final hose and disappeared. To Jan it had seemed like a lifetime. He looked at the others. Wells, shifting from one foot to the other, clearly tense but never allowing his gaze to waver, stared intently at the mire. Felicity, Jan could see from his vantage point, was physically shaking. Poor Helly was rocking and keening in a pitiful way, his eyes fixed on the spot where he had last seen Penny submerge.

Come on, Penny! Jan willed. *Up you come and it's all over! Let's get you to safety ...*

Oh NO!

A black, shiny hump had appeared in the centre of the gully. As Jan watched it, he could see the hump getting bigger. The leech was rising.

Jan lifted his head to shout a warning to Helly, but before he could do so, something green streaked across the top of the water, leapt into his arms and enclosed him in its five tentacles, gripping him tightly. It was Penny, terrified, her eyes large and frightened. Jan, keeping a careful hold of her, turned and sprinted from the side of the gully, calling to Felicity and Wells as he did so.

"Helly!" he cried frantically. "Get inside!"

They reached the Land Rover together, Wells gasping for breath and holding his chest. As one they turned to look back at the gully. The creature had slipped from the water and begun making its way up the slope towards them, its body undulating as it moved forward.

"Into the Rover!" commanded Jan, then, "Wait!"

The monster had stopped and slithered backwards a few feet. On it came again, but again it stopped and slid back.

"It can't get up the slope!" wheezed Wells, between gasps for air. "Something must have weakened it!"

The front half of the beast reared high in the air. The head, easily eight feet from the ground, displayed round, red, goggle eyes above a mouth full of sharp vicious-looking fangs. It flopped back down again with a loud splat, turned, and snaked back into the mire. As it disappeared, Jan, Felicity and Wells watched the rippling vegetation tell of its journey through the gully and out into the broad expanse of the grim mire.

They were a sorry looking bunch, these modern-day descendants of the Bronze Age Britons who sprawled exhausted among their forefathers' hut circles. Wells propped himself against the Land Rover, having almost, but not quite, recovered his composure. Penny had attached herself to a severely shaken Felicity, who held the pentepus tightly, whilst Helly, standing beside them, gently stroked Penny's round head. Mr Polly had perched on the bonnet of the vehicle and was bouncing up and down while occasionally turning his head and hissing loudly at the mire, then turning back to Penny and chirruping softly. Jan was on his knees gently rubbing one of Penny's tentacles, having apologised, through Helly, at least three times for putting her in danger.

Felicity, gradually recovering, gazed fondly at her little friend and planted a kiss on her damp head. *Penny Pentepus*, she thought, *you little minx! You are wallowing in this!*

It was Jan, gently rubbing one of Penny's tentacles, who noticed that one of the others was oozing a green liquid. "HG!" he called, "I think Penny is bleeding!"

Wells was on his feet in a flash. "Don't touch it! That blood is deadly poison to any other living creature!" He bent over the pentepus and carefully examined the wound. "It's fine. It's a superficial wound." Smiling gently, he said, "Penny, I want you to sit over here on your own, just for a minute while I see to this. Don't worry, you'll be perfectly alright."

Penny, gazing up at Helly, reluctantly complied. A minute ago she had been the centre of attention, now she sat alone, forlorn and frightened.

"I'll get some gloves and the first aid kit from the Land Rover." Wells moved around to the side of the vehicle. Suddenly he stopped and brought both fists down hard on the bonnet, sending Mr Polly into a paroxysm of squawking and hissing. "I'm a fool!" he roared, as he hammered the bonnet again. "An idiot! A total imbecile!"

Mr Polly had fled to Jan's shoulder. "HG, what is it?" Jan asked.

"Don't you see?" HG asked, his intelligent eyes gleaming, "We've had the answer all the time. I know how we can kill this beast, and so do you!"

It was Felicity who had the lightbulb moment. She flung her arms wide and exclaimed, "Penny's blood!"

"Penny," said Wells quietly as he knelt in front of her and beckoned Helly to sit by him, "I want to collect some of your blood."

Penny, alarmed, shuffled back a few feet.

Turning to Helly, Wells said, "Try to make her understand, Helly, I don't want to harm her. I want some of her blood so that I can kill the monster that tried to hurt her."

The mental interaction between Helly and Penny lasted much longer than usual. Neither moved a muscle while the exchange took place.

"Penny understand. Kill leech, HG!" cried an animated Helly. "Kill leech!"

Penny moved forward a little hesitantly and extended the wounded tentacle to Wells, who collected the blood in a vial, gently squeezing the tentacle to maximise the flow. Once he had as much as he dared take, he stoppered the tube and attended to the wounded appendage, cleaning and bandaging it before finally applying a rubberised outer cover. This, he explained to the others, would protect them from contamination.

"It's perfectly alright to make a fuss of the patient again," Wells announced, smiling indulgently at his charge. "Hugs, cuddles and kisses are in order."

And make a fuss they did. Penny was once again the centre of attention, the brave wounded little soldier.

CHAPTER THIRTY-SIX

*A*s they sat down to their evening meal, dusk was already beginning to descend upon the moor. Felicity pulled out a chicken leg from the picnic basket she had prepared but, taking one look at Mr Polly, she shook her head and replaced it. *I can never eat chicken or octopus again*, she thought.

They ate quietly until Jan broke into their reverie to ask whether the blood Wells had taken would be enough to kill the leech.

"I'm not sure," admitted Wells. "That's why we must, ultimately, incinerate the creature. I've filled two darts. If we can get both into it, even if the toxin doesn't kill the beast, it should at least stop it and prevent it returning to the mire. That will give us time to burn it!"

He stared in the direction of the mire and added as an afterthought, "And that's why the creature was so sluggish and couldn't get up the slope. One of its fangs must have just grazed Penny and the small amount of blood it ingested was enough to slow it down. Penny, you may have saved our lives today!"

Wells ran over the plan one final time. Everything was prepared. The hoses were connected to the propane bowser. The rancid chickens were in place near the edge of the gully. He had filled two tranquilliser darts with Penny's blood, and three 'torches'—created by taking several two-foot-long staves of wood and wrapping one end with many layers of hessian soaked in pitch—were stuck in the ground ready to light. These would be used to ignite the gas when the time came.

Helly, having removed his glasses, had taken up his position on the bonnet of the Land Rover, and declared he could see clearly to the far end of the mire. Penny was in the back of the vehicle, wrapped in a blanket with only her shining eyes peeking out. Mr Polly was snuggled in beside her, the night being cold.

The moon had risen at about eight thirty, and a little more than an hour after that, Helly startled everyone by speaking. "It's coming," he announced, pointing at the mire.

Everyone went on full alert. Felicity moved to the rear of the bowser ready to turn on the gas. Jan picked up the tranquilliser gun, already loaded with one dart filled with Penny's blood, and checked that the second dart was safe in the pouch on his belt ready to reload. Wells knelt next to the torches with a barbecue lighter, ready to ignite them.

Helly swivelled his head to the right. "Man coming!" He fumbled for his glasses and added, "with torch!"

Wells leapt to his feet, his eyes straining in the dark, but all he could see was the beam of the torch bobbing about as the man made his way along the northern edge of the mire. "Keep clear!" Wells called out in the direction of the light. "There's great danger here!"

The man with the torch ignored him and kept on coming. In the light cast by the moon, Wells could just make out the shock of white hair and the moonlight reflecting on his glasses. Pettigrew!

"Pettigrew? Get out of here! Get up the hill! You are in grave danger!" Wells waved frantically at the scientist.

From over his shoulder came Helly's calm voice. "Creature, very near."

Pettigrew stopped. He raised his fist in the air and shook it. "I want my monkey-boy back! And the other specimens you stole. I demand you return them, they're mine!"

He took another step forward, the tension in his face apparent. Something large and black appeared behind him. Wells screamed out another warning, but it was too late. The creature reared up, then struck! It lurched forward with alarming speed. Aiming for his shoulder, the monster's fangs buried deep into Pettigrew's flesh, releasing its poison. As the leech crashed to the ground, it brought Pettigrew down with it. The scientist screamed pitifully, thrashing and writhing—for only a mercifully short time—then lay still. Releasing its grip on Pettigrew's shoulder, the monster bit into his neck and, with a quick flick, severed the scientist's head from his body.

Centring its horrific jaws over the gory remnants of

Pettigrew's corpse, the creature began to feast. The almost indescribable horror of the sucking sounds was too much for Felicity, who had to turn away and regurgitate her supper.

Wells, who had closed his eyes momentarily in an attempt to blot out what had been unfolding in front of him, became suddenly steely calm. "Jan? Now," he ordered, his voice almost inaudible.

Instantly Jan, shaking with a combination of anxiety and adrenaline, sprinted forward and slightly to the side of the beast. He brought the tranquilliser gun up. He had never in his life known fear like this. He sucked in several deep breaths, trying to bring his shattered nerves under control, and then took aim at the point Wells had indicated.

He fired.

Fortune smiled. The dart hit the exact mark Wells had wanted, at a point near the underside of the leech, just behind the head. It emptied its contents into the beast.

Jan's shaking hands hampered his reloading of the gun, but he completed it just as the creature, stung by the impact of the first dart, was turning in his direction. As it reared up, Jan seized the opportunity to send the second dart into its soft underbelly before flinging himself to one side. He landed painfully, rolling over and over to avoid the monster's strike. The giant leech crashed down with a nauseating splat, its head only inches from Jan's face, the fetid stench from its gore-filled mouth making him retch. He threw himself to his feet and sprinted uphill, putting as much distance between himself and the foul creature as he could manage.

"Gas!" cried Wells, and Felicity opened the gas valve as he knelt down to light the torches.

As Jan reached the Land Rover, Felicity ran to him. The two embraced, both trembling, Felicity fighting back hysteria.

"Torches!" cried Wells, picking up his own and striding purposefully towards the leech. Jan and Felicity each grabbed a torch and joined him. Together, they strode towards the black abomination until Wells could hear the bubbling of the gas coming from beneath the water and popping around the creature.

"Now!" he yelled.

Simultaneously, three balls of flame arced gracefully in the sky, trailing burning pitch and hessian in their wakes. One fell behind the leech, one to the side and one actually landed on top of it. With an earth-trembling *WUMP* the entire gully erupted, sending smoke and flames leaping high into the night sky, the force of it throwing the three of them to the ground and sending the leech sliding back towards the gully.

Regaining their feet, they scurried up the hill to the Land Rover, where they were met by a frightened Helly. The hellventi jumped up to Wells and began patting his face.

"What on earth are you doing, Helly?" Wells was taken aback.

Felicity suddenly burst into uncontrollable laughter, caused partly by the hysteria which lay just under the surface, and partly by the fact that Wells's not insubstantial eyebrows and moustache were badly singed and still smoking.

After Jan had come to the rescue with a bottle of water and a packet of tissues, they sat together on the grass and joined Felicity in hysterical laughter, brought on no doubt by the kind of elation felt by every soldier returning from a dangerous mission. Helly joined them, waving his arms and making the guttural coughing sound that passed for laughter.

Once they'd managed to regain their self-control they sat quietly, watching the remains of the monster that had wreaked so much havoc on the moor slowly burn. It spluttered and shrivelled before their eyes until its burned-out carcass was less than half its original size.

Wells roused himself and walked to the bowser. After closing the gas valve, he re-joined his friends, and the four sat huddled together until the flames finally died out. On a whim, Jan, after shouting a warning to Helly, switched on the vehicle headlights, illuminating the entire gully. They cheered as what remained of the carcass sank slowly beneath the water.

The creature from the grim mire was gone.

CHAPTER THIRTY-SEVEN

Felicity leant against the old wooden gate and drained the last of her coffee.

"Thanks for that, Mrs Bickle," she said, handing her mug back to the farmer's wife.

Frankie Bickle, standing alongside his wife, removed his cap and scratched his head, staring in the direction of the barn. "I've never seen nothin' like this," he said, not for the first time. "It's quite incredible, is what it is."

"You'll have to start charging people, Felicity," Mrs Bickle laughed. "You'll make a fortune."

Felicity grinned, half an ear on the ferocious growling and snapping she could hear from inside the Bickles' huge barn. At the door, there was a growing pile of deceased rats.

"I'm certainly considering it. My Fossy is an environmentally friendly answer to any farmer's rodent problem. I should think if you borrowed her for a couple of hours once a week, you'd practically eliminate any issue you were having with rats in no time at all."

"I'd pay good money for that," Frankie Bickle said, rubbing his grizzly chin. "I don't hold with no chemicals, no how. How much do you think it would set me back?"

"Oh, Frankie." Felicity reached out and patted his arm. "I would never charge you. I feel the loss of your prizewinning bull was partly my fault."

The old farmer gazed at her quizzically. "Not sure how you work that out, my maid."

Felicity shrugged. "If not my personal fault, certainly the blame lies with my family." *Particularly my time-travelling great-great-uncle*, she thought.

Frankie looked none the wiser, so she left it at that. "In any case, I will bring Fossy over once a week on a Monday morning and we'll sort your rat problem out for you."

"Us'll pass your details along to everyone us knows from Tavi' market and drum up some more business for you, if you like?" Mrs Bickle offered. "You 'as to make sure you charges 'em, mind."

"I will," Felicity promised.

At that moment Fossy trotted out of the barn, her little stump of a tail held high, her black eyes shining as brightly as her coat, the rat in her mouth almost as big as she.

"Goodness me, that's a big bu—"

"Frankie!" Mrs Bickle chided.

"Brute. I was going to say brute."

Felicity giggled. Fossy ran up to them and dropped

the rat on her feet, freshly dead and not a drop of blood on it. Felicity, squeamish at the best of times, grimaced. She couldn't get used to the sight of dead animals herself, but Fossy definitely had a talent that she didn't mind exploiting for the benefit of the local farmers. "She always brings me the last one, for some reason," she told the Bickles.

"She just wants your approval, I suppose." Frankie Bickle picked the rat up by the tail and examined it. "Nice work," he told Fossy, and she sat down and waggled her back end in delight.

Felicity pulled a treat out of her pocket. "Good girl!" she told her. "There's a good girl."

Felicity pulled up into her drive and unclipped Fossy from her safety harness. The blessed little soul had been having a snooze after all her hard work. The combination of feeling tired out and the *Covid 19 Tomb Kickers* on her music system had lulled Fossy into the sweetest of dreams. Now she stretched and yawned in Felicity's arms, content to be carried indoors and deposited somewhere cosy.

They were met in the hallway by Mister Ogilvy.

He flicked his tail and stared up at the furry bundle in Felicity's arms. When they'd first brought Fossy home, Felicity had imagined that Mister Ogilvy would be jealous, but it quickly transpired that he remembered Aunt Maud's beloved little friend from old, and he'd been more than happy to see her again. Now the cat had a tendency to mother the little creature, and once Felicity had set Fossy on the ground, the pair of them ran off together so that Mister Ogilvy could give her a thorough tongue-washing after all of Fossy's exertions in the mucky barn this afternoon.

"Oggy, my darling, you make a very good mummy," Felicity called after them and unzipped her jacket, intending to hang it on a peg next to the door.

At that moment, Wells appeared at the top of the stairs, having just climbed down from the attic. Mr Polly sat on his shoulder, Penny danced alongside him and Helly, as usual, was in his arms.

"Fel-iss-it-tee!" Helly called and made a grabby motion with one hand.

Felicity gazed up at Wells and her eyes filled with tears.

He nodded at her, his face deadly serious.

"It's time," he told her.

CHAPTER THIRTY-EIGHT

As soon as the bell rang, Felicity sprang to the door, opened it and immediately felt a pang of disappointment. It wasn't who she had hoped it would be. But then what was she thinking? He wouldn't have rung the bell.

Instead, it was DS Alderson, so she wasn't too disappointed. He was a nice man, after all. Before he could explain his visit, she invited him in. As they walked through to the kitchen, he said, "I'm sorry to inter—"

"You're not!"

He blinked, puzzled. "Sorry? I'm not ...?"

"Interrupting me!" replied Felicity, smiling. "I hope you don't mind sitting in the kitchen. I thought we might have a cup of tea."

"That's very kind, thank you, Ms Westmacott."

"Please, just call me Flick."

"Flick? Sounds like someone—"

"Don't go there," Felicity warned.

"Oh! I'm sorry Ms West—Flick—I was—"

"Honestly, I'm the one that should apologise. It's just that I'm a bit sensitive about my nickname."

DS Alderson was beginning to wonder if he was ever going to get a chance to finish a sentence. "I'm sorry, I didn't mean to cause offe—"

"You're not causing offence, see? Sorry, I shouldn't interrupt. By the way, do you have a first name?"

DS Alderson smiled. "I do, as it happens. It's Sebastian, but people just call me Seb."

"Well, I'm 'people', so is it okay for me to call you Seb? Sebastian is a great name by the way."

DS Alderson chuckled. "Thank you, and yes, of course you can call me Seb."

"I'll tell you what, Seb," said Felicity, pouring the tea and handing him a cup, along with the milk jug and sugar bowl, "why don't I just shut up and listen instead of rabbiting on? You'll have to excuse me. I'm a little upset today."

"Sorry to hear that. Is there anything I can do?" Seb sounded genuinely concerned.

Felicity shook her head. "No, but it was nice of you to offer. Now! Are you here to give me information or arrest me? It must be one or the other."

Seb smiled. Flick was an easy person to like. Before he could continue, a cat shot into the kitchen pursued by a little terrier dog. They did a quick circuit around the table and then raced out again in the direction of the living room, although now it seemed that the cat was chasing the dog.

"Isn't that the little terrier from up—"

"From up on the mire? Yes, that's her. You'll have to excuse those two tearaways. They always have a mad half-hour every morning at this time."

"Was it 'Fossy' you called her?"

"That's right. The other one is Mister Ogilvy, named after a chara—"

"In *War of the Worlds*." It was Seb's turn to interrupt. "I remember that."

"You've read it?" asked Felicity, sounding only half surprised.

"Of course! What red-blooded lad hasn't read HG Wells? What a visionary. And a great historian as well!"

"Well, he did have the advantage of owning a time machine," smiled Felicity.

Seb guffawed. "Do you know, I never thought of that. You have a point there! If only, eh?"

"Yes, if only," replied Felicity, wistfully.

"But anyway, as much as I'm enjoying our chat, I really must get down to business." Seb suddenly sounded official again. "We think we now know the identity of your intruder."

Felicity experienced a prick of fear. Surely they couldn't know about Wells? *No of course not, that's absurd. Be calm.*

Seb carried on, oblivious of Felicity's inner turmoil. "We think it was one James Pettigrew, who termed himself Professor."

"Really?" Felicity asked, her eyes open wide.

"Yes, the official position is that we believe that he has

fled the country. I see you have a copy of this morning's *Mail*." Seb indicated the newspaper resting on the draining board. "No doubt you'll have read about the hoax perpetrated by Pettigrew and a reporter going by the name of Arnie Crabbe. We think that the fallout from that, coupled with the fact that the RSPCA was pursuing a prosecution against him for animal cruelty, led to him flee the country."

"Humm, I see," said Felicity, "and what's the unofficial position?"

"You're very shrewd, Flick. Off the record, right?" He waited until she nodded before lowering his voice. "Sgt Jock Galloway thinks Pettigrew may have drowned in Foxtor Mire. We found his notebook and a pair of spectacles that match the ones he wore along with a torch, just east of Whiteworks, right on the edge of the mire. In the notebook there was a sketch map of the location of the Gurney Farm. We think he might have intended to break in there but mistook your house for the farm, they being so close together."

"I see," said Felicity, keeping her face carefully blank. "Was there anything else of interest in the notebook?"

"Some nonsense about five-legged aliens, mini dinosaurs and ape-men." Seb shrugged. "Oh, and a reference to Mrs Gurney and a 'Miss Gurney', but there are no *Miss* Gurneys in Princetown."

"He wasn't the full shilling, then?" suggested Felicity.

"I couldn't possibly comment. Let's just say we think he may have been, er ... delusional." Seb placed his mug in the sink. "It's been lovely chatting to you, Flick, but I have a few more stops to make. I hope this information puts your mind at rest."

Felicity blew out her cheeks as she closed the door behind the DS. She had sailed a little too close to the wind once or twice there. Perhaps she should try to be a little more introspective.

She shrugged. What she really needed was a walk along the side of the infamous 'Grim Mire'.

On her return, she hauled off her boots in the hall and, after towelling down Fossy with her special towel, padded into the kitchen in her socks. She could have leapt for joy when she pushed open the kitchen door. Sat at the table was Jan, a wicker basket neatly covered by a tea towel in front of him. She flew into his arms as he stood up.

"Oh! It's so good to see you, Jan," she sang, then in a scolding voice added, "Where have you been, you big lug?"

"Sorry, Flick, Father's hurt his leg, so I'm working all hours at the moment. He's promised me a few days off when he's back on his feet again to make up for it. Mother sent this." Jan pointed at the basket. "She feels bad about gossiping about, well, you know what." He raised his eyes to the ceiling. "It's in the way of a peace offering."

"Oh, she needn't have worried," said Felicity, before asking eagerly, "What's in it?"

"Lunch!" said Jan triumphantly, whipping off the cloth.

Felicity supplied the tea—Jan's in the plain white pint mug she had bought for him at the pannier market in Tavistock—the cutlery and a plate each, upon which Jan deposited a sandwich. Well, not so much a sandwich, more a doorstep! Each one comprised two slices of homemade bread, cut thickly and spread with a generous layer of butter. The filling consisted of quarter-inch slices of crumbly vintage Cheddar smeared with copious amounts of Mary's own Devon chutney.

Felicity cut her doorstep in half and pushed one half to the side. "I'll have that for my supper," she said. "That's too much for lunch."

"Very wise," said Jan, who had also cut his sandwich in half but clearly had every intention of eating both parts. "There's pudding to follow."

Felicity received that information with mixed emotions. Pleasure, because no one made puddings quite like Mary Gurney, and despair because they were always so filling.

"Did you have to tell your Mother about our little friends in the attic?" asked Felicity.

"I told her your attic had been infested with pigeons, and that 'aliens' was our little fun word for them. And, having seen Fossy, she accepted that was what we were trying to find on the moor."

Jan carefully took out the pudding. It was a pie, beautifully golden in colour and smelling delicious. He cut it in half, then quarters. "Blackberry. I had to go and pick them this morning." He made Felicity laugh by mimicking his mother's voice. "Ged out there and pick me some blackberries you bad bey, make sure they still 'ave the wet doo on 'em an' don' 'ee bring back no red ones mind 'ee, or I'll take a broom 'andle to your back, me lad!"

He cut one of the quarters in half and eased it onto a plate. It oozed fruit and juice.

"Smaller piece for me, please," said Felicity.

Jan looked at her as if she had just sworn at him. "This *is* your piece," he said, and pointed to the unsliced quarter. "That's mine."

Taking a jar out of the basket, he unstoppered it and dolloped a spoonful of the contents onto Felicity's plate alongside her slice of pie. "Clotted cream, made from the milk of Master Dan'l Gurney's Jerseys. A present from his wife, Kathy."

After Felicity had cleaned her plate, she stared at the remaining slice of pie. She would wrap the half pie that remained in foil and place it in the fridge, but that single, lonely slice—surely she should eat that?

No! she told herself, she would be strong. She would keep it for later and enjoy it all the more.

After Jan had gone, Felicity surprised herself by doing some serious writing. She'd had a great idea for a new story, not a gothic horror this time, but a sci-fi instead. It would be about a young woman who finds herself having to look after some abandoned alien children ...

But then again, who'd read that? Maybe it wasn't such a great idea.

Picking up the threads of her half-finished ghost story, she immersed herself into the tale, the words flowing freely onto the screen.

It was a little after seven when she eased herself out of her captain's chair and stretched. Fossy and Mister Ogilvy copied her, which could only mean one thing. Exercise time. She let Oggy out into the back yard to sort out the mice in the barn, while Fossy accompanied her along the side of the mire for their evening constitutional.

Everything should have been fine, but after her return, Felicity felt empty. And not with hunger. Oggy had curled up beside her on the sofa, while Fossy stretched out in front of the fire. Her untouched sandwich lay on a plate on the coffee table and her slice of pie was still in the fridge. She drew her legs up and wrapped her arms around her knees, giving way to her inner feelings and allowing the tears to flow.

She was wiping her eyes, sniffling and still feeling sorry for herself when she heard a high-pitched whining noise.

Rrrrrrrr-rrrrrr-rrrrrrr-zzzzzzzzzzzz-eeeee.

The sound was followed by a bright flash.

Felicity sprang to her feet. She raced through to the kitchen and flung open the back door. Stepping out, she looked up at the barn. After a moment, a familiar red light shone from the upper window. Felicity could barely contain her impatience. She darted forward as soon as she spotted the man emerging from the barn. He stooped slightly, suddenly appearing older than he had before. Rushing to him, Felicity embraced him warmly.

"HG, I've missed you so much."

"And I you, my dearest Felicity."

"You haven't brought me any children?" she asked, her voice tinged with disappointment.

"There'll be no more children, my dear. Together with a number of the hellventi, I have established a nursery in TZB, at least for this area. There, they will attend to any orphaned children, not only of the sentient beings like the pentepus and iguanopteryx, but also of orphaned or abandoned morph-dogs and one or two other species of the lower orders. It is the culmination of my work with these beautiful people."

"And what of our children?" Felicity asked anxiously.

He placed his hand on her cheek. "Don't worry, my dear. All is well," beamed Wells, his bright eyes shining with remembered joy. "Mr Polly has returned to his flock and been allocated a perch in the highest tree, as befits his elevated position of traveller and adventurer. It's just over there by the Gurney farm."

Felicity looked that way, as though she would be able to see the little fellow roosting there.

"Dear brave little Penny has been accepted into a consortium of pentepus and is living very happily on the coast of what is currently South Devon. She is already establishing a reputation as a first-rate diver and fisher. No surprise there."

"And Helly?" asked Felicity. She couldn't help it; the tears began to flow freely.

"Ah yes, Helly," said Wells. He continued to smile but there was immense sadness in his eyes. "Helly has been adopted by a childless hellventi couple. As you can imagine, he has brought immense joy into their lives. He will never, of course, forget the parents he lost to the Morventi, but has already learned to love his new parents. He sent a message to you."

Choked with emotion and unable to speak, Felicity just nodded.

"He said to tell you that he is very happy, but sends his love and his thanks to you and Jan. And he says there isn't a day that goes by that he doesn't think of you."

Felicity wept on Wells's shoulder as he held her, patting her back.

"There, there, my dear. It's for the best."

When she had managed to regain some of her composure, she asked, "And what of you now, HG? What will you do?"

"I will retire. At least from time travelling, if not from writing. Each jump I make takes a little more out of me. I think that to carry on would be harmful to my health. I will make one more jump, back to Spade House, and then I will destroy the time machine and all of the plans I used to build it. I don't believe mankind is ready for a machine such as mine. It *could* conceivably be used in an indescribably horrible way."

"So, this is goodbye?" Felicity asked, heartbroken.

"I fear it is, my dear." Wells kissed her gently on the cheek as she embraced him once more.

As he turned to go, he suddenly swung back. "I

nearly forgot! A little gift to help you remember me." He pushed a small packet into her hands and walked slowly back to the barn.

Felicity waited until the flash told her that Wells and his time machine were gone forever. Her heart lurched with the loss of him from her life. She turned sadly for the house, making her way to the warmth of the living room.

All cried out, she sat in front of the fire for the longest time, hardly aware that it was dying down. Numb, she gently stroked Mister Ogilvy, lost in her own misery until finally he had had enough and meowed loudly, demanding his supper.

Felicity blinked and remembered the package. It lay in front of her on the coffee table. She plucked it up and examined it. It was clearly a book, wrapped in brown paper and tied with string in the old-fashioned way.

Opening the package, she ran her fingers over the rich texture of the green leather-bound volume, embossed in gold leaf on the front cover and on the spine.

The Time Machine
By
HG Wells

Inside the front cover was an inscription written in ink:

To my dearest 'Flick'
Fond memories of an amazing adventure

JEANNIE ALDERDICE & PETER ALDERSON SHARP

With love to the very end of time
Your exceedingly proud uncle,
HG

If you enjoyed *The Creature from the Grim Mire*, please consider leaving us a review. We love to hear your thoughts.

ALSO BY PETER ALDERSON SHARP

The Sword, the Wolf and the Rock: An epic historical thriller

Three implacable enemies fighting for a family they love.

Galilean zealots have risen in support of their new leader, Jesus Bar Joseph.

Known as 'the Christ', he is a prince of the line of David. After his crucifixion, his family find themselves in grave danger.

The leader of the zealots, Simon, known to his followers and enemies alike as the 'Rock' is a murderous, violent giant of a man whose sworn enemy is the Roman Centurion, Lucius Maximinus.

Maximinus, famed for his skill with a sword, had been charged with keeping the peace in Galilee. Working alongside him is his strange and brutal lieutenant, Titus, a loyal ex-gladiator believed by many to be half man and half wolf.

Within a short time these enemies find themselves on a gruelling journey, battling to protect one family, special to them all.

This is the bloody history of the first Christian family in the aftermath of the execution of Jesus Bar Joseph. The essence of this sweeping story is recognisable to all, but, containing treachery, rape, kidnapping, violence and murder, it is ***no*** bible story.

Coming Soon from Peter Alderson Sharp

The first in the Dragan Kelly series, *Cast No Shadow*

If you love James Bond, you'll love Dragan Kelly.

ALSO BY JEANNIE WYCHERLEY

The Complete Wonky Inn Series

The Wonkiest Witch: Wonky Inn Book 1

The Ghosts of Wonky Inn: Wonky Inn Book 2

Weird Wedding at Wonky Inn: Wonky Inn Book 3

The Witch Who Killed Christmas: Wonky Inn Christmas Special

Fearful Fortunes and Terrible Tarot: Wonky Inn Book 4

The Mystery of the Marsh Malaise: Wonky Inn Book 5

The Mysterious Mr Wylie: Wonky Inn Book 6

The Great Witchy Cake Off: Wonky Inn Book 7

Vengeful Vampire at Wonky Inn: Wonky Inn Book 8

Witching in a Winter Wonkyland: A Wonky Inn Christmas Cozy Special

A Gaggle of Ghastly Grandmamas: Wonky Inn Book 9

Magic, Murder and a Movie Star: Wonky Inn Book 10

O' Witchy Town of Whittlecombe: A Wonky Inn Christmas Cozy Special

Spellbound Hound

Ain't Nothing but a Pound Dog: Spellbound Hound Magic and Mystery Book 1

A Curse, a Coven and a Canine: Spellbound Hound Magic

and Mystery Book 2

Bark Side of the Moon: Spellbound Hound Magic and Mystery Book 3

Master of Puppies: Spellbound Hound Magic and Mystery Book 4 (TBC)

Dark Fantasy

The Municipality of Lost Souls (2020)

Midnight Garden: The Extra Ordinary World Novella Series Book 1 (2019)

Beyond the Veil (2018)

Crone (2017)

A Concerto for the Dead and Dying (short story, 2018)

Deadly Encounters: A collection of short stories (2017)

Keepers of the Flame: A love story (Novella, 2018)

Non-Fiction

Losing my best Friend: Thoughtful support for those affected by dog bereavement or pet loss (2017)

Follow Jeannie Wycherley

Find out more at on the website

www.jeanniewycherley.co.uk

You can tweet Jeannie

twitter.com/Thecushionlady

Or visit her on Facebook for her fiction

www.facebook.com/jeanniewycherley

Follow Jeannie on Instagram (for bears and books)

www.instagram.com/jeanniewycherley

Sign up for Jeannie's newsletter

eepurl.com/cN3Q6L

OUT NOW

The Municipality of Lost Souls

Vengeful souls don't stay dead

They taunt the minds of the living until they throw themselves from clifftops.

Yet death turns a profit when you drive ships onto rocks to plunder riches.

Agatha knows one thing for sure: respect the dead.

Especially those who did not die quietly.

Now, a lonely witch has conjured a young sailor's soul.

And woken them all.

Only Agatha knows the truth.

She hears it in the whispers drifting across the waves.

She hears it in the crackle of the flames.

And the marauders will stop at nothing to silence her.

Shh ... Listen ...

The Dead Are Coming ...

From the Amazon bestselling author of Crone comes a thoroughly original and spellbinding piece of storytelling. *The Municipality of Lost Souls* is a gothic ghost story set in 1860s England with characters destined to haunt you forever.

For readers of dark fantasy who love witchcraft, magic and a little spookiness. For fans of Daphne du Maurier, Laura Purcell, Michelle Paver and Stacey Halls.

Printed in Great Britain
by Amazon